This book should be returned to any branch of the Lancashire County Library on or before the date shown

SKELMERSDALE

T53

FICTION RESERVE STOCK

Lancashire County Library
Bowran Street
Preston PR1 2UX

Lancashire
County Council

Lizzie Steeples
by
Michael Yates
ISBN: 978-0-9935575-7-6

A copy of this book is deposited with the British Library

Published by

i2i Publishing. Manchester. UK.
www.i2ipublishing.co.uk

Acknowledgements.

I owe a tremendous debt of gratitude to a number of people who have helped me with this story. Here are some of them and if I have left anyone out, please accept my humble apologies.

In particular I would like to thank Andrew Savin for his generous help in guiding me through the minefield of the internet.

In addition I would like to thank Liz Lee and Emily Wilkinson for helping me to get 'Lizzie' onto Amazon in the first place.

Many thanks also to my son Jason who was there to help me to negotiate my way through a maze of technical difficulties.

I would also like to thank my dear wife Carol for her love and incredible patience over the last two years.

Thanks as well to my daughter Jackie and son-in-law Phil Marshall for giving me my two beautiful grandchildren Erin and Jake, who are the light of my life.

In addition I must mention Gill Quinlan and thank her for her help.

Also thanks to Lionel Ross at i2i Publishing for giving me the chance to realize my dream.

Lastly to my dear mother-in-law, Marian, who sadly died last year; she always believed in me and was always there for me.

Lizzie 4 Steeples

Chapter One

Monday November 2nd 1957

The gas lamps issued an eerie almost unearthly gloom, as the November smog began to lift and the rain continued to fall on the grimy cobble-stoned streets of the northern town of Thistlefield. With cotton mills and pits surrounding the area; the town had started to boom again after the war. The smoke from Taylor's mill belched out its' thick black cloud, as the hooter blasted the start of another working week.

The hooter from Taylor's mill woke Lizzie Steeples from a fitful and restless sleep. Unable to close her eyes for more than a few minutes at a time, sleep was the last thing on Lizzie's mind.

York Street was characteristic of the area. Rows and rows of run-down back-to-back terraces; their grim grey slate roofs already glistened with the steady patter of the early morning rain. Built by the wealthy mill and pit owners in the latter part of the nineteenth century, these humble dwellings were home to the multitude of workers that had migrated to the towns and villages from the countryside. Many had come in search of work and a better life. Conditions in the back streets were tough, and a better life became more of a fight for survival. The owners were only interested in profits, and although times were changing in favour of the workers, it was still a hard life in the factories and pits, as the rich owners drove the proletariat harder and harder in their quest for even greater profits.

The Steeples household was unlike most in the village. The terraced cottage where they lived was quite untypical of most of the two-up, two-down affairs of the area that most working class families lived in. Colly Ashcroft had managed to rent one of the bigger houses in the village. It had three bedrooms, a living room, a parlour and a back kitchen. The parlour and third bedroom was shared with Lizzie's brother Bob and his wife Alice.

Most were used to the harshness and deprivation of the times. A coal fire burned cheerily in the Yorkshire grate giving out a warm glow. The thin gauze of the gas mantle, the only source of light in the otherwise dim atmosphere, cast a yellowy glow in the cramped living room. Through the living room out the back, was the kitchen where a cold-water tap dripped incessantly into the brown stone sink causing a yellow stain, and up the yard was an outside privy that froze every winter. Sleeping arrangements were by no means ideal. Upstairs were the two main bedrooms. Lizzie's dad Colly occupied the main room, and Lizzie and the kids the other. Blankets had been a luxury that they could ill afford, and in the depths of winter, it was often Colly's thick army overcoat that had kept them warm.

Elizabeth Ashcroft, Lizzie to all who knew her, had been a bright buxom young woman of eighteen when she met Brooke Steeples, a dashing young second officer in HM navy. Three years of marriage, most of which he had spent in defence of king and country, and umpteen affairs later had put paid to that. She had borne him three children in as many years. With little or no money, and no help from her wayward husband, the harsh years had helped turn her into a gaunt shadow of her former self.

Her marriage was a sham from the start. She had been married only six weeks when Brooke waltzed off with the first of his many conquests, a doe-eyed blonde from the Welsh valleys. In all fairness, William, Brooke's father had tried to warn her that his son was a womanizer and that marrying him would be a mistake. William liked Lizzie and didn't want to see her get hurt, but Brooke was very persuasive, and very handsome, and at the time, she loved him. Lizzie was a positive and determined young woman, who thought she could change him, but men like Brooke never changed, all the warnings fell on deaf ears.

Lizzie and Brooke's family were at the opposite end of the social scale. Her family was typical working class. His was affluent. Brooke's family lived in a large detached house in Greenwood Village, a few miles away from Thistlefield. His father was a man of property. He was owner of an engineering company in Thistlefield, and he also owned houses in the town, and was part owner of the Black Bull pub in Greenwood Village. Among his other accomplishments, he was also a talented opera singer, and he had won many competitions and cash prizes all over the north of England singing the great arias of the renowned Italian tenors Caruso and Gigli. Brooke had been born into this affluent society, the younger of two brothers. With almost ten years between the siblings, Brooke was idolized by his mother. A wealthy woman in her own right; anything he wanted his mother gave him, she looked down on Lizzie from the outset.

In contrast, the house that Lizzie lived in was a typical working class terrace. It had been her dad Colly's house. He had rented it from one of the local landlords up until his death, when it passed to Lizzie. She kept it spic and span as best she could in the circumstances, but with the landlord refusing to do little or no repairs, there was always a smell of damp in the air. The gutters were clogged with muck and they hadn't been cleaned out in years. The windows rattled at the slightest hint of a breeze, and the roof leaked like a sieve. Lizzie knew that to complain only invited eviction. The unscrupulous landlords were only too eager to move in some other unsuspecting souls at an even higher extortionate rent.

However today her home was the last thing on her mind, as she sat in the lobby of the courtroom; it was the last place she wanted to be. She wanted to be a million miles from here. Today was the start of the trial that would change her family's life forever.

Chapter two

May 1938

Twice every year a travelling fair arrived in Thistlefield. It was usually about April or May and again in the autumn around October For some reason it always seemed to rain when the fair was due, but today that didn't bother Lizzie or her best mate Joanie Mathews; hail, rain or snow they were out to have some fun. All the local talent would be there. If you couldn't tap up when the fair was in town, you couldn't tap up anywhere!

Lizzie was a good-looking lass with long dark hair that had a natural kink, and dark sensuous eyes that offset her olive, almost Mediterranean skin, and a figure most of the Hollywood actresses of the day would die for. She was always a target for the local lads who positively drooled over her. Joanie on the other hand was the typical English rose. Fair complexion, peaches and cream skin, the most luxuriant blonde hair a girl could wish for, and the deepest blue eyes anyone had ever seen, topped off with the most perfect hourglass figure. She was the complete opposite of Lizzie.

The dashing young officer was with a gang of his mates on leave from the navy, larking about near the Waltzer. Brooke looked every inch a film star except he wasn't. Tall and athletic, with a shock of jet black hair swept back revealing a face perfectly honed and deeply tanned from his years at sea, he was a magnet for the local talent.

"Are you going on then Brooke or what?" Urged one of Brooke's shipmates; he was eager to show off in front of the group of girls hanging about the steps of the ride.

"In a minute," he said pulling a silver cigarette case from the inside pocket of his uniform and casually lighting up. "Fancy having a go?" He said drawing deeply on the cigarette looking in the direction of the gaggle of girls on the steps.

"Who me?" Said Joanie making her way up the steps.

"No, your friend with the dark hair. Fancy trying it out then?" He said his dark eyes boring into Lizzie.

Joanie nodded her head to indicate that she should. "Go on then Lizzie, he wouldn't have to ask me twice."

Lizzie was stunned, she'd had her fair share of boyfriends, but the really gorgeous ones usually ended up with Joanie, but here was this handsome hunk with the film star looks asking her if she wanted to go on the ride with him. "You mean me?" She asked sheepishly.

"Only if you like, I promise I won't bite." He smiled revealing perfect white teeth. Her life was about to change forever.

Despite the protestations of both her father, who thought she was too young and had only known him five minutes, and of William, who tried to warn her that son Brooke was a notorious womanizer his, she was bowled over by his ready charm and good looks. Within six weeks, they were married. She was eighteen; Brooke was twenty-two. By the time he was demobbed out of the navy, Lizzie had three hungry mouths to feed and a wayward husband to contend with.

Chapter Three

Jake was the first of Lizzie's three children; he was born in September 1939. It was like a production line of babies. Less than a year later Lizzie miscarried her second child, Lottie arrived the following August 1942, and little Jenny in July 1943. Lizzie felt like a prize heifer except they were better treated. Every time Brooke came home on leave, all he wanted her for was sex. It was a constant battle fighting him off, or succumbing to his advances in order to put food on the table. If he didn't get his way at home, there were always plenty of willing floozies. They were easily succumbed by his ready charm and deep pockets.

Maybe living with her dad wasn't ideal, but Brooke was away in the navy most of the time, and she didn't want to be far from her family and friends, what with war looming just around the corner. Brooke was constantly complaining that they should have a place of their own.

Their marriage was a disaster from the start and the mental scars were beginning to tell on Lizzie. They had only been married about six months when Brooke came home on leave with a beautifully wrapped gift box. They had been having a particularly bad time always arguing and fighting.

"What's in the box?" Asked Lizzie somewhat bemused. It was certainly unusual for him to bring anything home that might be for her these days.

"It's a present." He said quite casually. Lizzie's heart soared. Maybe he does think something about me after all she thought. "Can I have a look?" She said hardly able to contain her joy.

"Yes open it; I wanted to get your opinion on it anyway."

"My opinion. What do you mean my opinion?"

"Well you know I wanted to know if the style was right. I'm not much good with women's stuff. I've no idea about colour and size, you know things like that."

She couldn't wait to open the box. She didn't care what the colour was like or if it would fit, at last he had shown her that he loved her. Lizzie opened the box. Inside was the most exquisite dress she had ever seen. Carefully she took it out of its tissue wrapping and held it out in front of her. The black dress had a plunging neckline. There were silver sequins sewn onto the bodice, and it was tied at the back with a silver sash. It appeared to be silk but she wasn't sure, she'd never worn anything made of silk before. It must have cost a fortune. "Oh Brooke it's gorgeous. Can I try it on?" She said affecting a pirouette and spinning round on one foot causing the dress to billow out in front of her.

"Oh it's not for you. I just wanted your opinion on what you think of it," he said matter of factly. Lizzie was stunned; she let the dress fall to the floor.

"Hey be careful with that it cost a lot of money," he said stooping to pick up the fallen garment.

"What do you mean it's not for me?" She cried, the tears beginning to flow freely down her cheeks. "Who's it for then?" She sobbed.

Brooke was seemingly oblivious to his young wife's heartache.

"It's for a girl I've just met. She's about your build and not quite as worn. I just wanted to know what you thought." He said as if it were the most natural thing in the world to break your wife's heart whilst asking her about the style of his latest girlfriend's frock.

"Worn, worn. No wonder I'm bloody worn. You come in here and ask me if this."… She said picking the dress up of the floor and throwing it at him…

"This bloody thing will suit her, or if it's the right size. How do you think that makes me feel? When was the last time you bought me anything, or took me out anywhere? You're never at home, and when you are you never spend time with me; you're always out with some tart or other." She sobbed.

"How do you expect me to fancy you, the state you're in?" He snapped without any feelings for her at all. Lizzie was about six months gone and heavily pregnant. She no longer had the curvaceous figure of a few months ago, as her stomach swelled with the unborn child she was carrying. "It takes two you know, this didn't happen on its own." She said pointing to her swollen abdomen. Brooke looked at her with disgust. "You make me sick, I'm going out." He ranted.

"Well you'll have to leave me some money; we've nothing in the house."

"What about the money I gave you last week? What have you done with that?"

"I spent it, what do you think you've been eating for the last week, grass?" Lizzie shouted, now starting to find some of her old fire.

Brooke's temper was at boiling point. "Ask your dad for some. I'll not keep shelling good money out on this dump. I've told you before we should get a place of our own."

"I'd have been alright in a place of our own, the way you carry on. I'd have been on my own most nights wondering what the bloody hell you've been up to, as if I didn't know."

"Well can you blame me; Look at the state of you."

"How do you expect me to look; I'm your wife if it's not slipped your mind, I could look good if you brought me one of those fancy frocks you're so fond of buying for your fancy bloody tarts." She said unable to hide the indignation in her voice. "I already pay more than my fair share into this hovel as it is. Anyway I'm broke until next month, so you'll just have to wait." He said storming out of the house. Lizzie knew he was lying. His precious mother had seen to it that he wouldn't ever be short of money. She had put thousands of pounds into a trust fund for him along with shares from his father's businesses. The fund matured when he had reached the age of twenty-one, and the interest alone paid him a sizable monthly income.

It was well after six when Colly came home from work. The heat and the stink of toiling in the bleach works gave a man a voracious thirst, and Colly was one of the Platelayers Arms best customers. Lizzie heard her dad coming down the entry, the irons on his clogs sending sparks into the cool evening air as he staggered home. He hung his rucksack behind the back door, and went into the kitchen to swill his face in the brown slop stone sink.

"I've got your favourite for tea dad, tripe an' onions." She said trying to hide her red-rimmed eyes as she set the plate down on the kitchen table.

Colly sat down; he could see that she had been crying. "What's happened, is it him again? I told you before he were no bloody good but you wouldn't listen." He said his thick northern brogue spitting out an acerbic blast.

"Don't be daft dad; I've been peeling onions for your tea."

"Look lass, I might not be the most educated man in the world, god knows, but don't take me for a bloody fool. What's he done this time?" Lizzie couldn't hide anything from her dad; she had never known her mother, she had died bringing her into the world. Colly was all she had. "We rowed over money for the kids; that's all," she said.

"I'll bloody kill him," he raged slamming his fist on the table so hard that the plate bounced spilling the contents onto the kitchen floor.

"Leave it dad it'll sort itself out," she said not believing a word.

Chapter Four

The war had been over almost five years but things were still hard to come by in the winter of 1949. Everything was on ration. The residents of York Street were no different to any other street in the land, everyone was suffering. There was little to buy in the shops and that was assuming anybody had the money to buy what bit there was. Lizzie was up early as usual. Her shift at Taylor's mill started at 7:30am. She had no option, with little or no money from Brooke she had to work. She couldn't keep relying on her dad to put food on the table and clothes on the kids backs, they were her responsibility not his. Washing in the cold brownstone sink was no joke at six on a freezing cold morning; hot water was a luxury she couldn't afford, she would have to make do with the cold tap. She always boiled the kettle for the kids later; at least they could wash their hands and faces in warm water.

Joanie Mathews rapped on the back door, pushing the latch down before letting herself into Lizzie's kitchen. Her blonde curls tucked into her headscarf in an effort to keep the winter chill at bay.

"You ready Lizzie? If we don't get our skates on we'll be late an' you know what a miserable sod Joe Warmsley is."

"Be with you in a minute Joanie, just washing the kid's faces."

"Hello you lot. You lookin' after your mam then?" Said Joanie cheerfully to the brood of youngsters gathered round the sink.

"Hello Joanie." Squirmed Jake trying to wriggle out of his mam's iron grip, as she dug the flannel into his ears making the poor lad squirm even more. It was another typical day in Lizzie's life; up at six, light the fire in the grate that Colly had left set for her. He never lit the fire for himself preferring to leave it for Lizzie and the kids. Coal cost money, and there was little enough as it was.

"Come on you lot, off to Mrs Fishers," said Lizzie trying to galvanize some life into her young brood. Jake who had just turned ten had his balaclava pulled up over his nose leaving only his dark brown eyes showing and a wisp of dark hair sneaking out over his forehead. Jenny and Lottie were both dressed in identical pink bonnets with a white bob on top, and matching scarves were wrapped tightly round their necks to keep out the early morning chill. The short walk to Mrs Fishers was accompanied by the usual protestations from Jake on the need to go to school. The children safely dropped off, Lizzie and Joanie hurried up the cobbled street to Taylor's.

"How're things then?" Asked Lizzie patting Joanie's bulging stomach, heavy with her first child.

"Oh you know the usual, sick every morning, can't keep a bloody thing down, even a cuppa' sends me running to the lav heaving my guts up." She said trying to be cheerful. "Anyway how're you? Brooke still hanging around? I thought you'd divorced him years ago." It was always more than one question at a time with Joanie, It seemed she had to know everything at once, but she'd always been a good friend to Lizzie. "Yeah I did. Jake was only three when I finally got shut of him. He still comes round from time to time though. Since he took that job at his dad's place in Thistlefield, he's never away. I see more of him now than I did when we were married." She said sheepishly.

"Why don't you tell him to bugger off? Is he still carrying on with that tarty piece from the village? Why you put up with him is beyond me."

"What tarty piece from the village? I didn't know he was carrying on with anybody at the minute, not that it's any of my business anyway." Lizzie replied defensively.

Joanie could see that Lizzie was upset. "Oh didn't you know love, I'm sorry. Me an' my bloody mouth it'll get me soddin' hung one of these days. I thought you knew. My Arthur's seen 'im in the pub with her. A big brassy redhead, just 'is type. Still they're all 'is type aren't they love?"

Lizzie hunched herself deep into her coat. "Come on hurry up we'll be late," she said hurrying up the street.

Chapter Five

"Good morning ladies, glad you could make it," said mill manager Joe Warmsley looking at his pocket watch.

"Bugger off Joe, I'm not in the mood for your bloody sarcasm, get out me way, I need the lav," said Joanie angrily squeezing past him.

"What's up with her got her knickers in a twist again?"

"Leave her alone Joe, can't you see she's not feeling herself," said Lizzie in defence of her friend. Joanie had been trying to keep her pregnancy a secret, trying her best to hide it underneath her pinny. Up to now, she had managed it, but it was getting harder and harder, the further on she went.

"She's always on the bloody lav. I'm watchin' the pair of you. Anyway it's time you started its gone half past," he snapped unpleasantly.

Lizzie went into the card room. The dust was already causing her to cough as she covered her face with a scarf. Grime clung to every part of the building. Everything was covered in a layer of cotton and dust from the constant motion of the machinery. It was hard to make yourself heard above the perpetual noise and relentless clattering of the apparatus. Especially noisy were the spinning and weaving sheds. The only form of communication in most mills was a form of sign language, perfected and passed down by generations of mill workers; mothers to daughters, and fathers to sons. The air was thick with dust; there were no breathing masks, and no sophisticated extraction systems to clear the polluted air. The only extraction was through the open windows, and the only way to stop the dust entering your lungs was to wear a hanky or a scarf over your face.

The card room was one of the dirtiest places in the mill. The huge bales were fed through a huge carding machine. This combed the raw cotton by passing it through a series of rollers. The rollers took out the knots and impurities in the raw cotton before it was eventually fed into large cans where it came out as thick as rope, before it went onto the spinning room to be spun into cotton. This was Lizzie and Joanie's work place.

The open windows blew a draught of wintery air into the card-room, making it feel as if the women were working outside instead of enclosed inside their gloomy environment. Even in spite of the chill, Joanie was sweating as she fed the huge bales of cotton onto the rollers.

Lizzie; "I'll 'ave to 'ave a minute. I'm goin' outside for a smoke, I'll not be long."

"Try not to be too long, hey love. You know what his lordship's like."

Joe Warmsley wasn't the most popular boss at Taylor's. Lizzie had always tried to cover for her friend. She'd always been there for her especially when she first divorced Brooke. Joanie hadn't had an easy time since she got pregnant. She and husband Arthur had been trying for a baby for years but just when they had given up hope of ever having a family, bingo there she was, in the family way.

It was as if Joe had built in radar. Joanie hadn't been gone a minute when he appeared out of nowhere. "Where's your mate? Not skivin' 'agen' is she?"

"She'll not be a minute; she's just getting a breath of air. I told you she's been off colour lately."

"We don't pay wages so you can bugger off anytime you feel like it. If she's not up to it, I can soon replace 'er, there's a dozen more waitin' for her job." He said cynically not hiding the irritatingly self-satisfied tone in his voice.

"No need for that Joe, I'll keep her machine running 'till she gets back," said Lizzie smiling provocatively at him. She hated herself for playing up to the lecherous womanizer, but she felt she had a duty to look out for her mate. It seemed all the men she knew were tarred with the same brush, how soon they could get you into bed.

"When are you goin' to come out wi me?" He said grabbing her round the waist and pulling her roughly to him. She could feel the buckle of his belt pressing into her stomach as he ground his loins into her, his breathing heavy with lust. She turned away, the stubs of his yellow and blackened teeth and rancid breath repulsing her. "Not here Joe somebody might come in," she said forcing his dirty oil stained hands from her breast.

"When then? You keep sayin' you'll come out wi me but all I get is excuses."

"I've got three kids Joe, it's not easy, and my dad watches me like a hawk. I promise I'll come out with you as soon as I can sort something out with the kids. It's not that I don't want to Joe," she lied pulling away from his iron grip.

Just then, Joanie walked back into the card-room. "Hiya Joe, how's it goin'?" She said cheerily as if nothing was amiss.

"Where the bloody 'ell 'av' you bin? Get back to yer work yer lazy cow; any more slackin' by the pair o' you an' yer out." He snarled shaking his grubby thumb in the direction of the door, making it plain what he meant.

'What the 'ells got into 'im?' Said Joanie.

"The usual, I wouldn't go out with him," said Lizzie.

"You mean you wouldn't let 'im get 'is filthy paws inside yer knickers."

"That's about the size of it. He's been trying for months, ever since me and Brooke broke up."

"He's an 'orrible bastard that," said Joanie, not one for expletives. 'I wouldn't trust 'im as far as I could spit. You want to be careful of 'im Lizzie, he's a bad 'un an' no mistake."

"I know, but I need this job. Dad does his best, but without what I make here we could barely make ends meet," she said heaving another bale of cotton onto the already groaning rollers. "What about Brooke I thought he 'ad to pay maintenance to you an' the kids?"

"You must be joking he's not paid me a penny in months, to busy with his other women."

"But what about Christmas? It's only a couple of weeks off. Surely he'll not see you an' the kids short at Christmas."

"I'm sick of telling him. The kids are pestering me all the time about presents bless them. But what can I do, they're his kids too, but he doesn't bloody care, all he's bothered about is how soon he can get me in bed." Lizzie turned away her eyes brimming with tears.

"Come on love don't take on so." Joanie stopped for a moment. "You've not, you know, let 'im?'

'Oh Joanie I feel like a cheap whore, but it's the only way I can get anything out of him. If dad finds out he'll kill him and then me too like as not."

"I always knew 'e was a bastard, but I didn't think even 'e would stoop that low the bloody swine," said Joanie sympathetically'

'You don't know the half of it," said Lizzie dabbing her eyes. 'We'd better get this lot finished up before his lordship comes back," she said trying to put on a brave face.

"Bloody men. Who'd 'av 'em? ' Scoffed Joanie.

'Your Arthur's a decent lad though. You've got a good one there,' said Lizzie.

'Yeah I know." She said with a rueful smile.

Chapter Six

The maintenance office in Thistlefield was situated at the bottom of King Street. It was a soul-less grey-stoned building attached to the equally drab magistrates' court. It was where errant husbands were supposed to pay money in. This was money awarded by the courts in divorce cases for the upkeep and welfare of their offspring. Brooke though didn't think this applied to him and he was often late with his payments; that's if he bothered at all.

The freezing December air chilled little Jake to the bone. He stamped his feet to try and get some warmth back into his frozen toes. His worn shoes badly needed repair, but it cost five shillings at Mr Topping's cobblers to have them soled and heeled, and his mam hadn't got five pence to spare never mind five bob. His jacket was threadbare, and his grey school pullover had seen better days. It had been darned so often there was more darning in it than the original wool. He had rushed from St Thomas's school at four o'clock to the 'office' as his mam called it, in the hope that his dad had put his money in. Outside of the dreary building, he swung his arms and patted his shoulders to try and keep warm. He was thinking of the box of toy lorries that he'd seen the other day on one of his frequent visits to the town, in Oxley's shop window. There was a tipper truck, a concrete mixer, a milk truck complete with miniature urns, and an articulated truck complete with detachable trailer. He could have hours of fun with those, maybe even start his own haulage company one day, he dreamed. If only dad would put his money in. As usual, he was late. Every Friday was the same, he was never early, and that's if he came at all. Jake looked up and down King Street in the hope of seeing his dad's new Austin. He had been stood in the cold for over an hour his feet were so cold he could barely feel his toes. The licence plate PDD 482 would be stamped in his memory forever, the amount of times he had spent waiting for it to arrive. It was only a week to Christmas and there was no sign he or his sisters would be getting any presents at all this year. There was almost no coal for the fire, and it looked like there wouldn't be much in the way of a Christmas dinner. Maybe his granddad Colly would help out with the Christmas presents. He loved his granddad, but these days he seemed moodier than ever thought Jake as he wrapped his arms round his thin shoulders to keep out the cold. One minute he was as good as gold, the next he was ranting and raving all over the place. Maybe he'd just had too much to drink thought Jake, or maybe he'd had enough of seeing his mam suffer at the hands of his dad. He'd often heard his granddad swear about his dad telling his mam he were "no bloody good." For whatever reason he wasn't the same granddad he was used to.

It was twenty past five and the 'office' was getting ready to close. Jake went back inside to restore the circulation to his frozen feet. Alan Hastings the chief clerk behind the counter asked. "No sign of him yet Jake?" He was on first name terms with the youngster; he had known him that long.

"No not yet, maybe he's been held up at work; he's been really busy since they made him manager of that building firm," he said rubbing his frozen fingers together to create a bit of warmth.

It wasn't lost on Alan. "I'll give it another five minutes then I'll really have to shut the office," he said warmly to the young lad. It wouldn't be the first time his dad had turned up right at the last minute. It was almost as if the selfish bastard got some kind of kick out of making his kids suffer.

"Thanks," said Jake going back out into the street to see if his dad's car was anywhere in sight. The minutes ticked by slowly.

"I don't think he's coming tonight Jake. Here," said Alan pushing a shilling into his tiny frozen hand. "Go across to Evelyn's and get yourself a glass of hot Vimto, it'll warm you up."

The boy's eyes lit up at the sight of a whole shilling. It was more money than he could ever imagine. "Thanks Mr Hastings but I'll hang on for another five minutes if that's ok with you."

"Ok Jake, but I'll have to shut the office soon." Poor kid thought Alan, having a bastard like that for a dad.

"He never came mam, I waited 'till the 'office' shut but he never came."

"It's alright love." said Lizzie with a sigh. "Come over by the fire and get yourself warm you must be frozen through."

"I'm alright mam. I went to Evelyn's and got a hot Vimto. Mr Hastings give me a shilling; you can have it if you like. Evelyn said I could have the Vimto for nothing as she was closing up anyway and it would only get wasted." Evelyn knew Jake's dad as well.

"No you're alright Jake you keep it, maybe you can buy Jenny and Lottie a sherbet dab from the corner shop tomorrow," She said putting another rapidly diminishing lump of coal into the grate. At this rate, we'll be lucky to have enough to last the weekend she thought, as she poked the dying embers back into flame.

"Jake shout to your sisters to come in from the back yard, and tell Maureen and Charlie tea's nearly ready, and then nip down to the Platelayer's and tell your granddad his tea's on the table, there's a good lad."

Jake liked going down the pub where his granddad drank. Sometimes on a Friday, the men would give him a penny for a square iced lolly from Dolly Evans corner shop. He hoped he would get a penny tonight.

Lizzie lifted the large earthenware pot out of the oven in the Yorkshire grate and set it down in the middle of the kitchen table. The big pot sizzled and bubbled like a cauldron as Lizzie heaped the steaming stew into the hungry children's bowls.

"Can I have a piece of pie crust mam?" Said Jake, his mouth watering at the thought of the delicious pastry his mam had made to top off the stew. "In a minute. Go and tell your uncle Bob and auntie Alice I'm putting tea on the table."

"Hmm summat smells good," said Bob to his sister Lizzie.

"Aye it does that lass," said Alice. "Is there anything I can do?"

"No just sit yourselves down. Dad are you ready? I'm putting the tea out."

"Aye, I'll be there in a minute, I'm just swillin' me face." He shouted from the back kitchen.

61 York Street was bigger than most of the houses of the area. Being on a corner it had a bigger frontage than most of the others with a sizable front room that bordered Vere Street. The large narrow kitchen stretched all the way through from the front to the back of the house. In the corner of the kitchen just opposite the back door was a large brick boiler. On washdays this would be lit and all the heavy wash, sheets and bedding and the like, would be boiled ready for hanging out. A typical washday would see

sheets hung out across the street from house to house in their dozens, like an armada of sail waiting to go to war. Being on the corner, Colly's house had the luxury of an extra room at the front. It was usual to use this as a parlour or best room, and was only used for special occasions, such as weddings or more usually funerals, where often the bodies of the deceased were laid out. But on this occasion, it was occupied by Bob and his family. It was the best Lizzie could do for them in the circumstances since Bob had lost his job at the local foundry. Bob Ashcroft was a likable lad, but he was apt to be a bit work-shy. He'd got up late for his shift at the foundry one morning after a late night spent down the pub with his mates. When he turned in the foreman left him in no doubts that this would be the last time he would tolerate him being late. Bob being Bob wasn't one for being told what to do, and had promptly left the foreman dumped on his arse on the foundry floor nursing a black eye. Needless to say, he got his cards and hadn't worked since. It wasn't long before the house he was renting was in arrears with the rent and they were thrown out onto the streets. It had taken all of Lizzie's persuasive powers to get her dad not to see Alice and the kids homeless. Colly's front room was no picnic, but it was better than the street.

The evening meal was a noisy affair with four hungry mouths excitedly chattering about what they hoped to get for Christmas. The adults though weren't in as such good spirits as the children.

It was Alice who broke the melancholy mood. "Did Brooke put his money in?" She whispered to Lizzie not wanting to let Colly overhear.

"No little Jake was there 'till half past five but the bugger never came. Poor little thing was frozen through."

Alice tut tutted. 'How can a father see his kids have nothing' at this time of year?"

Colly had overheard Alice. "He's not a bloody man that bastard," he raged. The children stopped their animated chattering, startled by their granddad's sudden outburst of temper. They had rarely seen this side of him.

"Jake take the others into the front room and play, there's a good lad," said Lizzie fearing her dad's sombre mood.

"Aw mam we've not finished," Moaned Jake.

"Take it with you, and mind you don't spill anything on the floor." She said. Jake knew when not to argue especially when his granddad was in one of his funny moods. He knew they were better off out of the way.

"Dad don't go upsetting yourself," said Lizzie clearing the dishes from the table.

"Upsetting myself; I'm bloody sick of seeing you and the kids struggling week in and week out, while that bastard gets off scot free."

"We'll manage, we've managed before, and we'll manage again," she said scraping the leftovers into the fire causing it to spit and crackle as the scraps hit the dying embers.

"Why should you have to manage? He should pay what he owes you; god knows he's enough bloody money. They're his kids as well as yours. Anyway I'm goin' t' Platelayers," he ranted pulling the peak of his cap over his forehead.

Lizzie knew he was right, every week was the same, and she was always begging money off him for one thing or another. He never refused her or the children, but she sensed his patience was wearing thin with her errant ex-husband. These days Colly was spending more and more time at the pub; it was if he was trying to escape. He'd always liked a drink, but now it was as if he couldn't cope without one.

Lizzie was worried sick. "Bob go with dad see he's alright," she said pushing half a crown into his hand.

"Lizzie I can't take this." He said looking at the large silver coin.

'It's alright it's part of the coal money, I'll get the rest for next week when he's due." Bob had little or no money of his own. The dole didn't provide for drink, he could barely provide enough food for the kids. If it hadn't been for Lizzie's generosity when she could, he'd have forgotten what beer tasted like.

"Don't worry about the coal I'll not see us freeze." He said pecking her on the cheek as he hurried out after his dad.

"Get away with you, you daft h'aporth, go on, and keep an eye on dad for me."

He might be a bit work-shy but Bob had a heart of gold, and if he could do anybody a good turn, he would.

Chapter seven

At three o'clock in the morning, the railway coal yard was a damp desolate place to be. The only light illuminating the grimy yard, came from the distant lamps that threw deformed shadows over the piles of coal heaped in the deserted station sidings. At this ungodly hour, Bob and his mate Eric Braxton were crouched down behind two great mounds of best coal, their faces blackened with coal dust, as if they were on some top-secret mission for the commandoes.

"Christ, Bob," exclaimed Eric, blowing into his frozen hands. "How much longer are we goin' t' be? I'm freezing me soddin' bollocks off here." The temperature must have been minus three degrees in the coal yard.

"Shush, he's on his way round now," said Bob indicating towards the night watchman. He was ambling in their direction, his lantern swinging in the cold night air. "I've watched him for a week. He's round every hour till three o'clock. He gets to the corner there," said Bob pointing to a spot in the distance. "Has a quick look round and then he goes back to his cabin, stokes up the boiler, and he doesn't move again till six. That'll give us plenty of time to fill a good few sacks and get them on the cart."

"Where's the cart?" asked Eric clapping his hands together, in order to revive the circulation.

"Keep bloody quiet or we'll all end up in the nick. It's with Billy. He's on the other side of the fence trying to keep the horse quiet," whispered Bob.

"'Orse, what bloody 'orse? You never said owt t' me about a bloody 'orse," said Eric, his northern inflection thicker than a London smog. Billy Kendal was the third member of the band of unlikely thieves. He was trying his best to keep the moth-eaten horse from giving the game away, by constantly shoving the poor creatures head into a bag of oats.

Not to be deterred, Eric who wasn't the brightest star in the sky pressed on. "What do we need a bloody 'orse for anyway?"

"How else do you think we were going to move half a ton of best coal in the middle of the night? Stuff it in our pockets, you daft bugger," chuckled Bob.

The night watchman was only about thirty feet from where the two men where crouched. He swung his lantern and gave a cursory glance in their direction, before turning and heading back to the warmth of his cabin for a nip of the Scotch he'd got stashed away. It was too damn cold to be messing about outside at this time of year.

It was after five o' clock when they finally loaded the last of the coal onto the back of the cart. It wouldn't be long before the night-watchman was doing his rounds again.

"Phew that's the last of it." Said Bob with a sigh of relief. "All we've got to do now is shift it somewhere safe."

Billy was doing his best to keep the horse from giving the game away. The poor beast had been standing so long it continually stamped its hooves and snorted as if it were about to take its last breath. To make matters worse it started to rain, not heavily, but a steady drizzle, the sort that soaked you through and chilled you to the bone. The blanket that covered the horse was becoming increasingly wet and the unfortunate beast gave an involuntary shudder as the damp seeped into its skin.

"We'd best get goin' before old Betsy 'ere keels o'er on us," said Billy gently patting her nose.

"Aye, come on, let's get moving the old feller will be round again shortly and I don't want to be here when he comes," said Bob. "Eric throw that cover over them sacks, we don't need no prying eyes to see what we've been up to."

Old Betsy wasn't in the full flush of youth, and it took all of the old girls strength and a lot of coaxing and swearing from the three men to finally get her moving. "We should 'a brought a carrot," said Eric with stupid grin on his face.

"I'll give you a soddin carrot if you don't shut up and push," said Bob heaving at the cartwheel in order to get it moving. "If we don't get this thing going soon we'll all end up in the bloody nick, now stop yer gassin' and shove." Billy sat on top, while Bob and Eric heaved at the back of the over-laden cart. With a last mighty effort, they managed to get it moving. Slowly the cart inched its way out from behind the fence that had kept it hidden. Betsy gave another great snort and heaved as Billy flicked the whip to coax a last effort out of her. At last, it was moving but it was slow and cumbersome. The coal yard was badly pitted, and there were deep ruts that did everything to hinder their progress. At last, they made it to the gap in the fence.

"Nearly there now, if we can just get through here we'll be onto the road proper," said Bob. Suddenly there was a flash of light.

"What the bloody 'ell were that?" Said Billy still sat on top of the cart like some latter day shot gun rider from a John Wayne movie.

"Bugger me! It's the old feller; he's back on his rounds," exclaimed Bob. "Quick get through the gap afore he sees us." With a last shove, the cart went through the gap in the fence with a mighty crash, and onto the road.

"Hey, who's there?" Cried the night watchman running as fast as his old legs would take him, his lantern held out in his outstretched arm, swinging like a demented beacon.

"Stop thief." He shouted at the top of his voice. Betsy was going like the clappers now that she had a bit of firm ground under her feet.

"Gee up," urged Billy as he tried to coax more effort out of the aging nag.

"If we can get to the bridge a couple of hundred yards further on, there's a double sided gate just at the top of Vere Street, you know one of them big buggers that leads into the back of old Ma Jenkins's yard. She'll hide us till that daft old bugger stops his hollering. The way he's carrying on he'll wake the bloody dead," said Bob anxious to put as much distance between them and the coal yard as he could. Betsy was now doing a sterling job and the cart was rattling up the road as fast as her old legs would carry her.

The night watchman's bellowing had alerted the local bobby who was just about to go off duty. Eager to get home to a hot brew and a warm bed after a night walking his beat which included the coal yard, PC Freddy Jarrod was in no mood for chasing criminals, not at this ungodly hour in the morning. He had spent the night sorting out a brawl at the Kings Arms, where he had suffered the ignominy of a black eye. What he would say to his mates back at the station god only knew! Then he was called to assist in a domestic, where a woman and her six kids had been thrown out into the street, after her husband had come home drunk and threatened to burn the house down unless she cooked him his tea at two in the morning! To cap it all he'd been called to an address in Great George's Street. The neighbours said they had heard suspicious noises coming from the ginnel. When PC Jarrod arrived, he discovered that the noises were the neighbourhood cats, tipping bins over, no doubt chasing mice!! Now because a geriatric watchman was hollering his bloody head off because somebody was nicking a few hundred weight of coal, he was expected to go chasing the buggers all over the show at this hour in the morning, just as he was about to go off duty. "There were three of them you say. Which way were they going?"

"Up the road towards Potters Lane I think," said the night watchman rubbing his rheumy eyes tired from lack of sleep. "And you think they've been pinching coal."

"Oh aye, you can see where they've been. They must 'ave got at least a ton," exaggerated the old man. Poor buggers must have needed it if they'd got up at this hour to pinch it, thought PC Jarrod. He knew most of the locals on his beat. They weren't hardened criminals, by any means; mostly on the dole, drifting in and out of one dead end job after another, unable to find decent work after giving all for king and country. A bit rowdy after a night on the ale, and maybe a bit of petty pilfering but nothing serious, but still he had a duty to perform.

Bob and his gang of unlikely crooks were under the bridge and nearing the top of Potters Lane, the clip clop of Betsy's hooves echoing off the road as they turned into Vere Street. Billy jumped off the cart and rushed to the small gate that was built-in to the larger one.

Bob was at the top of the street keeping watch. "Hurry up," he hissed. There's somebody coming." He could hear the irons on the bobby's boots as he strode up the street. The large green doors groaned on their rusty hinges, as Billy and Eric coaxed Betsy through them and into the yard at the back.

"Bloody hell it's Freddy Jarrod he should have been in his bed by now," cried Bob rushing back to see if the horse was safely hidden away. "Keep her quiet, and I'll try and get rid of him. If he catches us with that lot, we'll all be up before the magistrates tomorrow."

Bob ran back to the corner just as PC Jarrod got there. "Morning Freddy; thought you'd be in yer bed by now," said Bob innocently gasping for breath.

"It's PC Jarrod if you don't mind, and might I ask what you're doing up at this hour?"

"Me officer, I'm just off to Toppin's to get a packet of fags I've run out," replied Bob casually.

"At this time of a morning," said Jarrod suspiciously. "You've not seen three men come past this way in the last few minutes have you?"

"Three men, what would three men be doing out at this bloody hour on a freezing morning?" Said Bob.

"Three men and a horse and cart to be precise," said Jarrod feeling slightly peeved, that he wasn't in his bed.

"Three men and a horse and cart; you sure you haven't been drinking officer?" Said Bob with a grin.

"You can wipe that silly bloody smirk off your face. Well have you seen anything?" said the disgruntled bobby.

"Oh aye they galloped past about ten minutes back chased by a hoard of blood thirsty injuns," laughed Bob.

PC Jarrod was not amused. He wanted his bed it was way past the end of his shift. "I asked you before. How come you're up at this hour?"

"Well you know how it is. One of the kids has been up all night, got the runs so I never got much sleep and I just fancied a fag."

Just then, there was a whinnying from around the corner. "What was that?" said Jarrod suspiciously.

"What was what?" said Bob beginning to hawk and cough violently. "Oh Jesus, I think I'm having a heart attack," said Bob hawking and coughing even louder and clutching his chest.

"Are you alright?" said the bemused bobby taking hold of Bob's shoulder as he doubled up in agony. "Yeah I'll be fine I just need a fag to get this bloody phlegm off me chest." he said continuing to splutter.

"You should give them things up they'll be the death of you," said Jarrod with suspicious concern.

"I know I'm trying but it's a hard habit to kick."

"Come on I'll see you home."

"There's no need. If I can just get me fags, I'll be ok. Toppin's is only up the road, I'll be ok."

"Well be quick about it. If you're not back home in ten bloody minutes, I'll run you in. Now bugger off, an' let me get to my bed, It's way past my bedtime anyway," said PC Jarrod tetchily, seemingly to forget the three men he was chasing and eager to be on his way home.

Bob waited for a few minutes until Jarrod was out of sight, before joining his partners in crime. "Phew that were close. I thought he were goin to collar us there for a minute," Said Bob to his two cohorts.

Chapter eight

It was Christmas Eve. Even though Bob's efforts had put a fire in the grate there was little else to be cheerful about. As usual, Brooke was late with his payment and it looked as if the kids would be going without presents again this Christmas. Jake had been stood outside the 'office' since nine o'clock in the morning and there was still no sign of his dad. His mam had given him a shilling to ring his dad's office in Thistlefield but every time he got through, he was told to ring back later as he wasn't in yet. It was late afternoon and he was down to his last couple of coppers if he didn't catch him this time, he wouldn't have enough money to ring again, best if he waited a bit longer. He'd been home a few times to report back to his mam, but the afternoon was drawing to a close and the light was starting to go. He decided to wait until the very last minute to give him the best chance to catch his dad in. It was almost four o'clock maybe another half hour then he would phone again. He looked up and down King Street for the familiar sight of his dad's Austin but there was no sign. He went back into the 'office'.

"Still no sign of him yet Jake?" asked Alan behind the counter. Jake just shook his head disconsolately.

"They said I should ring back later. He should be in by then." Jake looked up at the clock on the office wall. Ten past four, another twenty minutes and he would phone again. "Here go and get yourself a hot drink at Evelyn's, and I'll give you a shout if he comes." said Alan pushing a shilling towards Jake.

"No it's alright really. I prefer to wait here I don't want to miss him."

"Well, take it anyway you can still get one later if you like."

"Thanks," said Jake sheepishly taking the coin and stuffing it into his trouser pocket. The twenty minutes seemed to take forever finally, it was half past four. He would go and ring him again. He went to the phone box on the corner. Bugger there was somebody in there. He hung around outside the box. "Hurry up," he muttered to himself. He went to the side of the box and stared in. The woman could just about fit in the phone box, thought Jake. She was huge. Her fat bottom was poking out the phone box door. He was sorely tempted to kick her fat arse. She was animatedly chattering away to some unknown confidante on the other end of the line. She pushed Jake aside and tried in vain to close the door but her backside still stuck out like a beached whale. Jake waited patiently while the woman gabbled away to whoever it was on the other end of the line. At last, after what seemed ages, the woman put the phone back on the receiver. She muttered something about ignorant little boys and gave Jake a dirty look as she brushed past him, her fat posterior almost crushing him against side of the booth. His frozen fingers inserted the four pennies as quickly as he could into the slot. He dialled his dad's office number. It was ringing for ages. Please don't let them have gone home thought Jake. At last, someone lifted the receiver.

"Altitude Steel how can I help you," said the voice on the other end of the line.

Jake recognized Kathy his dad's secretary. "Is my dad there? It's Jake," said the timid voice.

"Hold on Jake I'll put you through."

At last, he thought I've caught him. "Dad its Jake. My mam says are you going to put your money in 'cause it's

Christmas and she hasn't got any money to buy presents or ood or anything," he said pitifully.

"Hello Jake, It's a bit late to get to the office now. I've been working late again and I've not been able to get away. Go home and tell your mam that I'll bring the money round to your house as soon as I leave here, there's a good lad."

"Ok I'll go and tell her straight away. You won't forget will you dad? It's Christmas day tomorrow."

"No I won't forget."

Jake ran back into the office. "Dad's bringing mam's money round to the house as soon as he finishes work," he said excitedly to Alan.

"That's good Jake I'm very happy to hear it."

"I won't be needing this now, will I?" said Jake excitedly, pulling the shilling from his trouser pocket and pushing it back towards Alan.

"You keep it son."

"Are you sure, my dad's coming round later an' he's going to give us some money."

"No I'm sure, you keep hold of it and have a nice Christmas."

"Thanks Mr. Hastings you have a nice Christmas too," said Jake galloping up King Street as fast as his young legs would carry him. He rushed in the back door of number sixty-one. "Mam, mam, I caught dad in. I spoke to him on the phone. He's going to bring the money round; he says it's too late to put the money in the office.

"You mean he never came to the office," said Lizzie in despair.

"No I spoke to him on the phone mam. He said he was going to bring the money round to our house 'cause it was too late to go to the 'office'"

Lizzie looked at the clock on the mantelpiece, it was ten to five now, and all the shops shut at six. If he didn't come soon he might as well not come at all. Slowly the clock crept past five and then onto quarter past, and still no sign of Brooke, not that she really believed he would turn up anyway. Jake was constantly in the window willing his dad to come.

"Mam, mam, he's here," said Jake excitedly as his dad's Austin pulled up outside the house.

Lizzie couldn't share Jakes excitement. She only felt anger and resentment as she had to depend on such a wastrel for her kids Christmas. "You took your bloody time. I hope you realize your kids have no presents and I've not a scrap in the house, and nearly everywhere is shutting for Christmas," she said bitterly.

"I couldn't get away any sooner. If we hurry we can still get to the town centre, some of the shops there stay open a bit later at Christmas," he said trying to appease her. Jake hoped his mam and dad weren't going to argue all night otherwise all the shops would be shut, and there would be no Christmas.

Christmas morning was all noise and pandemonium as the kids excitedly opened their meagre Christmas stockings. Lizzie had been up until the small hours carefully wrapping the few measly gifts that Brooke's money had bought. Lizzie had pleaded with him for a bit extra with it being Christmas, but as usual, any extra came with conditions. Lizzie was determined she wouldn't go to bed with him even if it meant they would have no Christmas. It was always the same, she was sick of behaving like a prostitute just to put food on the table. This time she was determined he'd have to find some other unsuspecting soul to gratify his carnal lusts.

Chapter nine

The New Year started much as the old one had finished. January 1950 was just as austere as the previous one. Lizzie was wrapped up against the biting cold as she trudged wearily up the street to Taylor's mill. The cough she'd had for the past couple of weeks had shown no sign of easing.

Joanie was worried about her. "It's time you went to the doctors with that cough, you've had it for weeks now, an' you've lost weight," she said, concern etched in her voice.

"I'm alright it's only a cough. I'll be ok when I've had a fag and a cuppa," she said trying to be cheerful. "Anyway you're the one to talk; how long before the baby's due?"

"Oh, a couple of months yet; it's due about the end of February beginin' of March," she said patting the ever-growing bump in her stomach.

"But you really should see a doctor. It doesn't cost anything these days. Not since the NHS started up a couple of years ago."

"I'll go in a few days if it doesn't get any better," she promised.

"Anyway how long are you going to be working? You can't go on forever, not with that in front of you," said Lizzie pointing to Joanie's swelling stomach.

"A couple of weeks at the most; Arthur wants me to finish straight away but I've told him I'll finish in a week or two. Anyway, somebody's got to keep an eye on you. Come on or we'll be late."

Lizzie was still working in the card room whilst Joanie had been given a lighter job in the spinning room. Joe had caught her coming out of the toilet one morning and spotted her bulging stomach. He had threatened to finish her on the spot. It was only Lizzie's intervention that had stopped him. She pleaded with him to let Joanie stay on a few more weeks. He agreed, but only if she would have a night out with him. She agreed for Joanie's sake and spent most of the night fighting off his amorous advances. Luckily, it had kept Joanie in her job. Lizzie dreaded going into work these days. The card room was hard heavy dirty work, and her health was making it almost impossible to do, that and constantly having to fight off Joe's advances, these days was no picnic.

She had asked Joe for a lighter job. However, Lizzie was told that there was only one vacancy in the spinning room so she agreed Joanie could have it.

Half way through her shift Lizzie went outside to get a breath of air and a smoke. Smoking was banned in the card room as a loose spark could set off a major fire risk.

She was in the yard when Joe spotted her. "Lizzie I'm glad I've seen you. I think there might be a job goin' in the spinnin' room in a couple o' weeks. I've been talkin' to Joanie an' she tells me she's packin' in soon. The manager in the spinning shed's a good mate of mine. I could put in a good word for you if you like."

"That'd be great Joe. I could do with a lighter job; this one's getting a bit heavy these days. Do you think I'll have a chance?"

"You will if I say so. But course you don't get anything for nothing in this life," he said with a smirk. Lizzie knew what was coming. There was always a hidden agenda with Joe.

"Joe I've told you what dad's like. He watches me like a hawk."

"Well your dad's not here now is he?" he said coming closer to her. "Come on give us a kiss." His hot rancid breath stinging her eyes as his lips brushed hers.

"No, not here Joe, somebody might see us," she said pushing him away.

"In here then." He said pushing her into the waste cotton store. She stumbled and fell backwards onto the floor. Joe was on her in an instant. His thrust his greasy hands up under her skirt and tried to pull down her knickers. He fumbled with his trousers as he feverishly tried to undo the buttons. Lizzie tried to fight him off and punched feebly at his face, her strength almost gone. He slapped her hands away; knocking the cigarette she had been smoking into a pile of loose cotton waste. Moments later, it began to smoulder, but Joe in his lustful frenzy hadn't seen it. Lizzie did her best to fight him off but she was weak from her illness and he was to strong. He forced his hand between her thighs and tore the flimsy garment down below her knees. The sight of her nakedness only seemed to enflame his lust even more. Lizzie screamed but there was no one to hear her cries. She scratched at his face but he slapped her hand away as he tried to force himself upon her. The cotton waste was well alight by now and smoke was billowing from the store. Lizzie choked as the smoke and fumes engulfed the store. Joe realized there was something up and hastily buttoned up his trousers. He ran outside to find a group of workers gathered by the door wondering what was going on.

"What's up Joe?" asked one bemused spectator, as the smoke continued to billow out of the room. "A bloody idiot decided to 'ave a smoke in there an' dropped a fag end in the waste,' he said pointing to the store. "Has anybody called the fire brigade?"

"Yeah somebody saw the smoke and called them. They're on their way now," said another onlooker.

"Is there anyone else in there?" said a woman with her hair wrapped in a scarf.

Just then Lizzie stumbled through the door, her eyes were streaming and her face was black from the smoke and fumes.

"It's Lizzie Steeples," cried the woman in the headscarf. She was coughing and choking; her clothes were dishevelled as she collapsed in a heap on the floor of the yard. "Quick somebody get the nurse," said the woman cradling Lizzie's head in her arms. "It's alright love the nurse she'll be along in a minute try not to move."

"He tried to rape me," she gasped.

"You what? Who tried to rape you?" said the woman.

"He did; Joe Warmsley." She coughed.

By now, the entire spinning shed had been evacuated to the yard.

Joanie found Lizzie. "What happened? What's goin' on?"

"Oh Joanie he tried to rape me." She sobbed.

"Who tried to rape you? Has anybody sent for the doctor?" said Joanie bending over her stricken mate.

"Shush, love the doctor he'll be here soon."

"Who tried to rape you Lizzie?" asked Joanie again.

"It were Joe Warmsley. I was having a smoke. The next thing he's telling me there might be a chance of a lighter job in spinning shed. Before I could blink we're in the cotton store and he's on top of me. I tried to get him off but he was just too heavy," she sobbed.

"It's alright love." She said patting Lizzie's hand. "The nurse is here you'll be alright now."

"Come on love let's get you into the surgery where I can get a better look at you," said Nurse Johnson sympathetically.

Joe was still bent over coughing and spluttering trying to find an ally in the gathering throng. His reputation was well known especially amongst the female members of the crowd.

"I caught her smoking in the cotton store," he said defensively to no one in particular. "I told her to put it out, the next thing I know she on me like a wildcat. I tried to defend myself, but she bloody near tore my eye out." He said pointing to the scratches raked down one side of his face.

"You most likely deserved it you dirty bugger." Rasped a female voice he could hear but not see amongst the crowd of people.

The fire brigade arrived and soon had the blaze under control. Apart from a few bales of cotton and a few blackened walls in the cotton store, there was very little damage. The main damage was Lizzie's reputation. She had just accused Joe of rape.

In the surgery Lizzie had been examined by the nurse, but because she had inhaled so much smoke and fumes, nurse Johnson had insisted that she be taken to hospital for a thorough check-up. Lizzie protested insisting that she was all right, but Nurse Johnson was having none of it and packed her off to the local infirmary. Several hours later, she was allowed home, but only after she had been examined by the doctors and had her chest x-rayed.

The manager's office wasn't the most cordial place in the world, it was essentially a place of business, but this morning it was even more forbidding than usual. It wasn't every day that one of Mr. Grizedale's employees accused one of his managers of rape!

Underneath her coat Lizzie was dressed in her best frock. Even though the office was heated by a roaring fire in the grate, Lizzie had buttoned her frock right up to the throat. She didn't want Mr Grizedale to think she was some wanton hussy.

Sam Grizedale stood in front of the fire, his huge frame blotting out most of the heat coming from the grate. He was a big man probably near twenty stones in weight, with a rotund face. The jowls on his cheeks hung down like pieces of raw meat. They were criss-crossed with fine thin purple and red lines, the consequence of an over indulgence of rich food and fine wine. His ample stomach was held in by a waistcoat threatening to burst open at any moment.

"Well are you going to tell me what this is all about?" asked the manager his voice surprisingly gentle in a man so large.

"I caught 'er in the cotton store 'avin' a smoke an' when I challenged her about it she went for me," said Joe before Lizzie could get a word in edgeways.

"That's not true. You came on to me and when I wasn't having any you jumped me," said Lizzie eager to defend herself.

"You're not supposed to smoke anywhere near cotton waste at all," said Grizedale sternly.

"I told 'er that," lied Joe.

"You're a bloody liar. You never said anything at all and there's no 'No Smoking' sign," said Lizzie.

"Were you having a smoke?" Asked Grizedale softly.

"Yeah, but I was outside at the time. I wasn't in the cotton store," persisted Lizzie.

"She was inside Mr Grizedale," lied Warmsley again. "An' when I asked her to put it out she just swore at me. The next thing I know when she sees I'm not 'avin' any of it, she's all over me askin' me to kiss 'er an' everythin'. I told her not to be stupid and put the fag out an' get back to work."

"That's a bloody lie and you know it, you lying bastard," raged Lizzie. "Ask Joanie Mathews she'll tell you what the lecherous pig's like."

"Now now, Mrs Steeples, let's keep the proceedings civilized," said Grizedale gently. Lizzie's sudden outburst beginning to convince him that Joe was right.

Joe could sense that he was gaining favour with Grizedale, and pressed home his advantage. "Mrs Mathews is bound to stick up for her sir. They're as thick as thieves the two of 'em. I'm always catchin' them skivin' off. I've had to warn them both on several occasions about their time keepin'," he said condescendingly.

"Is this true Mrs Steeples?" said Grizedale beginning to lean towards Warmsley.

"Well he's told us a couple of times but Joanie's having a baby and she needed a break. But we always got the job done," said Lizzie fearing things were not going her way.

Not to let the advantage go Warmsley pressed on. "Almost every morning I catch at least one of them off the job. I have to say sir that it'll be a great relief when Mrs Mathews leaves in a couple of weeks."

"Why, where's she going?" asked Grizedale innocently.

"Oh didn't you know sir. She's pregnant, but she didn't elect to tell anyone. I only found out myself the other week, and so I put 'er on lighter duties in the spinning room. I didn't want 'er lifting those 'eavy bales an' causin' 'er any damage to 'erself an' the baby sir," he said sanctimoniously.

"Does that sound like someone who would rape an employee?"

Sam Grizedale left the warmth of the fireplace to go and rest his bulky frame in the overstuffed chair behind his desk. Elbows resting on the desk top, he made a pyramid of his pudgy fingers, he seemed to be deep in thought. "Mrs Steeples would you go and wait outside for a few minutes please," he said his voice just an octave above a whisper, "I need to speak to Mr Warmsley in private."

Lizzie got up and left the room. She had a bad feeling that Grizedale was taking Warmsley's side. The corridor outside the manager's office was cold and draughty, the brown and cream walls were grim, but the chill that Lizzie felt wasn't coming from the draught, but from inside her as she feared the worst.

"Well Joe, are you going to tell me what happened?" said Sam Grizedale easing himself over towards the fire.

"It's like I told you Sam. She was 'avin' a smoke an' when I told 'er to put it out she went for me."

"But what about the alleged rape; that's a pretty strong accusation to make for someone just having a smoke."

"I told you before what she's like. Every time I catch 'er she comes on to me so's I'll let 'er off."

"You mean this isn't the first time that this has happened?" questioned Grizedale.

"Sam 'ow long 'ave you known me? You took me on as a young lad straight from school, when you were just spinnin' room manager, an' I was just a snot nosed kid from the streets. Taught me everythin' I know. 'Ave you ever known me to bother any of the women in this place? It 'appens all the time. The women turn in late, or make a balls up an' the next thing y'know they're offerin' it to you on a plate. Lizzie Steeples is one o' the worst, always bloody skivin' off. Thinks if she offers to drop 'er drawers she can get away wi' it. I tell you Sam I'm bloody sick of it."

It was some twenty minutes later, that Lizzie was called back into the office to be told the grim news that she dreaded.

"Mrs Steeples; were there any witnesses to the alleged attack yesterday?" said a grim faced Grizedale now sitting behind his desk.

"No, you know there weren't. There were only me and him," said Lizzie pointing angrily in Warmsley's direction.

Sam Grizedale seemed a little uneasy as he shifted his bulk out of the chair. "Mr Warmsley and I have discussed the case in some detail. It seems that your employment record is, how shall we say, a little lapse. It would seem to me that Mr Warmsley and yourself are at constant loggerheads and find it impossible to work together. In view of the seriousness of the allegation against him, and the possibility of further disruption to the workforce I have no alternative but to terminate your employment with this company forthwith.

"If you wish to pursue the matter of the alleged assault further, you would have to take it up with the police. That of course is your prerogative," he said focusing his gaze directly at Warmsley who was looking anything but comfortable.

"Of course any wages that are owing to you, you can pick up at the end of the week," he said shuffling a bunch of papers that were lying untidily on top of his desk. He looked decidedly uneasy but he had to back his manager. He couldn't let an accusation like this disrupt the company. He liked Lizzie and believed she was a good worker but he couldn't afford the scandal and he reluctantly had to let her go.

Lizzie was stunned she never thought for a minute that she would end up losing her job. "He's a bloody liar; he's nothing but a lying bastard. He tried to rape me," she cried. "I need this job. How am I going to feed my kids?"

"I'm sorry Mrs Steeples, I really am but I have no choice." Joe smirked as Grizedale shouted through to his secretary's office, "Mrs Purlock would you please escort Mrs Steeples from the premises?" he said as he turned his back on her as she was led from his office in tears.

Chapter ten

Lizzie didn't know how she was going to break the news of her job loss to her dad. She had no allies at home now that Bob had managed to get a job labouring in a local engineering factory, and had put down a month's rent in advance on a house not far from the works. She only had Colly to rely on, and he was becoming more and more unpredictable every day. When Jake and the girls came home from school, they were surprised to see their mam home from work so early.

"You're home early mam, didn't expect to see you 'till later," said Jake rooting in the larder in the hope that there might be a biscuit left over from yesterday's tea.

"I wasn't feeling too well so the nurse told me to come home," she lied. "You've not been well for a while. Are you sure you're ok mam?" said Jake concerned for her. "I'll be alright lad it's just a stomach bug I've picked up. I'll be right as rain in a day or two."

It was a week now and she still hadn't told Colly that she had lost her job. Just how much longer she could go on deceiving him was anyone's guess. It wouldn't be to long before events at home changed all that.

As usual Friday was Colly's night at the Platelayers Arms. He liked his ale but when he'd had a drink or two he became increasingly morose. "Put another in there an' a whisky chaser to follow," he drawled, pushing the pint pot towards Lenny Stockley, the landlord of the Platelayers.

"Why don't you get yourself home Colly. I think you've had more than enough for one night," said Lenny eager to avoid one of Colly's infamous outbursts.

"You refusing to serve me after all the bloody money I've spent in this place."

"I'm telling you as a friend. You've had enough, now get yourself home and get a good night's kip."

"I'll go t'Crown they'll serve me in there an' you can bugger off Lenny," he snapped, glaring at the landlord through glassy eyes.

He staggered up York street and crashed through the back door to find Lizzie in the kitchen. "What's for me tea lass?" he droned as he slumped on the kitchen table, hardly able to sit up straight.

"I've not got you anything I didn't expect you home until later. You usually go straight up when you get in from the pub," said Lizzie defensively not wanting to upset her dad.

"Well I'm hungry an' I want summat to eat. Is that too much to soddin' ask for?" he said, sending a pile of plates crashing to the floor in a temper, the noise of which brought the kids rushing down the stairs to see what the clattering was.

"What's up mam?" said Jake holding his terrified sisters hands.

"Why are you not in bed? You should be in bed at this time o' night," Said Colly wagging his finger at the frightened children.

"What's up granddad? Why are you shoutin' at us?" said Jake not used to seeing his granddad in this sort of mood.

"You should be in bed. Now go on be off wi yer afore I lose me temper."

The children began to cry. Jake tried to hide his tears; he was the eldest and he didn't want to cry in front of his sisters, but he'd never seen his granddad like this before.

"Mam what's the matter with granddad?" asked Jake tearfully.

"It's alright love, go on back up to bed an' take Lottie an' Jenny with you. I'll be up to tuck you in, in a minute."

Colly slumped at the table unable to sit up straight. Lizzie banged a steaming mug of tea down in front of him. "Here get that down and try and sober up. Was there any need to shout at the kids like that? Poor little sods don't know what's happening to them these days. What with their no-good father never on time with his money and now I've lost my job at the factory, don't you think they've enough to put up with." Lizzie could have bitten her tongue off; she didn't want her dad to know, at least not yet, not this way. She wasn't sure if he'd heard her, but it was done now he'd find out soon enough anyway.

"What do yer mean, yer've lost yer job?" he said drunkenly reaching for the mug and spilling half the contents onto the floor. "I had a row with one of the gaffers and I got the sack."

"What do yer mean a row? Why did yer get the sack?" He said sobering up pretty quickly now. Lizzie didn't want to go into details, not at this time of night.

"He accused me of smoking in the cotton store and the boss believed him instead of me and I got the push." She said revealing all she was prepared to do at this hour. Hopefully he wouldn't have to know the whole truth. He'd more than likely blame her anyway.

Chapter eleven

Lizzie felt more desperate than ever. It had been more than a month since she had lost her job at Taylor's. She had tried most of the other local mills, but most of them had no vacancies. There were jobs, if she could travel outside of Thistlefield, but she would have to find somebody to have the kids from about five thirty in the morning, and Mrs Fisher the local child minder bless her could only manage them from about seven. Her dad couldn't have them, he had to be at the bleach works for six, and anyway he was difficult enough to deal with these days without the burden of the kids to worry about. Joanie had told her there might be a job going at Matlock's mill, but it was a couple of miles out of town in Littleton. She decided it was worth a try. At the moment her life was just about as miserable as it could get. True to form Colly blamed her for losing her job and told her he couldn't be expected to provide for her and the kids, as that was her ex-husband's responsibility. She couldn't argue with him on that, but it was almost impossible to get Brooke to pay his money on time. There was never enough food in the house. What bit there was she gave to the children and her dad, often going hungry herself. She was behind with the rent, she owed the gas and all the local shops wouldn't let her strap anymore. Her health continued to suffer and she was losing weight at an alarming rate. Matlock's was her last hope.

It was a Wednesday morning. Lizzie was on her way back from Matlock's. For once she felt that her luck was changing. The mill manager had been impressed by Lizzie and told her that there would be a job going, but not for a couple of weeks. She was disappointed that there was no job right away, but happy that she would be back at work in a few weeks. With the few shillings she had left in her purse, she went up town to Littleton market to buy a few things for their tea rather than risk shopping in her own locality. She was ashamed that she still owed most of them money. If her dad ever found out he would kill her. He had never had much but he had always paid his way. He had never owed money to anyone in his life. He would rather give up drink than owe money to neighbours and local tradesmen. The shame would be more than he could bear.

Lizzie was almost out of the front door when she spotted the gasman further up the street. She quickly stepped back inside, not sure whether he had seen her or not. She hid behind the large sideboard that dominated the front room. Moments later came a loud banging on the door. She tried to make herself smaller as she crouched behind the dresser. The banging became louder and more insistent.

"Come on love I know you're in there, I've just seen you. I need to empty the meter," bellowed the gasman not caring who saw or heard him. Lizzie continued to hide refusing to come out until he had gone. One or two of the neighbours had come to see what all the racket was about. "I know she's in there. I've bloody seen her," said the gasman to Lizzie's neighbours.

"Not like Lizzie, not to open the door," said Mrs Trowbridge, Lizzie's next door neighbour. "She might 'ave gone to pick up the kids from school," she volunteered.

"What at eleven o'clock in the morning," he said stuffing a paper through the letterbox informing her that if the meter wasn't emptied and the gas bill paid in the next seven days, they would be cut off.

Lizzie looked at the bit of paper with dread. How could they empty the gas meter. She'd emptied it weeks ago not long after she left Taylor's. The kids had been hungry, and there was nothing in the house. She had picked the lock with a hairpin, and took the money that had been feeding them for the past three weeks. She had hoped to get another job, but the job at Matlock's only started in two weeks. She had been hoping to get back to work before now and put the money back before anyone discovered what she had done. Sadly, it was too late; they would be cutting the gas off next week. What her dad would say she dare not think about.

In desperation, she rang Brooke. "I need you to let me have my money early this week, and next weeks as well, you owe me two weeks anyway." She pleaded.

"I can't get to the bank I'm busy this morning," he said.

"Brooke I'm desperate, we've nothing in the house and I've nothing to give the kids," she said not wanting to reveal the real reason she needed the money so badly, although it was true there was very little in the house.

"I've told you I'm busy this morning."

Lizzie hated herself. "How busy? Too busy for me?" she said huskily. She was almost sick with disgust.

Jake and his sisters came home from school to find Lizzie in the kitchen sobbing her heart out. "What's up mam? Are you alright?" said Jake, hurt to see his mam so upset.

"No it's nothing love, I trapped my fingers in the cupboard drawer and it hurts a bit, that's all. Now why don't you take Jenny and Lottie out into the yard and play and I'll shout you when tea's ready," she said, her hand pushed deep into the pocket of her pinny, clutching the one-pound note, and the one ten shilling note that Brooke had given her. It wasn't even one weeks money for the kids. She felt so degraded.

"Mam's always crying these days," said Jake to his sisters. "I wonder what's wrong with her."

"Maybe she's ill," said Jenny.

"She's not going to die is she?" cried little Lottie tearfully.

Chapter twelve

William Steeples or 'Owd Decker' as he was popularly known around the pubs in and around Thistlefield, from his habit of always having a deck of cards in his pocket. The back room of the Black Bull that William part owned, was full with spectators watching the illegal card game. Gambling on licensed premises was against the law, but William Steeples always had a game going, at least once or twice a week. Up to now he had always avoided the law. Mainly because one or two of the local constabulary liked a game themselves, and always gave him the nod when there was likely to be a raid. He scooped the pile of notes and coins from the table, there must have been about twenty or twenty-five pounds in the kitty. There were at least four five-pound notes, a couple more one-pound notes mixed with a few ten-shilling notes, and the rest in coins of various denominations. A small pot by his standards.

"Well gentlemen thank you for the game." He said to the group of men gathered in the back room of the Black Bull pub. "If any of you are interested I shall be appearing at the Crown public house in the next few weeks," he said to the punters he had just relieved of their hard-earned cash. William was a talented singer and often performed in the pubs in and around Thistlefield. He had also appeared at the Dunston Opera House, which was the largest town nearest to Thistlefield, playing to packed audiences in the likes of The Pirates of Penzance, and other notable Gilbert and Sullivan operetta's. "Where I shall of course, give you a chance to win your money back," he said cheerfully stuffing his winnings into his wallet.

"You'd better you old bugger," said Tom Arnold, an old adversary of William's good-naturedly, "I've lost nearly three quid tonight."

"Stop your crowing Tom you can afford it. Anyway you know I'll always give you the chance to win your money back. It's not my fault you're such a lousy poker player." He laughed.

As well as being an excellent singer, William was a noted gambler. Poker and brag being the games he excelled at most. He was also an avid student of the turf, and liked nothing better than to empty the local bookies pockets whenever the opportunity arose.

Tom laughed. "That'll be the day when I get the better of you." William downed the last dregs of whisky and pushed the empty glass away. "Where is it you're at?" asked another of 'Owd Decker's victims.

"The Crown, just off York Street, you can't miss it."

Chapter thirteen

Lizzie was at her wits end. It was a week since she'd had the letter about cutting the gas off, and Colly didn't know anything about it. Her dad would never live it down. He'd always paid his way he had never owed a penny to anyone in his life. Lizzie had packed the kids off early to Mrs Fishers, in the hope that she could avoid the gasman. She busied herself with the household chores until tiredness overtook her. She hadn't slept a wink the previous two nights worrying, it wasn't long before she slumped in the chair in front of the fire and fell into a fitful sleep.

A sudden hammering on the front door disturbed her. She shook herself awake. Unable to grasp what was happening she jumped up out of the chair and ran into the back kitchen. The hammering on the door continued unabated, causing neighbours on either side of Lizzie to come to their doors to see what the commotion was all about.

"Come on love open the door, we know you're in there," said one of the two burly gasmen.

"What's up?" asked a bemused Mrs Trowbridge.

"This is Mrs Steeples address?" said one of the men seeking confirmation from the neighbour. "Have you seen anything of her this morning?"

"Yeah Mrs Steeples lives here. She might be out. I think she took the kiddies to Mrs Fishers this morning. She looks after them while she goes to work," replied the neighbour.

Lizzie could hear the snippets of the conversation. She crouched down not daring to show her face. She tried to peer out of the front kitchen window to see what was going on, but she couldn't see anything. She stood up to get a better view, but as she did her elbow caught the worktop and sent a pile of pans and crockery crashing to the floor. "What was that?" Exclaimed one of the gasmen. "I told you there was somebody in there. Come on open the bloody door or we'll have to break it down," threatened one of the men angrily.

Lizzie was too tired, too weary, and too exhausted to care anymore, and let the men in. The older of the two men stared at Lizzie. Her emaciated body thin beyond reason. She stared at him. Her once glossy hair hung from her head limp and lifeless, and her dull sad eyes gazed at him from behind two rings so dark they were almost black. The olive glow of her face was gaunt and puckered, and the skeletal skin was grey.

The elder of the gasmen could see the state Lizzie was in. Softly he asked, "Where's the meter love?"

She pointed to a cupboard in the corner. "In there," she said; her voice barely a hoarse whisper. "But there's nothing in it. I opened it to feed the kids," she sobbed. "I was going to put the money back as soon as I got a job. I've got a job now, but I couldn't get one round here, and the kid's dad he hardly ever pays his money. I'm so sorry." She wept wretchedly.

The younger of the two men looked at his mate. "Look at the state of her Joe. We can't cut her off. Christ what a bloody mess. What're we goin' to do?"

"I've no option lad, I'll 'ave to report it. She's done the soddin' meter. There should 'ave been £5-4s-9p in the box, it's empty." He mouthed softly to his mate.

"Can't we put it in for her?" whispered the young lad kindly.

"Have you got £5- 4s-9p?" he said. He turned to Lizzie. "I'm sorry love but I'll have to cut you off. I'll have to report it. I don't want to do it but if I don't report it, I'll probably lose my job.

"What'll happen to me?" said Lizzie the tears streaming down her face. "I don't know love; it's not up to me."

"Will I go to jail?"

"I don't think so love. More than likely you'll probably end up in court and get a fine I'm really sorry love, try not to worry." Lizzie just looked up and nodded her head. "Ok." She said the tears streaming down her face.

Colly came home from work to find the house in darkness, and only the firelight illuminating the living room. Lizzie was by the grate stirring a pot of stew slowly cooking in the oven, the only thing she was able to prepare since the gas had been cut off. "Hello lass. 'As that gas mantle gone agen? They don't last two minutes them buggers do they." He said unaware of the situation.

"Oh dad they've cut the gas off." She cried.

"What? They've what? They've cut the gas off. Why?" asked Colly in disbelief.

"I couldn't pay the bill dad," sobbed Lizzie, the torment drawn in every line of her face. "I give you money for the gas. 'Ow come we've bin cut off?"

"Dad I'm so sorry." She could barely look at him.

"Come on lass," said Colly, beginning to soften a little. "Folk get cut off all the time round 'ere. I'll give you the money an' you can pay the bill in the morning, an' we'll get it back on."

"Dad I've done the meter. I'll 'ave to go to court," she said, her back to him, hardly daring to look him in the face.

Colly grabbed her by the shoulders and angrily turned her to face him. "You've what?" he raged his fury fuelled by the ale he'd consumed earlier. "You've done the gas meter." He bellowed at the top of his voice hitting her so hard across the face, that she went sprawling across the kitchen floor.

The commotion brought Jake and his sisters running into the kitchen. "Mam, granddad. What's up?" He said seeing Lizzie slumped on the floor her hand over her cheek where her father had hit her. "Yer mam's a bloody thief lad. I'm off down t'platelayers," he said. "That's if I can 'old me 'ead up."

Chapter fourteen

The Crown was packed to the rafters. The crowd was noisy and raucous but good humoured. It wasn't every day that they got a singer of William Steeples calibre to entertain them. They waited eagerly for his appearance, anticipating the entertainment to come. William though had more important business to attend to. He was in the middle of a poker game and the noisy throng would have to wait a little longer.

The back room of the Crown was hushed as 'Owd Decker' held his cards close to his chest. Tom Arnold felt at last he had the chance of a winning hand; it would all depend on this next cards. 'Owd Decker' had been winning all night; Tom sensed at last he had the winning hand. He looked down at his cards, three nines, a four of hearts and a six of diamonds. He hadn't had three of a kind all night. "Two," he said trying to read the faces of the other players round the table. He knew from bitter experience that William could read a face better than he could read his own hand. He threw the four and six onto the table. The dealer, a middle-aged bank clerk with a bad chest and a rasping cough from too many cigarettes, dealt Tom two cards. He picked them up from the table, not daring too look. He turned them towards him, his hands nervously covering the cards not wanting prying eyes to see what he had got. He could scarcely believe his luck; the dealer had dealt him the nine of hearts, and seven of spades. He could barely contain himself. Four of a kind, the best hand he'd had all night. He sipped his drink trying to stay calm, the sweat forming on his brow and upper lip.

"How about you William?" asked the bank clerk stifling a cough. A thick blue haze of tobacco smoke filled the atmosphere of the tiny back room of the Crown. The air was tense with anticipation as the two men tried to out-psych each other.

"I'll play these," said William confidently puffing on the Havana firmly clenched between his teeth. He spread his hands over the backs of his cards keeping them close to his chest like a Mississippi riverboat gambler.

"Bob what about you? Are you in or out?" Wheezed the dealer.

Lizzie's brother Bob looked at his cards. He was unknown to most of the players sitting round the table. He wasn't a regular at the card table but from time to time he chanced his arm. He'd heard about the game on the grapevine, it was an opportunity too good to miss.

"Arthur you in or what?" asked the dealer to one of the other players sat round the table.

"No, too rich for me, I'm out," he said throwing his cards onto the table.

"Ted what about you? You in?"

"No, I'm out," said Ted raising his hands with a sigh of resignation.

"It's down to you son. What're you going to do?" Asked the dealer. Bob looked at his cards as if uncertain which way to go. He hesitated just for a moment and looked at the pot of money in front of him. There was more than three weeks wages plus what he'd managed to scrounge on the table. He was up against two of the most ardent gamblers in Thistlefield.

"Well," said the dealer.

"I'll play these," said Bob.

"In that case I'll go five and I'll raise it another five," said 'decker' throwing two five-pound notes into the pot.

"That'll cost you ten, to stay in the game, gents," he smiled sucking on his cigar.

"I'm in," said Tom throwing ten pounds into the kitty, confident he had the winning hand.

Bob looked at his hand and fingered the notes he still had left in his pocket. "I'll go ten and raise it another ten," he said throwing two ten pound notes onto the table.

There was a gasp from around the room. "Bloody hell," cried one boozer.

"That'll cost you twenty quid to stay in the game," said Bob with not a flicker of emotion.

Tom looked at his cards the confidence of two minutes ago rapidly ebbing out of him. "Damn it," he said slamming his cards angrily down on the table, "I'm out."

"Looks like it's just you and me then son," said William with a mischievous smile on his face. "Tell you what; let's cut all the buggering about. There's twenty-five and I'll raise it another twenty-five. If you want to see me it'll cost you fifty quid."

The tiny room went deadly silent; you could hear a pin drop as Bob felt in his pocket for the money. He dearly hoped he hadn't bitten off more than he could chew. He peeled off ten five pound notes from his rapidly diminishing stake, and threw them onto the table. "What've you got?" he said his stomach churning.

"Flush, four five six seven eight of clubs," said William confidently spreading the cards out before him. The hand drew gasps from the assembled crowd. Not much could beat a flush, only a higher one.

Bob seemed to hesitate as if he was resigned to losing.

"Too much for you hey son," said 'decker' as he started to draw the pot towards him.

"Just a minute." The revellers hushed as Bob slowly spread his cards out before him. Without warning, they broke into a rapturous round of cheering. Ale tankards beat a tattoo on the tabletops threatening to reduce them to matchwood as the applause continued unabated.

"Jesus, he's got a royal," declared one of the onlookers.

"Bet owd' 'decker' never expected that," said another.

William stared at the flush of diamonds. Ten through to the ace. He shook his head in dismay, it wasn't very often that he was out bluffed in a card game, but he had met his match today. "That was some game you played there young man, I like your style." He said patting Bob good-naturedly on the shoulder. "I'm sure I've come across you before?"

"You might have, my sister married your lad. Lizzie Ashcroft as was. Lizzie Steeples these days," said Bob stuffing the money into his wallet.

'I'm not really a card player; I'm more for the horses. I got a tip the other day. Red Ace at Doncaster. I had a tenner on it at 100-8. won over a hundred quid."

"A man after my own heart. I like a bet myself. Be sure to let me know if you get another one." He said leaving the room.

Chapter fifteen

It had been over a month since Lizzie had let the gasmen in. She had been working at Matlock's for two weeks and she dreaded every day she came home, wondering if the postman had delivered the mail. But each day nothing had arrived. Maybe the gas board had decided to let her off, knowing she had only took the money to feed the kids. Her dad had paid the gas board the money back. There hadn't been any real harm done, she wasn't a criminal. Today though her worst fears were realized. As she opened the door, the letter was on the mat staring at her. She looked repeatedly at the official looking brown envelope, not daring to look inside. Lizzie put it down on the table and stared at it as if it were some alien being. She went to the drawer and pulled out a long bladed knife. Hands shaking she slit open the envelope. It was there in black and white. She had been summoned to appear before the local magistrate's court. She kept looking over and over again at the letter informing her that her case would be heard in just over a week's time. She read the summons for the umpteenth time not believing that she had to go to court. She wasn't a criminal. Real criminals, thieves and murderers went to court, not her. She had only wanted to feed the kids. She clutched the letter to her chest and began sobbing uncontrollably.

Colly could hardly face going out, his daughter a thief, and for a few shillings in the bloody gas meter. Why hadn't she asked him? He would have seen her all right. More to the point why hadn't that bastard ex-husband of hers paid what was due to his kids? One of these days that bastard would get his due desserts.

Holding court in one of his favourite bars, Brooke was unaware of Lizzie's sorry plight. Not that that would bother him, he had more pressing matters on his mind, like how he was going to woo his latest conquest into bed. Not that he had any trouble as a rule, but this one was proving to be more of a challenge than the usual crop of trollops he was used to bedding. Brooke was oblivious of another pair of eyes watching him from across the room, he was too busy plying his latest admirer with drink, hoping he might get lucky later, and get her into bed. Bob had gone to the Old Dog Inn on the promise of a tip running at Catterick the following day. He ordered a pint and watched as Brooke turned the charm on to his latest floozy. Barely able to contain his anger, Bob took a long draught from his drink.

"Give us a couple of minutes will you Charlie, there's somebody I've got to see, I'll only be a minute." Pushing his way across the crowded bar he made his way to where Brooke was persevering with the nubile blonde. "I wouldn't take what this bastard 'as to say too seriously, if I were you darlin', he's poison," said Bob, the venom in his voice hard to disguise.

Startled Brooke turned to face his accuser. "B..'Bob I didn't know you drank in here. W..' what'll you have?" he stuttered. Although Brooke was an ex-navy man, he wasn't the most resolute of souls when it came to facing up to anyone, especially an irate brother-in-law.

"Nothing from you, you bloody excuse for a man."

"Brooke who is this man?" asked the stunned blonde visibly shocked by Bob's outburst.

"I'm 'is brother-in-law love. Did you know his ex-wife is in court next week, because this louse wouldn't feed his kids?" he said staring directly at the over made-up tart. "He gave her 30 bob to go to bed with him and then left her in the lurch. She was so desperate she did the gas-meter to feed his kids and now she's in court." Bob snatched Brooke by his collar. "I've half a mind to ram this down your bloody throat," he said pushing his beer glass into Brooke's face. Brooke was visibly shaken and the sweat was beginning to form on his brow. A meaty hand on Bob's shoulder alleviated what was fast becoming a dangerous situation. "Leave it Bob, come on let's get out of here before there's real trouble," said his mate Charlie.

"You've not heard the last of this," snarled Bob as Charlie dragged him away, as all eyes in the pub focused on the ruckus in the corner.

"What was all that about?" said the tart clearly shaken.

"It's nothing just a misunderstanding that's all. He was drunk as usual. Finish your drink and we'll get out of here."

"Not on your bloody life. I'm not getting mixed up in any domestic between you and your ex-wife." She empted her glass and left.

Chapter sixteen

Thistlefield's magistrate's court was a cold foreboding place. Lizzie shivered as she sat in the waiting room expecting the next name to be called would be hers. Joanie her best friend had gone with her to give her a bit of moral support. She told Lizzie not to worry as her solicitor Mr James Sylvester, had got her cousin Walter Shaw off on a similar charge. This was only a magistrate's court she had said and not a court for hardened criminals. Serious crimes were dealt with at the assizes or crown courts not here. Owing to the extenuating nature of her offence, Mr Sylvester was sure she would only get a fine and a probable term on probation. This was where justice was dispensed for minor infringements of the law. Most cases dealt at the magistrates were for minor theft, disturbances of the peace, wife beatings, drunk and disorderly and the like. Although in the eyes of the law, breaking into a gas-meter was a serious crime, it wasn't first degree murder, or theft of the crown jewels.

What if she was found guilty? She thought. What would happen if she did face a custodial sentence? They would take her kids off her, wouldn't they? The thoughts were racing through her head as she waited nervously for her case to be called. Her solicitor Mr James Sylvester had been suggested by Lizzie's best friend Joanie. He had got her cousin Walter off a similar charge of theft. He had been looking for a new overcoat. After trying on several garments in various establishments, he walked out of one of the local tailors shops in town, with an overcoat without paying for it. Mr. Sylvester had pleaded that the poor man had been suffering from a bout of depression. This had been brought about explained Mr Sylvester due to his client losing his job at the local gas works. Being a proud and reliable breadwinner for his family, Mr Shaw had fallen into a bout of depression.

He also argued that his client was of previous good character, and had no previous convictions. Mr Sylvester pointed out during his shopping trip he was suffering from depression, and that he was therefore unaware of his actions at that time. The court had been persuaded by Mr. Sylvester's arguments, and Mr Shaw had been given a six month suspended sentence. He was fined £2/10 shillings, ordered to pay the cost of the coat, 5 guineas, and court costs of £3/15 shillings plus a fee of 10 guineas to Mr. Sylvester, and subsequently left court a free man without a blemish on his character.

Bob had gladly agreed to pay Mr. Sylvester's fees. 10 guineas was nothing as the tip from Charlie had paid dividends and the £20 on Devils Dawn had paid handsomely at odds of 8-1 and had netted Bob over £160 after deductions. Bob omitted telling Lizzie where the money had come from, knowing how much she hated the thoughts of any sort of gambling. He just told her now that he had got a job and he had been able to put a bit away every week, for emergencies. As this was an emergency, he was only too happy to help. Lizzie had been too worried to question the truth of it; she was just hoping to keep out of jail.

Her reverie was soon broken by the court usher. "Mrs. Elizabeth Steeples, Mrs. Elizabeth Steeples."

"Yes," said Lizzie nervously, almost a whisper.

"Court number two," said the elderly court official.

"Don't worry everything will be alright," assured Mr. Sylvester.

Lizzie was led into the witness box where she swore to tell the truth the whole truth and nothing but the truth.

"Would you state your full name and address?"

"Elizabeth Steeples, 61 York Street, Thistlefield."

The gas company's solicitor, Mr. Martin Cartright, pressed hard for a custodial sentence as a deterrent to further thefts. He argued that there had been a spate of thefts from meters recently, and if the problem wasn't nipped in the bud, it would soon become an epidemic. He was hoping that the court would deliver a custodial sentence, and therefore deter others from taking the same path. Lizzie became extremely anxious as his arguments were very forceful. When he had finished his closing speech, Mr. Sylvester rose to his feet and addressed the bench.

"Your honour, I have listened to my learned friend's arguments and under normal circumstances I would indeed press for a custodial sentence. But these are not normal circumstances." Looking down at a few scribbled notes on his legal pad, he went on. "Here we have a young woman of previously unblemished character, through no fault of her own appearing before you today." Lizzie sat in the witness box staring at the floor. Mr. Sylvester went on. "At Christmas, Mrs. Steeples had no money for food or presents for her three children, up until 5-30pm when her ex-husband condescended to call with £3-15 shillings which was his duty to pay towards the upkeep of his children. He offered no extra help towards their Christmas fare, and nothing in the way of presents for his young family. It was only a last dash to the town centre shops with a very miserly amount of money, that saved this poor woman's and her children's Christmas at all."

Mr Cartright jumped to his feet. "Your honour where is this leading?"

The magistrate, the honourable Captain Charles Bridgeford somewhat testily said, "Yes Mr. Sylvester, could you please tell us where you are going with this line of testimony."

"Your honour, I'm trying to point out that my client is no more a criminal than you or I, and that her actions were borne out of desperation rather than that of a persistent criminal. Her misdeeds were due wholly to the actions or rather the inactions of her ex-husband to provide for his children." The arguments went on for another twenty minutes until both sides had exhausted all their differences of opinion.

Finally, a little after 3-30pm, Mr. Bridgeford delivered his verdict.

"Will the defendant please rise?" said the court usher.

"I have listened with great interest to the case both for and against Mrs. Steeples, and I've reached the conclusion that the wrong person is here in the dock today." James Sylvester couldn't help but smile to himself as he heard the words.

Mr Bridgeford went on. "Although what you did was in itself a crime, I can understand the reason behind it. If I may be so bold as to say, that an animal in the wild would do no more, or no less to feed its family than you have tried to do for yours. Indeed I have to say that listening to Mr Sylvester's persuasive testimony, and the sorry circumstances that have surrounded this case, I have come to the conclusion that it isn't you that should be before me today, but your ex-husband for driving you towards the action that you felt compelled to take."

The grin on James Sylvester's face was now beaming from ear to ear.

"However a crime has been committed," said Mr Bridgeford, somewhat pensively, rubbing the bridge of his nose deep in thought. "And as such must be punished lest we send the wrong message out to the public at large. Therefore I am going to impose a custodial sentence of three months." The grin on the face of James Sylvester disappeared as quickly as an ice cube in the sun. Lizzie buried her head in her hands visibly shaken. "Oh God, no. What about my kids?" She cried.

"However." Went on the magistrate. "I'm going to suspend it for twelve months and place you on probation for twelve months." He turned to Lizzie. "You're free to go, and I don't want to see you in my courtroom again."

Chapter seventeen

With the shame of the court case still hanging over her, Lizzie felt that her every move was being watched by her neighbours. She found it hard to take the snide remarks from people she once regarded as friends. Her only friend these days seemed to be Dr Oakfield, whom she had been seeing more and more of these last few months. Lizzie had had the persistent nagging cough for weeks, and during the past few months it simply wouldn't go away. The large detached house in the suburbs of Thistlefield served as Dr Oakfield's surgery, as well as his home.

Lizzie hadn't been waiting long when the kindly face of Mrs. Oakfield appeared from the hatch in the surgery's waiting room. "Mrs Steeples doctor will see you now if you would like to go through." Mrs Oakfield spoke just above a whisper, not wanting to disturb the other patients waiting for her son's attention. Although well in her seventies, Florence Oakfield was small and slightly built, with a mind as sharp as a tack. She still worked full surgery hours as his secretary/receptionist, and she was also a qualified dispensing chemist. She had carried on from when her husband had had the practice, and when he died she continued her duties for her son. This was normal practice in many small towns and village surgeries. Although in the larger towns and cities, chemists were springing up in every high street. However it was still normal practice for surgeries to dispense their own medicines, especially as it was a bus ride to the larger towns where there was likely to be a chemist within easy reach.

The green leather seat in the waiting room wasn't built for comfort, and Lizzie got up rather shakily and made her way down the corridor to Dr Oakfield's room. It was the cream painted door at the end of the corridor. She wondered to herself how she must know every inch of the surgery; she had been there so often in the past few months.

"Come in," said the warm voice of Dr Oakfield. Lizzie pushed the door open and went into his surgery. "Ah Lizzie what can I do for you?" Knowing full well what the problem was as he read her medical notes, before she had even opened her mouth.

"It's this damn cough doctor I just can't seem to shake it off."

"Did you finish that linctus that I prescribed for you last month?"

"I took it all, and for a while I thought it was going to work, and then the other day this." She showed him the handkerchief spotted with flecks of blood.

"How long has this been going on?" he asked.

"About three or four weeks ago I noticed a little speck, but because I'd had a bad dose the last time I put it down to that. Then it seemed to clear up, and I thought no more about it, then the other day it started again, and it just seems to have got worse."

"And I don't suppose you've taken my advice and given up smoking, or at least cut down," he said as gently as he could, not wanting to sound like an admonishing father.

"I've tried but things have been so hard, what with my ex-husband not paying his money on time. Everything's so expensive. I've managed to get another job but I'm up at the crack of dawn and it's after six every night when I get home. I'm so tired all the time I need a smoke just to relax."

He understood Lizzie's craving. It had been almost ten years since he'd had his last cigarette. He hadn't touched one since he'd seen his father die prematurely from lung cancer, but the craving was always there.

"Where is it that you're working now?" He asked.

"I got a job at Matlocks. Was doing all right 'till I met up with one of my old bosses." She said.

"How do you mean?"

"Do you remember when I used to work at Taylors a few years back, and I got the sack. Well a bloke called Joe Warmsley, he was my boss. Well to cut a long story short I heard he left Taylors, I don't know why, but I never cast eyes or ears on him since I left. Then all of a sudden I find out he's managed to get himself a bosses job at Matlocks."

"And what has all this got to do with you meeting up with this Warmsley fellow.?" Dr Oakfield implored.

"Well I got a job in one of the weaving rooms, a bit noisy but not so dusty. Warmsley found out I was working there and transferred me into the card-room back among all the muck and dust."

"And how long ago was this?"

"Probably about three months," she said a harsh cough racking her body.

"That's about the time you started to see me. I'd better have a look at you, would you get up on the couch please."

Ten minutes later Lizzie was still in the doctor's surgery.

"I'm arranging for you to go into hospital for some x-rays and some blood tests. It's nothing to worry about. Once I get the results then maybe we'll be able to get to the bottom of this. Meanwhile I'm going to prescribe something a little stronger to help that cough of yours. And Lizzie I strongly advise you to give up that job of yours and try and stop smoking."

Chapter eighteen

Jake was growing into a fine young lad. At going on eighteen he had left Thistlefield secondary modern almost two years earlier. Although he had a good head on his shoulders and picked things up quickly, academic life had never been Jakes favourite thing. He had always preferred sports and games to maths and English. When it came to sports, he was always the first name on the sports masters' lips, and was a regular choice when it came to representing the school at football or rugby. Jake had never been the biggest lad at school, but he could hold his own with anybody.

It was the end of the week. Jake worked at one of the local factories. He was an apprentice fitter but he didn't really like it. Apart from the fact that the money was really poor, he was only on £3 10s a week barely enough to get him to work and back. By the time he'd tipped up to his mam bless her, for his board, she tried to give him a pound a week for himself, there wasn't much left for going out.

He hated the one day a week he spent in the local technical college. It reminded him too much of school without as many lessons, and he still had homework to do. Everybody told him he needed a trade so he was stuck with it. Jake decided he'd do the homework tonight after his mam's cig run. He'd hardly been home five minutes before he heard his mam's voice from the back kitchen.

"Is that you Jake love?" Wheezed Lizzie, barely able to catch her breath. Jake knew what was coming. It was the same every Friday. Once his mam's money had run out by the end of the week, he had to go and search the streets for dog ends so that she could have a smoke. Bad enough that she had to smoke at all in her condition but dog ends!

"Jake love could you go and see if you can find me a couple of dog ends, I've run out of cigs." This evening was proving to be more difficult than usual. Lizzie clung to the kitchen table as the pangs of pain tore through her chest as she struggled to get her breath.

"Mam are you alright?" asked Jake fearful that his mother was going to collapse right there on the kitchen floor.

"I'm alright lad; I'll be right as rain in a minute. Go and tell your sisters to wash their hands ready for tea," she rasped as another painful spasm tore at her tortured lungs.

Jenny and Lottie had been listening to their mam's choking cough on the stairs, afraid of coming into the kitchen, fearful of what they might see. Not for the first time would they come down the stairs to find their mam bent double heaving her lungs out gasping for breath!

"Is mam alright Jake?" asked Jenny her dark eyes brimming with tears.

"Course she is," replied Jake trying his best to reassure his sisters that there was nothing to worry about. Lottie though, the elder of the two girls wasn't convinced that her mam was all right.

Jake pulled on his coat and went in search of the streets near his home, hoping he might find a few half smoked cigarette ends for his mam. After a fruitless search of the streets, a despondent Jake finally returned home with a couple of dog ends for his mam.

"I could only find a couple, mam," he said, the sadness in his voice hard to ignore. "I'll try again later on tonight, when the men are going to the pubs; they always throw bigger dog ends away when they go to the pub." Little did he know that by the end of the week certain events would change his young life forever?

Chapter nineteen

The Black Bull inn was bursting at the seams, which was usual on a Friday before a big race meeting the following day. This was where all the local tipsters sold their so-called precious information on the following day's races. Most of it was useless and most of the punters ended up broke on the promise of the following day's good things. An exception though was William Steeples, better known to the locals as 'Owd Decker.' He was in the know. He had contacts all over the north and if his money went down, he was usually onto a winner!

Bob was there with his best mate Eric, trying to get hold of Dixie McGovern. Dixie was one of Bob's most reliable sources of information on all things relating to the turf, but as usual, an enthusiastic crowd all-vying for the latest good thing always surrounded Dixie. He had once been a successful jockey, but his love of a pint had caused his weight to balloon and he was soon forced to prematurely retire from the saddle. These days found him handing out tips to any unsuspecting idiot that would pay. Sometimes though, he had red-hot information, but it was only for the chosen few.

"Excuse me gents there's someone I've got to see," he said in his broad Irish brogue as he pushed his way to the back of the bar where William was sat.

"Decker me old mate. How the hell are you?" He beamed, being one of the privileged few to call him by his nickname.

"Dixie, how are you doing?" The ex-Irish jockey motioned William to go through to the back room where there were less prying eyes and even less flapping ears. Once safely ensconced in the privacy of the landlord's back room, they were assured they wouldn't be disturbed and could get down to the days business, for a cut of course.

Dixie wasted no time in coming to the point. "Tomorrow's big race at Newbury; the Bodsworth Brewery handicap hurdle over 2 miles 1 furlong."

"Bloody hell, Dixie, that's a bloody cavalry charge; there'll be at least 25 or 30 runners," said an exasperated William. The Bodsworth was one of the most competitive handicaps of the season and it wasn't unusual for a long priced winner to go in.

"I know and that's why this'll be the coup of the season so far."

"I don't know Dixie we don't usually go in for these types of ventures." said William cagily. The types of ventures William went in for; the result was usually known beforehand!

"Well if you don't want to know there's plenty more that will," he said cocking his head to one side, a cheeky grin on his ruddy face a result of too many winter mornings in the cold and too many pints of Guinness. "I've never let you down before, have I?"

"That's bloody debatable," said William, a look of doubt on his face. "Ok then let's be having it."

"Money first," he said holding out his pudgy hand.

William took out his wallet and took out a five-pound note handing it over. It was Dixie's usual fee for information.

Dixie held up his hands as if trying to push an imaginary force away from him. "Sorry Decker but this one'll cost you twenty."

"What!" shouted William. "Twenty bloody quid; you must be bloody joking, you must think I'm made of soddin money."

"Come off it Decker, everybody knows you're bloody minted, you tight old bugger. Do you want the horse or not?"

Reluctantly William took out three more five-pound notes from his wallet. He knew Dixie's tips were usually on the money. "What makes you so sure this horse is such a sure fire thing?" he said keeping hold of the money tightly in his fist.

"Do you remember about two years ago there was a horse out of Sid Hardy's yard, four year old at the time, won a couple of bumpers then went on to win a good maiden at Chepstow. Well as you know, Chepstow is a pretty stiff course undulating, with a long run in. Well this beast absolutely romped home from some decent animals. One of them Dashing Blade went on to run second in that year's champion hurdle, only beaten two lengths. Well this bugger beat Dashing Blade by no less than twelve lengths next time out and was fancied for the champion hurdle after that."

"Well how come it didn't run?" asked William, getting a bit agitated at the length of the tale.

"It broke down in training, pulled muscles in its back or something. Anyway it's not seen a racecourse for nearly three years, but Sid entered it in a little handicap at Huntingdon about six weeks ago, just to get a weight for tomorrow's race. Huntingdon is a fairly easy track and he was just giving it a pipe opener, you know just to blow the cobwebs away. It absolutely cantered home from some decent animals. According to the head stable lad, it was pulling the jocks arms out at the end of the race, and was hardly blowing, anyway it's cherry ripe for tomorrow it's only carrying 10st 4lbs. My mate recons it's got over a stone in hand of the handicapper, but it won't have after tomorrow."

"What's the soddin thing called for God's sake?"

"Money," said Dixie holding out his hand. William rather grudgingly handed over the rest of the money.

"Pickpocket," said Dixie stuffing the money into his trouser pocket.

"Sounds bloody appropriate," grunted William as he left the room feeling that he'd just had his wallet lifted.

Bob finally caught up with Dixie. "Are you sure that'll win? It's not seen a racecourse for years."

"I've told you Bob it's been set up. I've just told Decker and I never give that old bastard a dud. Anyway after the Bodsworth, it'll shoot up the handicap. That's why the money's going down tomorrow. Have I ever let you down before?" Bob and Dixie went back years. Dixie came over from Ireland when he was about eighteen to escape a poverty-stricken existence. He was the youngest of a family of ten and life was harsh in post-war Ireland. He had tried his luck in stables over there but a disastrous affair with the trainer's wife had seen him pack his bags and head for England. In fairness, it wasn't all his fault. He was a young lad far from home, and she was a buxom thirty-five year old who wanted to show him the ways of the world. She was a wonderful teacher until her husband heard their throes of passion in the stables, one day, when he made an uncharacteristic early return from the gallops. Maybe he already had his suspicions, but that was the end of Dixie's career in Ireland. He'd met Bob not long after on the building sites, and Bob had taken the young lad under his wing, so to speak. So from time to time Dixie had kept Bob in the know, when anything good was going down.

Chapter twenty

Jake was trudging wearily down the street when he saw his uncle Bob coming out of the platelayers arms. It was obvious he'd had a few; he was staggering all over the place and singing at the top of his voice. He spotted his nephew and shouted over to him, "Jake lad, what're you doin' out at this hour?"

"Hello uncle Bob, mam's sent me to look for dog ends, she's run out of fags."

"Here take these," he said pushing a packet of woodbines into his hand. "Better than dog ends; an' I can always get some more tomorrow, cos tomorrow I'm gonna be rich."

"How are you gonna be rich, uncle Bob?" asked Jake putting the packet deep into his shabby coat pocket.

"Shush," he said putting his hand to his mouth. "Can you keep a secret?"

"Course I can," replied the youngster. "What is it?"

"I know the winner of the big race tomorrow. Pickpocket," he giggled drunkenly. "An' I'm going to have twenty quid on it."

"Twenty quid on Pickpocket. You've not got twenty quid Uncle Bob. That's a fortune."

He put his hand in his pocket and pulled out his wallet. "There see, how much do you think's in there?" He said, showing Jake his wallet stuffed with cash.

"Put it away Uncle Bob somebody might see," said Jake his eyes bulging at the sight of more money than he'd ever seen in his whole life. This was a rough area and the sight of a drunk with more money than sense, was a magnet for any chancer passing by to relieve him of it. "Come on I'll help you home."

As if on cue, a straggly youth had been watching from the pub doorway; probably no more than eighteen or nineteen, but wiry and streetwise. "What's up mate? You havin' problems with your old man then? 'Ere let me 'elp you get him 'ome."

"It's all right we can manage thanks," said Jake, putting his arm around his uncle's shoulders and trying to get him upright.

"No problem mate," he said putting his arm out as if to help him. Suddenly his hand made a snatch for the wallet, but Jake was as streetwise as him and saw it coming. "Your wallet uncle Bob, he's after your wallet," shouted the young lad.

Bob might have been drunk, but he wasn't completely senseless. Quick as a flash, he grabbed the lads arm and smashed it down across his knee breaking his ulna. At the same time Jake aimed a powerful kick into the thief's groin, sending him crashing to the pavement howling in agony. The noise brought several people out of the pub to see what the commotion was all about. Bob was suddenly sober and wasn't about to hang around until somebody called the Bobbies. Holding onto Jake they scurried off as fast as their legs would carry them.

It was only minutes from home but it seemed like Jake would never get his uncle there. To cap it all, it started to pour with rain. At the corner of York Street, a drenched Bob, heaving from the exertions of escaping from the fracas at the pub, suddenly stopped and emptied the contents of his stomach into the gutter.

"You alright uncle Bob?"

"I'm alright now lad. Come on, let's get 'ome before we catch our deaths."

Chapter twenty-one

Lizzie woke early; the wracking cough had kept her awake for most of the night. All she needed was a fag and a cup of tea, and she could face the world again. Jake had heard his mam get up and followed her down the stairs. "You're up early lad, what's the matter; your sisters got their feet in your face again?"

"Mam Uncle Bob says he's goin' to be rich after today."

"Don't take too much notice of what your uncle Bob says Jake, he's been telling us he's going to get rich for years, but it's not happened yet, nor is it likely," she said taking a deep drag on the cigarette that only started a fresh bout of coughing.

"But he says he knows the winner of the big race today at Newbury. I'm going to have a bet on it. I've got a few bob put at one side that I've been saving so I'm going to put it all on Pickpocket." At once Jake realized he'd let the cat out of the bag. It was supposed to be a secret.

"Pickpocket who's pickpocket?" asked Lizzie not fully awake yet.

"Nothing' mam just somebody tried to pick Uncle Bob's pocket last night in the pub, but I saw him and warned Uncle Bob, that's all."

"Well don't you go betting any money on them stupid animals; you'll come to no good, mark my words."

Jake breathed a sigh of relief. His mam hadn't suspected anything; he'd got away with it thanks to his quick thinking.

"Is there a brew in the pot Lizzie? My throat's as dry as a camel's arse."

"What's all this rubbish about you getting rich today?" said Lizzie as she pushed the steaming mug of tea towards her brother.

"Oh that. Just some lads I met in the pub 'avin' a laugh," said Bob, trying his best to shrug off the accusation.

"I don't want our Jake to get mixed up in anything like that, you hear me. Money's tight enough without him wasting it on bloody horses." She rasped as another fit of coughing tore through her lungs.

Chapter twenty-two

It was half past one and the five-pound note was burning a hole in Jakes trouser pocket. Where was uncle Bob? He was desperate to get his money on Pickpocket. He felt today was going to be his lucky day. He was convinced that later, he was going to be rich. He ran down to the Platelayers arms; his uncle was always there on a Saturday afternoon. Two scruffy-looking men were hanging about the steps of the pub.

"Have you seen my uncle Bob?" asked Jake desperately.

"Who's yer uncle lad?" said the drunk, obviously the worse for wear, hanging on to his mate for fear he might fall over.

"Bob Ashcroft, he always comes to the pub on Saturday afternoons."

"Can't say I know 'im. You know 'im Bert?"

"Can't say as I do. Why don't yer just 'ave a quick look for yerself?"

"I'm not eighteen yet and I don't want to risk the Bobbies seeing me; can you have a quick look and see if he's still inside the pub, mister. I really need to find him. My mam's sick and there's nobody to look after her, everybody's out," he lied convincingly.

"Go an' 'ave a quick shufty Tommy. Ask if anybody knows, who was it again lad?" wheezed Bert to his mate.

"Bob Ashcroft," said Jake. Minutes later the drunk came out of the pub.

"Sorry lad but he's not in there. Why don't you try the Queens Head just down the road, he might be in there," said the drunk, taken aback by the Jake's apparent plight.

"Thanks mister," said Jake sprinting down the road as fast as his legs would carry him. After a frantic search of the pub, there was no sign of his uncle. He sat on the steps of the Queens Head contemplating what to do next. He'd never put money on a horse before. He didn't even know where the bookie's was. Reluctantly he set off for town, sad that he'd missed the chance to get his money on Pickpocket. He wouldn't be getting rich any time soon.

Chapter twenty-three

He was just coming from under the railway bridge, when he spotted his uncle Bob coming out of the Victoria pub.

"Uncle Bob," he shouted at the top of his voice, running as fast as his legs would take him. "Uncle Bob, am I too late?" He cried his lungs almost bursting with the effort of trying to be heard above the roar of the Glasgow express thundering across the bridge.

"To late for what lad?" asked his perplexed uncle.

"I want to bet on Pickpocket. I want to put this fiver on it to win. Am I too late?"

"Where did you get money like that to bet on horses?" said Bob suspiciously. "I've been saving it up for a few weeks just in case something came up. But I want to bet on Pickpocket so's I can help mam out when it wins," said Jake urgently.

"But there's no guarantee that it'll win lad. Backin' 'orses is a mugs game. I've seen many a lad go broke on the promise of a quick buck on a slow 'orse," he said patting young Jake on the head.

"Please Uncle Bob, put it on for me then I can help mam when it wins."

Bob stoked his chin solemnly. It wasn't often Dixie gave him a dud and what harm would it do the lad. If it won he'd have a good few quid in his pocket, and if it lost, well he'd learn a valuable lesson, and not go wasting money gambling. He'd always been a gambler but that didn't mean he wanted his nephew to go the same way as him. "Give us yer money 'ere, but this is the only time. An' if it loses don't come cryin' to me ok."

"I won't uncle Bob I promise," said Jake relieved to get the money on.

Chapter twenty-four

Lizzie had nothing in the house; it looked as if she would be scraping the dripping from the bottom of the chip pan again for the kid's teas. She looked in the mirror her gaunt face stared back at her. Haggard and drawn before her years, she now sported a huge bruise under her right eye, and her lips were badly split. Earlier she had been in touch with Brooke to ask him if he could lend her any money, as she had nothing for the kids' teas. Jenny was still at school, and legally he was still liable to pay maintenance for her but not the eldest two. He said he would come round and sort something out.

Lizzie was in the kitchen when he called. "Brooke I've nothing in the house and the kids have nothing for their teas," she wailed. "Why do I always have to come begging to you? They're your kids as well as mine. I'm sick and tired of always chasing you to help out with them."

"I've been busy you know how it is, and anyway I don't have to pay for Jake and Lottie they're both working," he said, his clipped tones beginning to irritate her.

"Well can you help me or not?"

"Here," he said reaching into his wallet and pulling out some notes. "There's an extra ten bob there if you're nice to me," he said a lascivious look on his face. He never ceased to amaze her. After all the time they'd been divorced, he thought he could just walk back into her life any time he wanted.

"Bugger off. What do you think I am? Some bloody tramp you can pick up off the street."

"Come on Lizzie, there's nobody in; we could go upstairs for half an hour."

"You think you can buy me for ten bob," she raged. "Here take your bloody money," she said, throwing it back in his face. "I'd rather starve than go upstairs with you. And you'd better get out before our Bob gets back, or he'll throw you out on your arse, you soddin excuse for a man."

Not to be deterred he took another note out of his wallet. "Lizzie I'll give you another pound just for half an hour upstairs," he said waving the money in front of her face. She snatched at the notes but overbalanced and fell into his arms.

"See I knew you couldn't resist me," he sneered, pawing her breasts and trying to lift her skirt at the same time.

"Get your filthy hands off me you dirty pig."

"You know you don't mean it, come on, let's go upstairs." She could feel his hot breath brushing her cheeks. She lashed out and gouged a deep scratch in his face.

"You bloody bitch," he snarled and thumped her in the face splitting her lip, and bruising her under her eye. He dragged her shouting and screaming up the stairs and threw her onto the bed. The more Lizzie resisted the harder it seemed to urge him on. He savagely ripped the skirt from her waist and tore her underwear away, before straddling himself between her legs. Lizzie screamed as he brutally entered her. She tried to resist, but Brooke was powerfully built and she was powerless to stop him. She whimpered in pain, as he thrust cruelly between her thighs. He was determined to satisfy his lust. Lizzie was so weak she could barely catch her breath; she could do nothing but lie there listening to his animal grunts as he finally spent himself and rolled off her.

It must have seemed like hours when Lizzie heard Alice's voice at the bottom of the stairs. "Lizzie are you up there love?" she shouted.

Jake was in the back yard, unaware that his mam was upstairs.

"Jake, where's your mam love?" she asked.

"I don't know, Aunty Alice, I've been in the yard.'

"Lizzie are you there love?" she shouted again.

Lizzie tried to straighten her clothing, smoothing out her skirt which Brooke had thrown on the floor and trying to find her torn underwear. She could sense someone was calling her, but she was in a daze, she could hardly remember what day it was. Was it night already? How long had she slept? Questions kept fogging her mind. What had happened? Had Brooke really raped her, or was it just her imagination. The bruises on her thighs and between her legs quickly told her that it wasn't. She tried to get dressed but her legs felt like jelly, and she fell to the floor with a thump.

The sudden noise brought Alice rushing up the stairs followed closely by Jake.

"Lizzie love, are you all right?" Lizzie was slumped on the floor sobbing her heart out. "Lizzie whatever's the matter? What's happened?" cried Alice, putting her arms around her sister-in-laws shoulders.

"It's Brooke he's, he's raped me." she stuttered. "What is it with me every time I want something, it's always let's go to bed," she cried.

"What do you mean love? What's happened?" said Alice trying to ease Lizzie back on her feet. "First it were Joe Warmsley, and now Brooke," she sobbed. "What were Joe Warmsley and Brooke doing?" asked a bewildered Alice.

"What's up Mam, what's happened, why are you crying?" asked Jake.

"Go downstairs love and put the kettle on. I'll see to your mam. You could do with a good strong cuppa couldn't you love," she said hugging Lizzie close to her. "Go on love she'll be alright I promise. And plenty of sugar in that tea, there's a good lad."

Jake went to make the tea but stopped at the bottom of the stairs.

"They both raped me; Brooke's been doing it for years and then again today" he heard his Mam tell Aunty Alice. "Because I wouldn't go to bed with them they raped me. I wanted a lighter job in the factory," she sobbed pitifully. "Card room were too heavy for me. He said he would fix it but only if I went to bed with him."

"Who said he could fix it for you? Lizzie I'm not following you love," said Alice.

"Joe Warmsley one of the bosses at Taylors It was about five years ago. The kids were a lot younger. Jake was only about thirteen and I needed the job. When I refused to have 'out to do with him he knocked me back into carding shed and I dropped my fag. Place caught fire, and he said it were my fault as he'd caught me smoking in there."

Jake couldn't believe how anybody could hurt his mam like that, especially his dad.

"When I told old Grizedale that he'd tried to rape me, he concocted a story as how I was a skiver and was always coming on to him."

"Who's Grizedale Lizzie, I don't understand?" asked Alice.

"He was the manager at Taylors. He believed him and I got the sack, and now I've had the same treatment off Brooke. What is it with me Alice do I look like a tart or summat?"

"Course you don't love," said Alice squeezing Lizzie's shoulders, and wiping the tears from her eyes. "Bloody men, filthy buggers the lot of them only got one bloody thing on their minds."

"I've brought your tea, plenty of sugar just like Aunty Alice said. Are you going to be alright Mam?"

"Course she is love, she's just a bit upset that's all. She'll be alright once she gets that cuppa down her, won't you pet?" said Alice trying her best to alleviate the situation.

"Don't worry about me I'll be alright," she sniffed through tear-stained eyes. "I've got nothing more than a few cuts and bruises; I'll be alright love honest. You go and look after your sisters, there's a good lad."

"Just wait 'till Bob 'ears about this he'll bloody kill him."

"No, please Alice, don't tell our Bob, I don't want any trouble."

"But you can't just let them get away with it love. They deserve jailing the filthy pair of them."

"I know but who's going to believe me? It'll be my word against theirs and it's not like I've any proof is it. Please just leave it. Oh I feel so dirty and used," she sobbed.

"It's not you as should feel dirty and used love, it's those dirty bastards. If I ever get my hands on them I won't be responsible for my actions," she raged.

Chapter twenty-five

Jake was waiting outside Platelayers arms. He'd been there for more than an hour. It was half past three the race must be over by now he thought. It was run at half past two so it must be over. "Hey mister, how did pickpocket get on in the big race this afternoon?" he asked the gruff looking man coming out of the pub.

"Pickpocket. Who's pickpocket?" He grunted his mind obviously not on horseracing.

Not to be deterred Jake was determined to find out the result. A fat looking bloke was sauntering to the pub engrossed in his paper, 'He'll know,' thought Jake. "Hey mister who won the big race this afternoon?"

"The big race; what big race? an' why would a young whipper-snapper like you want to know summat like that eh?"

"Me and some mates saw the race in the paper this morning," he said. "And we all picked a horse out, and the one who picks the winner gets five bob each off the rest of the gang," he lied convincingly.

"Well I don't know for sure but it were a big-priced un, I can tell yer that. So if yer picked the favourite, it's like as not, you'll not be collectin' five bob each from yer mates," he laughed.

"Well what won it? Do you know?" Jake was beside himself, he could barely keep a limb still. He knew he wasn't on the favourite so what had won the race? "Please mister do you know what won?"

"Hang on a minute son an' I'll go an' ask inside the pub, somebody in there's bound to know." Jake waited for what seemed like an age. He went to the door of the pub and opened it only to be shooed away by an angry looking barmaid, who looked like she'd had one too many gins and too many late nights judging by the veins showing on her bulbous nose and purple cheeks.

"Get off with yer," she screeched. "A young lad like you shouldn't be in a place like this. What'll yer mam say?"

"I'm waiting for somebody; he'll be out in a minute," countered Jake hoping the man hadn't forgotten he was waiting.

"Who are yer waitin' for lad?" asked the woman, the tone of her voice somewhat surprisingly mellower than her earlier outburst. Maybe she just felt sorry for him or maybe it was just her maternal instinct kicking in. "What's 'is name lad?"

"I don't know. He were just a fat bloke reading a paper with a grey coat on."

"There's plenty o' fat blokes with a grey coat on, readin' a paper in there lad. Was there 'out else that you can remember about 'im?"

"I think he had, like a white silky scarf thing round his neck too, tied in like a knot."

"I think I might know who it is, wait 'ere a minute." Minutes later she appeared at the door with the man. "Is this 'im?" she asked Jake. "This young lad says he's been waitin' for yer. Is that right?"

"Aye, that's right Mabel."

"Well hurry up, a young lad like that shouldn't be 'angin' 'round pub doors."

"Thanks missus," said Jake hoping his wait had not been in vain.

"That's alright love just make sure you get off 'ome as soon as you've done eh," she said with a friendly wink.

"I will missus and thanks. Well what won the big race?" Jake could barely contain himself. He just had this feeling, if the favourite hadn't won, then he had a chance that it might be his horse.

"Well it weren't the favourite, I can tell you that much," said the fat bloke.

"Well what were it then?" pleaded Jake.

"Summat beginning with 'P' I think. Pink Locket or summat; I know my bugger finished nowhere as bloody usual." Jakes heart sank he hadn't seen Pink Locket, that was his five quid down the drain. "Are you sure that's what won, Pink Locket?"

"Pretty certain, son. Aye, number 16, Pink Locket, 40-1, bloody bookies benefit."

Suddenly Jake perked up. Number 16 that was his horse Pickpocket; he was sure of it. "Mister can I have a look at your paper?"

"Aye 'ere you are lad." He quickly turned to the racing page sure enough Newbury 2-30 the Bodsworth brewery handicap hurdle number 16 Pickpocket. It must be the same horse. He eagerly scanned the rest of the runners in the 2:30. There was no other horse that sounded like Pickpocket in the race, and certainly no Pink Locket. It must be Pickpocket. "Mister was that horse not called Pickpocket?" he asked.

"Aye now you come to mention it, aye it was Pickpocket. It picked my bloody pocket alright. I suppose yer mates they'll have to fork out the five bobs now eh," he laughed.

"Aye they will that," chuckled Jake under his breath. But I'll have more than five bob with my winnings. He thought.

Chapter twenty-six

Five years earlier 1952.

Lizzie sat in the doctor's surgery, twisting her handkerchief nervously between her fingers. The racking cough that had plagued her for the last few months wasn't getting any better. Poor food and even worse living and working conditions had seen to that. The house was damp all the time, and in winter there was barely enough coal for the fire since dad had gone. Brooke never paid his money on time and if he did it was always after a trip upstairs. If it hadn't been for the pittance she earned at Bensons mill they would have starved. The problem was that these days she was becoming weaker and weaker. She was finding it harder to breathe, and the job at Matlocks in the cardroom was slowly killing her.

In truth, she had a pretty good idea, what the prognosis was going to be.

"Mrs Steeples you can go in now," said kindly Mrs Green, the doctor's receptionist.

"Lizzie come in, please sit down. How have you been since your last visit?"

"Struggling, if I'm honest doctor. I can hardly get my breath these days. I'm gasping for breath just going up the stairs."

"Well I'm not surprised. I've got the results of the tests we did a few weeks ago, and I'm afraid to say it's not good news." He said shuffling a sheaf of papers in his hands. Lizzie shifted uneasily in the chair, twisting her hanky even tighter round her fingers, almost cutting off the blood supply, dreading to hear the doctor's next words. "They've found a shadow on one of your lungs, I'm very sorry," he said apologetically.

"A shadow, what do you mean?"

"Well in a nutshell you have tuberculosis. You have scar tissue covering most of your left lung. That's why you've had difficulty breathing. I'm sorry to be the bringer of bad news, but it's what I suspected all along, but we had to do the tests just to be sure." Lizzie slumped forward her head in her hands. "Does that mean I'm going to die doctor?" She cried.

"Lizzie I won't lie to you."

"How long have I got?"

"Well the scar tissue is fairly advanced."

"How long doctor? Weeks? Months? Will I see my kids grow up?" The tears were streaming down her pale cheeks.

"Without treatment about six months at the most," he said.

"Six months." It was like being hit with a sledge hammer; little Lottie and Jenny, her babies, and Jake growing into a fine young man. It couldn't be happening to her. Would it be that she would never see them grow up, or get married, and have families of their own? Would she never see her grandchildren?

"And with treatment, how long?"

"The treatment nowadays is very successful. But it would mean several months in a sanatorium, but if all goes well you could live a normal lifespan."

"And is this treatment available?" She said recovering her composure a little.

"It is but not in the northwest. I could refer you to Dr Allenby he's one of the leading specialists in the treatment of TB. However his clinic's in Chelmsford just outside of London. If you agree you would have to go to London for the treatment. You would be away for several months."

"And what's his success rate?"

"I'll not lie to you Lizzie, the treatment in an advanced case like yours I would say at best 60-40. But Dr Allenby has had some remarkable results, and treatment is improving all the time."

"And the alternative is I've got about six months at the most."

"I'm afraid that's about the size of it Lizzie. Still you don't need to make up your mind straight away. Go home take a few days but don't leave it to long, we need to act as quickly as possible. In the meantime I'll give you a prescription for something to make your breathing a little easier, and to help you sleep at night."

"Thanks doctor but I've made up my mind. I'll go for the treatment. Can you set it up for me?"

"If you're sure. But what about the children?"

"Don't worry about them I'll ask their dad to look after them for a few months; Jakes going on thirteen he'll help out as well. He's a good lad," she said hating the thought of being without them for God knows how long. They should be all right with their dad though. He had bought himself a fine big house in Greenwood village not far from his parents' place. Surely they would help to take care of their grandchildren for a few months while she had treatment. She would have asked her dad Colly, but he had been drinking steadily for the past few months and she didn't trust him to look after the kid's properly. Her only option had been Brooke.

Chapter twenty-seven

"Where're we going dad? asked Jake, from the front seat of his dad's car.

"Mam says we're coming to stay with you for a bit while she's in hospital."

"Well just at the minute Jake, I've got a lot of business on and I won't be able to look after you for a little while, so I'm dropping you off at some friends."

"Is it granddad's house? Will we all be together?" asked Jake already fearing the worst.

"Well just for a little while Lottie and Jenny will be staying with some very nice people not far from you."

"Where will I be staying then?"

"We want to stay with Jake," cried Jenny.

"I want my mam. When's she coming back?" sobbed Lottie, burying her head in her older sister's shoulder.

"It's only down the road. You'll be able to see them every day. You mustn't get upset, it won't be for very long, and then your mam will be back."

1957

That was more than five years ago. Jake had never forgiven his dad for dumping them in a children's home. He had never forgotten his sister's anguished cries, especially young Lottie. She was only ten and was like a little doll as they dragged her and Jenny screaming for their mam into that bloody awful home. He was thirteen and had been close to tears, but had refused to let them see him cry. He promised he would see them soon, and not to worry.

Since then Jake had grown into a fine-looking young man. At almost eighteen he was broad shouldered, muscular and agile, with a shock of almost blue black hair, tawny skin, and the most intense blue eyes, almost certainly inherited from his mother. He was more than capable of holding his own against lads older than himself. His time in the home had quickly taught him how to look after himself. One night not long after he'd been in there, one of the older lads had come over to his bed, and tried to force Jake to fondle him. Jake was having none of it, and promptly grabbed the lad's member as hard as he could and twisted it so hard he almost tore the head off.

The resulting screams brought the head of the home rushing breathlessly into the boy's bedroom. "What the hell's going on?" he asked clearly flustered at being wakened at this late hour of the night.

"It's alright Billy's just having a nightmare; isn't that right Billy?" said Jake glaring at the panic stricken youth.

"Yeah I was having a bad dream that's all, I'm ok now though," he said nervously, rubbing his tender crotch. The sweat was pouring down his face.

The man slapped the youth hard across the head and dished out the same punishment to Jake. "Well get back to sleep all of you, you've got school in the morning," he said grumpily as he went back to bed. For the rest of the time he was in the home, no one ever picked on him again.

Chapter twenty-eight

1957

Lizzie liked working at Benson's mill. It gave her a wage every week and she was glad to meet up with her old mate Joanie again. Her operation had been a success and now more than five years later she was feeling better than she had done for years. The only downside was she missed her dad. His bouts of heavy drinking had finally taken its toll. The thoughts of his grandchildren in a kids' home had probably been too much. Jake had come down stairs one Sunday morning to find his granddad with his head in the gas oven. Whether it was intentional or not was never really proved. The official verdict was suicide whilst the balance of his mind was disturbed. However, Lizzie was convinced it was the constant pressure of seeing her and the kids struggle. She had somehow managed to put it behind her and was at last starting to get her life back on track.

The worst was behind her. She had gained weight and the colour had come back to her cheeks again, and she was glad not having to rely on young Jake all the time.

Joanie drew deep on her fag, looking up at the clear blue sky end enjoying the warm spring day as the sunshine warmed her face. "I thought you'd given them up when you were carrying little Alice," said Lizzie who would have killed for a smoke, but she hadn't touched one since her operation.

"I know I must be daft, but it's a hard habit to give up" she said taking another drag before crushing the dog end under her foot." Have you heard who's starting next week love?" she said with more than a little consternation in her voice.

"No who?"

"Joe Warmsley."

"Your kiddin' me. How the hell has he got a job here? I thought he'd buggered off over to Yorkshire, Leeds way or somewhere like that. Last I heard he'd took up with some young lass over there and got a couple of kids."

"Well according to Arthur he saw him in the pub last week and he's coming back here. He's left the woman he was with and the kids; lost his job apparently. Arthur says the factory went bust. I don't know for sure. But he says they were looking for a supervisor here and he somehow got the job. I'm sorry love but I thought you should know. I'm sure nowt will come of it."

"Yeah thanks Joanie, thanks for telling' me." Somehow, at the back of her mind she knew she hadn't heard the last of him.

Chapter twenty-nine

Jake fidgeted anxiously as he waited for his uncle Bob. Today was going to be another profitable one; he could sense it in his water. Over the last few months, Jake and his uncle had made quite a killing betting on Dixie's tips. The latest was a horse called 'Blowtorch,' a forgotten nag out of Barney Mulligan's yard over in Yorkshire. Barney only had a small string but was legendary for setting up a betting coup. 'Blowtorch' had last run at the Cheltenham festival earlier in the year where, only for a stumble coming over the last in the county hurdle, it would have surely won its race. Nevertheless it was beaten less than two lengths in a blanket finish after being almost on the floor and ran on to be a creditable fourth. Barney decided that was it for the time being, and put him away for the rest of the winter.

Today was the day that 'Blowtorch' was going to do the business according to Dixie. He was due to run that afternoon in a two mile Henry 2nd stakes at Sandown. According to Dixie, it would be a pretty competitive race and Blowtorch's odds should be around the 20-1 mark, as he was running against top notch proven stayers on the flat.

At last, Jake saw his uncle. "Where've you been? I've been on pins the last hour," grumbled Jake.

"Patience lad. I've had to spread the money around a bit; can't put that much on with one bookie. They'll get suspicious and the odds will drop like a stone. Two hundred quid is a lot of money to spread around it takes time."

"You've got it all on though."

"Aye every penny, but I've had to go all over town to do it."

"What'll we make if it wins?"

"If it comes in at its present odds we'll make two thousand quid each. Most of the lads I've got it on with are givin' 20-1, but it depends on the race, it could come in a bit or it could go the other way and drift. It depends on what the punters back on the course."

"Two thousand quid," thought Jake. It was a fortune. If the horse won they could open that club they were always talking about. What they could do with that sort of money!

All ears were tuned to the radio, crackling high above the bar of the vault of the Black Bull. The vault was stuffy, the early June temperature was in the low seventies outside, but in the pub it was nearer eighty degrees as the punters gathered round the radio waiting impatiently for the start of Sandown's two mile, group two, Henry 2nd stakes. The commentator said that they were lining up behind the tape and the starter had raised his flag. Any second now they would be off thought Jake, wedged between his uncle and Dixie trying his best to keep out of sight of the landlord.

"No," exclaimed the commentator. One of the horses was refusing to line up. He couldn't quite see which it was at the moment, but it looked like the blue and orange colours of number eleven Blowtorch.

"Oh no," gasped Jake thinking of the two hundred quid about to go down the drain if Blowtorch didn't run. After what seemed like an age the starter brought them into line again. This time Blowtorch lined up with the rest the starter dropped his flag, they were off. The race began at a frantic pace with the lead changing hands at least half a dozen times in the first four furlongs. Sandown was a one mile five furlong right handed oval track with a long run in and a stiff uphill finish. It suited a horse that was a good galloper and had plenty of stamina. According to Dixie, Blowtorch filled the bill on both counts.

The radio crackled as the commentator gave the eager listeners a yard by yard account of their horse's position. "And leading with just over a mile to travel is Blue Danube from, in second place Slipstream, closely followed by Tallboy, with a group of about six or seven bunched up behind the front three. Two lengths behind these comes the favourite Black Prince, who is now making a forward move." He said animatedly.

"Where's Blowtorch?" moaned Jake worriedly.

"Bringing up the rear are Golden Idol, River Boat, Blowtorch, Silver Streak and in last place Sundial."

"He'll never win from there," Groaned Jake.

"Patience lad," Said Dixie. "He's got a hell of a kick 'as this fella; don't rule him out yet. He likes to come off a strong pace."

"The favourite, Black Prince is now making significant progress from the rear of the field, and he's just behind long time leader Blue Danube, who is beginning to tire."

"Come on Blowtorch," mouthed Jake to himself, his fist clenched nervously.

"They're entering the final four furlongs, and Black Prince is challenging Blue Danube for first place. Making a run from the back is Golden Idol and River Boat, and starting to pick up the pace is Blowtorch. They're in the final two furlongs and Black Prince is beginning to wear down Blue Danube who is tiring rapidly and is falling back into third place." There were groans from some of the punters who had obviously backed Blue Danube. "Also making a good run is the well backed Tallboy who has now gone into a clear second place, only a length behind Black Prince. Fighting for the minor placings are Slipstream,

Golden Idol and River Boat. These seem to have the race between them the rest seem to be out of it."

"Oh no that's two hundred quid down the drain," groaned Jake.

"They're in the final furlong and Black Prince is having to fight to keep the lead. He's being strongly challenged by Tallboy who is upsides of him with Slipsteam in third. These three have got the race between them.

"With less than half a furlong to go it's neck and neck. Brad Kelly is going for everything on Black Prince he's got 'is nose in front again, tallboy is slipping back and Slipstream is making a renewed challenge under Seamus O'Flynn, but wait there's been a bump. It looks as if Black Prince has bumped into Slipstream and impeded his run. Wait; here comes Blowtorch he's absolutely flying. There's less than a hundred yards to go, Black Prince is just in front by a nose from Slipstream alongside, with Blowtorch and Micky Devlin riding like a man possessed on the outside finishing like an express train."

"Go on Blowtorch," shouted Jake punching the air from the back of the vault.

"Its Black Prince from Slipstream and here comes Blowtorch. They've gone past together I can't separate them, but I think the favourite might just have held on from the flying Blowtorch but it's hard to tell from this angle. But there was a bit of interference in the last half furlong and I think there might be a steward's inquiry. Yes as I thought, the flag has gone up it's a photo finish, and there's also a steward's inquiry. We're going to have to wait a little longer for the result of this one," announced the commentator.

Jake was beside himself, he couldn't bear to listen to the radio any longer and went outside to get some air. After what seemed a lifetime he heard a roar from inside the pub. He rushed back in to see his uncle being patted on the back by his mates. "Well what's happened?"

"I told you that he had a hell of a finishing kick didn't I," said Dixie with the broadest grin you had ever seen on his face. "You mean we've won."

"Aye, a nose from Slipstream and Black Prince. Black Prince finished second, but was demoted to third for interference. But that had nowt to do with our lad he got up right on the line."

"How much have we won then uncle Bob?" asked Jake excitedly hardly able to contain himself. "Well he came in at 25-1 so I make that more than five thousand quid."

"Bloody hell," was all Jake could say?

Chapter thirty

Joanie rapped on Lizzie's back door. "It's open, come on in," said Lizzie.

"We're going to be late. It's already past seven o'clock and the bus leaves at ten past," said Joanie.

"Be with you in a minute. Come on Lottie love get a move on lass we're going to be late."

"How do you like working for a living then duck?" asked Joanie cheerfully.

"It's ok," replied Lottie miserably, trudging slowly to the bus stop.

"What is it love? The early mornings; you'll get used to it won't she Lizzie. How long you been here then?"

"Nearly three months."

"Blimey I didn't think it was that long, time flies. It doesn't seem five minutes since you left school."

Lottie had left school that summer. She had turned fifteen and Lizzie had got her fixed up at Bensons. It was only a light job. She was working in the spinning room bringing empty bobbins for the spinning machines, and generally brushing the floors and keeping the dust down. It wasn't the best of jobs, and the money was poor, but it was a job. It would be a year or two before she could go on the machines themselves. At least it was a wage coming in. With Jake working with his uncle Bob at the club they'd opened, and Lottie with a part time job working at a drapers in Thistlefield, things had been getting a little easier at home, but lately Lottie hadn't been herself. For a few weeks now, she had been moody and withdrawn. Lizzie was at pains to get anything out of her. Maybe it was the early mornings, but she had her doubts.

The factory hooter sounded just as they got off the bus. A crowd of workers rushed the gates trying to get to their work before they got docked a quarter of an hour's pay for being late.

"Mam I don't feel well this morning I think I'll go home," said Lottie being forced into the factory yard by a horde of anxious workers, eager not to lose any of their wages. "What's up with you? You've been in a funny mood for the last week."

"Come on duck, it'll soon be break time an' you can tell your aunty Joanie what's up," she said sensing the youngster's gloomy frame of mind.

"It's nothing why don't you just leave me alone," she said pushing past the two women into the factory. "She's really got it on her this morning. You don't think its lad trouble do you love?"

"I'd thought of that myself, but she's not even got a boyfriend as far as I know Joanie, but I'm pretty sure that's not what it is."

"Well summat's got into her that's for sure. You'd best keep your eye on her, you know what young lasses are like when it comes to lads, their Mams are always the last to know. Come on we'd best get in before we're late."

Lottie was pushing the skip laden with bobbins round the noisy spinning room. It was hard to hear yourself think with hundreds of spinning machines clattering away like a dozen trains all rushing through the station at once. She was busy filling the machines, when a figure brushed up beside her.

"Oh you made me jump. I didn't see you there Mr. Warmsley," she said, her young cheeks flushing a bright shade of red. He smiled at her, his rotten teeth yellow and black from decay protruding through lascivious lips, almost turned her stomach.

"There's some bobbins down at the end of the room on the floor below, I'll show you where they are. I need you to bring them up."

"It's alright I know where they are, I'll go and fetch them in a minute," she said trying to ignore his lecherous gaze. "No these are different we've not had these before I'll show you which they are come on."

The tiny room was covered in dust and there was raw cotton spread all over the floor. She had been here before.

"There aren't any bobbins in here," said Lottie nervously trying to back out of the dusty room.

Joe shut the door to the storeroom, causing Lottie to jump with fright. "Come on give us a kiss. If you're nice to me, I'll see that you get a job on the spinning machines. The money's twice what you'll earn fillin' boxes," he said pulling the frightened girl towards him.

"No leave me alone." She almost got the door open but his rough hands slammed it shut throwing the dead bolt at the same time. He pulled her back savagely and threw her to the floor. She screamed out but no one could hear her. He was on her in a moment. His filthy hands were all over her young body. Pawing her budding adolescent breasts and clawing at her clothes as he tried rip off her underwear. She fought him but he was too strong.

"No please," she begged. "Please don't." But her pleas fell on deaf ears as he grunted and gasped on top of her spreading her legs as he spent his lust. When he had finished Lottie just lay there crying. Tears streamed down her face. He buttoned up his trousers and tucked his shirt in. "That wasn't so bad was it? If you hadn't been so bloody hysterical you might even 'ave enjoyed it," he said cruelly.

Lottie whimpered in pain. It wasn't the first time Warmsley had molested the girl. "Just you wait 'till I tell my mam about this, you'll end up in jail you filthy pig," she sobbed angrily smoothing out her dishevelled clothing, and trying to straighten her hair.

Furiously he grabbed her and pinned her against the door, the iron latch digging into her frail body through the thin cotton of her flimsy dress, which he had so very nearly torn from her young body. "You tell anybody about this an' you an' yer mam will be lookin' for more than another job, understand," he said viciously his foul breath wafting over her like an overflowing privy.

"Just you wait 'till my uncle Bob hears about this he'll bloody kill you," she rasped defiantly.

"You tell anybody what's happened 'ere today an' it's me as'll be doin' the killin' girly, you 'ear me," he snarled, his arm pushed brutally against her throat so that she could hardly breathe. "Now get back to yer work an' remember not a bloody word."

Chapter thirty-one

The jamboree club was throbbing with the sound of people having a good time. It had always been Bob's dream to own his own drinking establishment, and now thanks to their win on Blowtorch he had made it a reality. He and Jake had pooled their money and bought the place at a knock down price. It had taken most of the money they had won, and now almost three months of hard graft to get it back into shape but now they were reaping the rewards. Lizzie didn't really approve but for once, it gave her brother a purpose in life; better than drifting aimlessly from dead end job to dead end job. At last he would be able to make something of himself, and hopefully make something of Jake as well.

Jake stayed in the background fetching and carrying for his uncle and quickly learning the ropes. He soon picked up the day to day running of the club. His formal education had been limited, but he was streetwise and as sharp as a tack. With his uncle in tow, not many got the better of them, when dealing with club business. Lizzie only wished she could say the same about Lottie who was becoming more and more withdrawn every day. Going to work had become the bane of her life, and it was a battle every day to get her daughter to go. She had lost more than a few shifts in the last few weeks and the bosses at Bensons were starting to get fed up with her bad timekeeping. Much more and she would be in danger of losing her job.

The queue for the lunchtime break seemed to get longer every day. Freddie Marsden was feeling peckish. Being an apprentice fitter at Bensons certainly gave a young fellow an appetite.

"By 'eck. You got a worm or summat? That'll be two bob love," said big Elsie on the till.

"Two bob. I thought it were only one an' six," said Freddie starting to blush. "Sorry lovey but that's a two shillin' dinner you've got there. Steak an' kidney pie, two veg, chips, gravy, bread an' butter, jam roly-poly an' custard plus a mug of tea that's two bob."

"But I've only got one an' six," he said, his eyes boring into the canteen floor.

"Can't you see the lad's embarrassed Elsie? Here love, I'll lend you the tanner, but I want it back mind. Money doesn't grow on trees," said Joanie coming to the young lad's rescue.

"Thanks missus. I'll pay you back Friday when I get my wages. Where do you sit?"

"Over there," she said pointing to the table where Lizzie and Lottie were already sitting. "There's a spare seat if you want it, but I expect you'll want to sit with your mates."

"No. We're on separate sittings for breaks. It's in case of breakdowns you know, somebody always on call," he explained. Secretly he had been trying to get an excuse to meet Lottie for a few weeks, but had never had the nerve to ask her. This was a perfect opportunity. "Well if you're sure I wouldn't be in the way."

"No I'm sure you wouldn't be in the way. Kids they must think we were born yesterday," She smiled to herself.

Chapter thirty-two

Brooke pulled up outside Lizzie's door. His excuse was that he was entitled to see his kids, but in truth it was Lizzie he was after. He was like moth drawn to a naked flame he just couldn't help himself. It had been more than thirteen years since the divorce and although he had never re-married, he still called. He was a serial womanizer; it was just in his blood.

Curtains twitched, as he pulled up outside her house and switched off the car engine. Lizzie dreaded it. He seemed to have built in radar calling when there was no one in. In the early years before the kids got older she had always managed to keep at least one of them in with her, but now they had friends of their own and she couldn't shackle them to her apron strings any longer. Lizzie tried not answering the door, but his persistent hammering soon had the neighbours gawping through the curtains or coming out into the street to see what all the fuss was about. She had no option but to let him in. Lizzie, like Brooke had never re-married and had no regular man in her life preferring to keep them at arm's length. They had caused her enough problems to last her a lifetime. Ever since Jenny had started work, his visits had been getting more and more frequent. Jenny had become very friendly with young Frank the mechanic at Bensons. Lizzie had been grateful that he had started to bring her out of herself. The downside being she was left more and more on her own, and with the club occupying Bob and Jakes time these days she was feeling more and more vulnerable.

"How many times have I told you not to call?" she said hoping the irritation in her voice would get through her ex-husbands thick skin.

"You know you don't mean it," he said grabbing her round the waist and pulling her to him.

"Will you leave me alone," she cried. "I don't mind you coming to see the kids, but I'm not jumping into bed with you every time you call."

"Come on Lizzie we were good together," he said pulling her closer to him. He was powerfully built and she could barely breathe as his hot breath crushed her lips. She pounded his shoulders with her fists, but it had little effect, it only seemed to spur him on. She thought of how many times in the last year he had assaulted her. Assault was the only way you could describe his advances. It wasn't love, and it wasn't passion not passion in the true sense, it was lust pure and simple, nothing more. She punched his face and caught him a glancing blow to his nose causing it to bleed. Momentarily he stopped and wiped the blood from his face. Angrily he punched her in the face knocking her to the floor. Brooke jumped on her ripping her skirt off. Lizzie tried to pull the skirt back on but she was weak from the blow. She just lay there and whimpered as he tore her underwear off and brutally entered her. He grunted and groaned and in a moment it was over, as he spent himself. He didn't utter a word as he did up his trousers, he just looked at her and grunted something inaudible and left her lying there. She felt used and dirty. Her head was spinning from the punch he gave her when she tried to resist him, and her eye was black and blue, already starting to swell. It was several hours later that she was awakened by Lottie coming home from the cinema with Frank.

"Mam what's up are you ok?" Lottie was shocked by her mother's appearance. "Mam are you ok?" She said shaking her mother by the shoulder. "What's happened? Have you fell or summat?"

"Shall I call a doctor? She looks in a right state," said Frank.

"Mam are you ok?" Lottie asked for the umpteenth time. Lizzie started to come round a little, but her head was still spinning and she felt sick inside. She tried to straighten her clothes, and pulled the heavy woollen cardigan tight around her shoulders as if it might keep any unwelcome intruders at bay. "I'm alright love I must have fell over," she uttered defensively.

"You don't look alright. Are you sure you're ok?" Lizzie stumbled towards the chair but before she could reach it, she fell over hitting her head on the side of the fireplace.

"Mam," cried Lottie in despair as she crashed to the floor. "Frank call the doctor quick, there's a phone box at the end of the street, and then tell our Jake."

Two hours later Lizzie was in the accident and emergency ward of St Mary's hospital. She was still unconscious. Because of the extent of her injuries, the police had been informed.

"Any chance we can speak with Mrs Steeples?" asked Detective Constable Diana Linley.

"Not at the moment I'm afraid," said the young junior doctor in charge of the A and E department at St Mary's. "She's still unconscious. She's had a very nasty bang on the head, and she's also got extensive bruising on her back and on her ribs. Some of the bruising is older and some of it is more recent. I would say that some of it has been done in the last few weeks maybe even longer. She's also got a lot of bruising on her thighs."

"Bruising on her thighs; you mean there's been a sexual assault. Has she been raped?" said DC Linley.

"Well we can't be certain at this stage, but there has certainly been some recent sexual activity possibly in the last few hours. Whether it was with her consent or not, we won't know until she wakes up."

"How long is that likely to be?" asked DC Linley.

"Hard to say with this type of injury; could be a couple of hours, could be a couple of days, we'll just have to wait and see but my guess is you won't hear nothing for at least twelve hours.

Jenny and Jake had been waiting anxiously pacing up and down the corridor waiting for news of their mother. Jake had arrived as soon as he got the message from Frank that his mother was in hospital. "What's up with her? Why are the police here?" he asked the duty doctor.

"Your mother has had a nasty fall but not to worry. We've given her a thorough examination and we've also taken some x-rays of her head and chest. There's nothing broken, but the x-rays show that your mother had some scar tissue around her lungs."

"Yeah she has TB a few years ago, went down south to have it treated, came back ok though. It's not come back has it?" said Jake, fearful that his mam might have had a relapse.

"No I'm sure she's going to be alright. What she needs now is plenty of rest."

"But that policewoman said she'd been raped. When did it happen?"

"We're not even sure that it is rape yet, but there has certainly been some sexual activity recently that's for sure. Surely, your father should have been informed. Where is he? He should be here," the young doctor went on.

"Mam and dad were divorced years ago," explained Jake. "They hardly see one another these days."

Jake wanted an explanation, turning away from the doctor; he went to find the police officer. DC Linley was just coming out of the matron's office when Jake spied her.

"Officer is it true that mam's been raped?"

"I'm sorry sir you are?"

"Jake, Jake Steeples, she's my mam. Is it true she's been raped?" he asked the pain clearly etched onto his young face. "Who'd do summat like that? Not to mam, she's suffered enough already."

DC Linley wasn't sure how to proceed. Rape wasn't something you discussed with someone's kids, especially when it was the lad's own mother. Shouldn't your dad have been here?" asked D C Linley inquisitively.

"Same as I told the doc, they've been divorced for years. He only see's her now and then, and that's when he comes to see us, which is rare these days." Jake was unaware of his dad's visits to see his mother when they were out.

"Really and when was the last time you saw your dad then Jake?"

"Don't rightly know, a week maybe two I'm not sure. Why what are you getting at? You don't think it was my dad do you?"

"Do you know if your parents were on good terms Jake?" said D C Linley making notes in her diary. "How do you mean?"

"Did they argue? Or fight?"

"She was always on at him to pay his maintenance. He never paid on time; they argued about that a lot."

"Anything else? Did she have any boyfriends that your dad might have been jealous of?"

"Mam never had any boyfriends, as far as I know. What are you getting at? Are you trying' to say mam was a tart or summat? You should be out there trying to catch the animal who did this to her. So help me I'll kill the bastard if I get my hands on him."

"Please Sir, don't do anything you might regret. I'm sure that we'll apprehend the culprit in due course, leave it up to the law to deal with."

"Well you'd better be bloody quick cos if I get to him first..." He left the sentence unfinished brushing past DC Linley and into the corridor to find Lottie.

"Oh Jake have you seen our mam? Who'd want to do that to her?" she said squeezing Jake's hand so hard she made the poor lad wince.

"It's alright Lottie, mam's tough, she'll be ok," said Jake.

She turned to the doctor. "Can we see her just once more before we go?"

"Just for a minute, then I think you should go home and get some rest," said the doctor kindly.

Lottie almost wept when she saw her mother. Her face was black and blue, and her head was covered in bandages. She went over to the bed and squeezed her mother's hand. "Oh mam what's happened? Who did this to you?" she cried.

"Come on Lottie lets go home there's nothing you can do here; you'll just have to wait until she wakes up," said Frank gently, putting his arms around her shoulders and ushering her out of the door.

Chapter thirty-three

Lizzie woke with a start; it had been more than a month since her attack. The police had been round on several occasions but she had refused to press charges against her former husband. What was the point? Who would believe her? Folk would only say she egged him on. It was six o'clock and the alarm had woken her from a troubled sleep. She was due back at Bensons but the thought of going back there filled her with dread. Lottie was still playing up but she was no nearer finding out what was wrong, and that louse Joe Warmsley had been sniffing round. She was sick of fighting him off. Every day was the same. What with Brooke, and now him, his lecherous advances were beginning to get her down. Joanie called round at the usual time but the journey to work these days was anything but pleasant.

The morning passed quickly as Lizzie got back into the swing of things. At least being busy kept her mind occupied. She was crossing the factory yard when Joe Warmsley saw her. "Lizzie can I have a word?"

"I've nothing I want to say to you unless you're about to crawl away and die somewhere," said Lizzie sharply, trying to get past him. "Come on Lizzie. Why don't you be nice to me? I can make life really easy for you if you'll only give me a chance."

"I just want you to leave me alone, that's all," she retorted angrily.

"Why don't you come out for a drink with me tonight? Me an' you, we've just got off on the wrong foot that's all. I'm not so bad when you get to know me," he said placating trying to win her over. "I've not a lot of friends, an' I know I've wronged you in the past, but I'd like to make it up to you."

"You must be bloody joking. I've not forgot what happened at Taylors. You raped me, and all I got was the bloody sack."

"I know I got carried away an' I was sick about it after. I never wanted it to 'appen an' I'd 'a done anythin' to put it right. I was really sorry. I never wanted you to go."

"You got carried away. I'll say you got carried away. You told Grisdale that I started the fire; that I was always off the job, and the best of all that I was always coming on to you. All you've done since I started here is to try to get me to go to bed with you," she scoffed.

Joe pleaded with her. "I always fancied you Lizzie. I thought you fancied me, and well I know I shouldn't 'ave done what I did, an' I'm sorry". Lizzie almost began to believe him; his story was almost plausible. Maybe it was her. Maybe she was being too hard on him, but he had raped her and she had lost her job, and now he was trying it on again. Why would he change now? Lizzie was determined not to let her guard down, men like Joe Warmsley wouldn't change. A leopard didn't change its spots.

"Well why didn't you say summat back then? No you let everybody think I was just a cheap tart and that I set fire to the cotton store when all the time it was your fault."

"I wanted to but I suppose I couldn't face the consequences. I know I was wrong an' I could 'ave gone to jail, but I was scared Lizzie. You 'ave to believe me, I've regretted it every day since. I went over to Leeds after Taylor's shut down hopin' to put the past behind me, but that didn't work out either. Every time I try an' get into a relationship with a woman, summat always seems to go wrong. I really like you Lizzie an' I wish I could do summat to convince you that I'm really sorry for what happened."

"Well you could start by leaving me alone and not pestering me all the time."

"Ok. Can we at least be civil to one another while we're at work."

"Suits me," said Lizzie pushing past him into the factory.

The hooter sounded for the end of the shift and hundreds of workers all made their way to the buses waiting in the factory yard to take them home. Lottie was pulling her coat on when she spied Frank running across the yard towards her. She and Frank had been going out for a few months, but lately the relationship had become a little strained.

"Lottie are we alright for tonight?" he asked. "There's a couple of new films showing at the Ritz. One's a new Norman Wisdom comedy and the other's one of them Carry On's; should be a good laugh. I wondered if you fancied going?" Lottie had been distant with him for a few weeks lately, and the poor lad was at pains to know why.

"I don't really feel like going out tonight thanks. I think I'll just have a night in."

"But we've not been out in ages. What's up Lottie? Are you going off me or what? If you are I'd sooner you tell me," he said nervously fidgeting with his snap bag. "No it's nothing like that I just don't feel like it, that's all."

"Well is it ok if I come round then? We could just go out for a walk and maybe call at the chippy. You know, just get a bit of fresh air. You've not been outside of the house for ages and you're starting to go pale," he smiled. She looked at his handsome face, a smear of oil or grease on his cheek where he'd forgotten to wash it off and his tousled hair falling over his twinkling eyes.

"Well if you don't expect riveting conversation or anything I suppose a bit of fresh air would do me good." She smiled.

Chapter thirty-four

Friday and Saturday nights were always busy at the jamboree. Bob and Jakes' investment of their horse winnings seemed to be paying off, business was booming. This particular Friday 11th October, it was especially boisterous. There was a crowd in on a birthday do or anniversary. Bob wasn't sure, but they were spending their money and in his opinion that was all that mattered. They had invested everything they had into the Jamboree and Bob was determined to make it work. If a group of women wanted to spend their money in their club then that was all right by him. The noisiest group was a bunch of lasses from Bensons.

"Come on who's having a dance then?" said Sandra Mason, a buxom young lass with peroxide blonde hair obviously the worse for wear.

"Sit down Sandie, it's barely nine o'clock and you're already three sheets to the wind. Yer makin' a right show o' yerself," slurred her mate who was none too steady herself.

"Come on it's my birthday today. I'm eighteen and I want to dance." She staggered to her feet, but promptly fell back down into her seat with a piercing shriek of laughter.

"What's goin' on over there"? asked one young lad enviously eyeing up the group of women.

"A birthday party or summat," volunteered Jake who was busy pulling a pint. "See that lass with the blonde hair." He indicated pointing the newly pulled pint in her direction. "I think it's her birthday."

"Oh right. I think I might go over there an' see if she wants to dance."

"Go on Tommy mate I dare yer," urged one of his mates.

"They'll eat you alive that lot and spit out the crumbs," sniggered another.

"I hope so," laughed Tommy making his way over to where the crowd of women were sitting.

"Who'll eat you alive?" slurred Joe Warmsley standing with the gang gathered round the bar.

"Let 'im be Joe. Tommy's goin' to see if one o' them lasses wants a dance that's all."

"I'll just go over an' show 'im how it's done then." Joe had been in the club since early evening. He had been drinking heavily and had been drowning his sorrows all night.

"Leave it Joe," said Tommy grabbing Warmsley by the coat and dragging him away from the bar.

"Get yer 'ands off me or I'll knock yer bloody 'ead off you little bastard." He turned viciously and punched the lad in the face splitting his lip and drawing blood. He staggered towards where the women were sat. "Well ladies what 'ave we got 'ere?" He smirked, leaning over the women, his pint slopping out onto the table.

Sandra clumsily tried to get out of her seat but fell back awkwardly kicking the table over, spilling the drinks all over the floor.

Jake was there in an instant. "What's going on here?"

"I want to dance but these miserable sods won't dance with me," said Sandie, her skirt rising up around her waist showing an ample expanse of flesh.

Joe's eyes ogled the girl, her near nakedness sending his brain reeling at the thoughts of what he'd like to do to her. "I'll dance wi' yer lass come on," he said dragging Sandra onto the floor.

"Leave her alone she doesn't want out to do wi' you. Just bugger off. I know you don't I?" piped up Betty

Johnson one of the women in the group, who had pushed between Warmsley and Sandra.

"Can't say as I've 'ad the pleasure love."

"No an' yer not bloody likely too either. Yer work at Bensons don't yer? Yeah I know you. I've seen yer many a time; yer a boss or summat, yer work in't spinnin' shed."

"Aye that's right love, I'm supervisor," he said, his eyes still fixed on Sandra's exposed flesh. "What yer doin' 'ere then? On the prowl?"

"Same as you I expect. Avin' a good time. Now what about that dance."

"She doesn't want t' dance. Why don't yer just sod off an' leave her alone," said Betty pushing Warmsley angrily away. Joe lunged viciously at her just as Jake forced his way between the two of them.

"Is everythin' alright here?" he said elbowing his way between Joe and the women. "I just want to dance that's all," said Sandra.

"You 'eard her she just wants to dance, no 'arm in that is there?"

"Not wi' you she doesn't. I 'eard about you from Taylors. That's where I remember yer from," said Betty now in full flow. "I thought I'd seen yer before, an' what yer did t' that young woman. They should a' locked yer up an' thrown the soddin' key away yer dirty bastard."

"I don't know what you 'eard missus but it weren't true," he said suddenly lunging at Betty and grabbing her by the throat. Jake rushed between the two of them.

"Come on you, out," he said grabbing his arm and dragging him off the terrified woman. Joe swung round and caught Jake full in the face. His nose exploded covering Joe in a shower of blood and gore. Jake was a powerful lad, his muscles were like cords of wood honed by years of hardship and having to fend for himself. Moments later he hit him with a pile driver that knocked him off his feet.

"Go on Jake flatten the bastard," urged the group of lads. "Yeah go on Jake belt him," they yelled.

Jake was on him again in seconds pummelling Joe around the head. "If you come near me again, I'll kill you, you bastard," he snarled as his uncle pulled his raging nephew off the stricken man.

"If I were you I'd get going while you can still walk," said Bob, doing his best to restrain his furious nephew.

"Nothin' was ever proved. I was cleared of doin' owt wrong. Nobody can point a finger at me," he ranted as he staggered out of the pub and off down the street clutching his battered face.

"What the bloody hell was that all about?" said Bob clearing up the mess of broken glasses and spilled drinks.

"I've no idea, I think he was trying it on with one of the lasses and she weren't having any," said Jake making his way over to where the women were sitting. "Sorry about the disturbance. Are you ladies all right? We don't normally get any trouble in here. I'll get you some fresh drinks, on the house of course."

"Aye we're alright love. Thanks for getting rid of that louse. He's bad lot', 'im. It's not the first time he's tried it on with one of the lasses. He were just the bloody same at Taylors. He attacked a young woman there, but the bastard got away with it. Sorry about the language love, but that man really gets my goat," said Betty angrily. "It were that young woman back at Taylors I felt sorry for, the one that he tried to rape. Poor lass ended up gettin' the sack because of that piece of filth." She ranted on pulling a comb through her dishevelled hair.

"Who was that then?" asked Jake.

Lizzie 135 Steeples

"I think her name was Steeples; aye, Lizzie Steeples."

Chapter thirty-five

The ladies' toilets were crowded with girls touching up their makeup before the last dance.

It was fast approaching midnight and the ones not lucky enough to get a taxi or a ride home would have to walk. Better to look appealing in the hope of getting a dishy young lad to escort you, rather than walk home alone. Sandra was putting the finishing touches to her mascara. She flicked her hair and touched up her lipstick. She stood back and admired herself in the ornate gilded mirror. Not bad she thought. Just turned eighteen, who could resist her girly charms?

Lottie and Frank held hands as they strolled down the dimly lit path near the canal. Just under the bridge, Frank pulled Lottie towards him and pressed his lips to hers.

"Frank don't somebody might see us," she said nervously turning her head slightly so his lips brushed her cheek.

"There's nobody here to see us. Anyway I want to know why you've been acting so funny lately. Is it summat I've done? It's quiet here, that's why I brought you this way," he said.

"No it's nothing you've done Frank."

They walked a bit further along the path, the moon casting eerie shadows along the bank from the trees as they moved softly in the breeze. Frank put his arms round Lottie and pulled her closer for a kiss.

"Don't Frank. I don't feel like it," she said pulling away from him.

"Come on Lottie tell me what's up. If you don't want to see me again just tell me, at least put me out my misery."

"It's not you it's me," she cried.

"What do you mean it's you? What's the matter?"

"I'm pregnant. I'm having a baby," she cried.

Frank was stunned he didn't know what to say. "But how? We were always careful, we always took precautions."

"It's not yours Frank," Lottie broke down and sobbed uncontrollably. She blurted out the whole sorry story of how Joe Warmsley had raped her and threatened to kill her if she told anyone.

"I'll kill him if I get my hands on him," said Frank.

"Please Frank don't tell anybody. Even my mam doesn't know," she sobbed. "I'll understand if you don't want to see me again. I can't expect you to take care of somebody else's bastard. Anyway there's a woman at work, she says she knows somebody that can help me get rid of it," she cried.

"Don't worry Lottie; you've no need to get rid of it if you don't want to. I'm going to take care of you no matter what. I love you and there's an end to it," he said pulling her closer to him. "And don't worry I won't tell anybody."

Suddenly there was a rustle in the bushes as if a bird or something disturbed the night.

"Oh what was that?" cried Lottie clutching hold of Frank tightly. "Shush. I thought I heard summat." They moved a little closer to where they thought the sound was coming from. "There it is again."

"Frank I'm scared let's go home," she said trying to drag him back up the path to a more illuminated area.

"Come on I think there's somebody down there," he persisted.

"But Frank what if it's thieves or murderers they could be waiting for us. Come on lets go."

"Wait here then I'll just be a minute. I'm sure I heard something," he said striding bravely towards the noise. He crept amongst the thorny undergrowth, parting the branches as they plucked at his clothes and scratched cruelly at his skin, edging nearer to where he could hear the soft whimper of a voice.

"Oh my God! Lottie. Here quick, hurry up there's somebody hurt down here."

Lottie rushed to his side fearful of what he'd found in the gloomy thicket. "Who is it? What's up with her?" cried Lottie shaking with fear as she stared horrified at the young girl lying spread-eagled in the bushes.

"I don't know but there's blood everywhere. Quick call an ambulance and then the bobbies, there's a phone at the top of the street. I'll stay here with her till you get back."

"But who shall I say it is if they ask?"

"I don't know her name, but I'm sure she works at Bensons," said Frank.

Chapter thirty-six

The walls gave off an eerie glow from the fluorescent lighting that reflected back into the mortuary. Basic and functional, the white tiles on the walls added to the starkness of the room. In the centre stood a stainless steel gurney; on one side a channel running down to side to catch any bodily fluids that might escape during a post-mortem. Detective Chief Inspector Bradley's footsteps echoed in the chill room. He walked slowly to where the pathologist was waiting by the refrigerated containers, accompanied by Jack Mason. He had reported his daughter missing when she hadn't returned home earlier that evening from her birthday party. An inconspicuous nod of the head and the pathologist pulled open the drawer. The cabinet opened smoothly revealing the body covered in a crisp white sheet. The pathologist pulled back the cover exposing the upper part of the young girl's body. Her face was colourless and ghostly. Her lips had taken on a bluish hue, and there was some bruising around her eyes. Her blonde hair was streaked with dried blood, and her curls were matted and unkempt.

"Is this your daughter?" asked DCI Bradley quietly, turning to Jack Mason. He was a tough man. He'd spent half his life down the mines, and the rest labouring on the building sites when the pits closed. He gasped, as hard as he was, he couldn't stop the flow of tears from flowing down his cheeks as he gazed unbelievably at his daughter's body.

"Yes," he said, his voice reduced almost to a whisper. "Why? Why would anyone want to do this to my girl?" DCI Bradley took Jacks arm and led him out of the room.

He had done it many times before, but it never got any easier.

"We will get whoever is responsible," he said gently knowing that nothing he could say could mend the hurt that Jack Mason was feeling.

"The girl died just after two this morning, a couple of hours after she was found," explained the pathologist. "She died of a massive trauma to the brain. Some sort of heavy instrument, a hammer or a club, something of that nature. She had also been drinking rather heavily, but we'll know more when I open her up."

"Had she been sexually assaulted?"

"Yes, there's bruising around her thighs, and traces of semen in her vagina."

"Thanks doc, you'll let us know if you find anything else," said DCI Bradley leaving the mortuary.

The incident room was packed. "Well we know the time of death. So somewhere between eleven and midnight on Friday night was when the attack took place. Somebody in that club must have seen or heard something. Jackson you'll come with me to the club. The rest of you I want you to talk to her mates. Find out if she had a boyfriend. If she'd had a row with anybody or if anybody had a grudge against her."

Jake was behind the bar when DCI Bradley and DS Jackson walked into the jamboree. They showed him their warrant cards. "We're investigating the death of a young girl in the early hours of the morning, and we wondered if you might be able to shed some light on it for us. I believe she was in here last night with a group of friends?"

"Which girl was that then? I've not heard about anybody dying," said Jake.

"Aye there were dozens of girls in 'ere last night. Always is on a Friday. It's a very popular night," said Bob, changing one of the whisky optics behind the bar.

"She was celebrating her birthday. She'd just turned eighteen," explained Detective Sergeant Jackson.

"Yeah I know the one you mean; blonde, curly haired lass. Got a bit tipsy wanted to dance with everybody," said Jake rubbing his bruised face.

"Did she dance with anyone in particular?"

"Well most of the time she just kept falling over. She'd had a few. But there were this one lad. He was with his mates at the bar. Tommy summat but I couldn't tell you his last name. He said he were going over and ask her to dance. A few of his mates were egging him on like. Anyway there was this other bloke, older than the others, said he was goin to ask her. His mates told this bloke to leave off but he wouldn't be told. Next thing he's over by the table and all hell breaks loose. We had to chuck him out didn't we uncle Bob?"

"What happened?" asked DCI Bradley.

"One of the women recognized him from some other factory and told him to leave the lass alone, but he wouldn't. That's when it got nasty and we threw him out."

"Is that where you got the bruises sir?" said DCI Bradley pointing to Jakes face. "Aye the bugger copped me one right on the hooter."

"Do you happen to know his name?" said DS Jackson.

"Joe summat or other, but Betty Jackson, she was one of the older women in the group, she recognized him. She'll know who he is," said Jake.

Chapter thirty-seven

Sunday morning was always a lie in and then a big fry up. It was a tradition started by Colly. Since her dad's death Lizzie had tried to carry it on. "How many rashers do you want Jake?" she said, pushing the crispy bacon round the frying pan.

"I'll have four, and two eggs and a piece of fried bread as well, I'm starving," he said, stirring another spoonful of sugar into his mug. "What about you Jenny?"

"Just some toast for me mam. I'm not that hungry."

"Lottie what'll you have love?"

"Nothing I'm not hungry either."

"But you've eaten nothing proper for days. You're wasting away love. Come on try a bit of toast, and I'll put you a nice fried egg on top." At the mention of the fried egg Lottie put her hand to her face and ran from the kitchen. Lizzie ran after her. She caught her throwing up in the outside privy. "How long has this been going on then?"

"I don't know what you mean?"

"You, throwing up and off your food; you've eaten nothing for days proper. How late are you?"

"What do you mean?"

"Come on lass you've been moody for the last month or so. I know the signs. When did you last come on?"

"I don't know what you're on about. I just feel a bit off colour that's all."

"Who's is it? Is it Franks?" Persisted Lizzie.

"Is everythin' alright mam?" asked Jake from the back door.

"It's alright love go back to your breakfast. Don't let it get cold."

"Come on Lottie back into the house. Tell me what's going on."

"Jake put the kettle on and made a fresh brew; me and Lottie are going into the parlour so we don't want to be disturbed, is that understood?"

"Ok mam whatever you say," replied Jake wondering what the hell was up.

"Ok Lottie are you going to tell me or am I going to guess what's up?"

"Oh mam, it's not Frank. We've always been careful when we've slept together." Lizzie was shocked by Lottie's revelation.

"You mean you've been sleeping with him? What do you mean it's not Frank? Call me a fool if you like love but am I missing something here? What do you mean it's not Frank? Jesus Lottie you're barely fifteen love."

"It's not Frank who's got me into trouble mam," cried Lottie.

"Well you don't get pregnant unless it's the immaculate conception; so whose is it then?" Lottie told Lizzie the whole story. Ten minutes later Jake took his ear from the door, somebody was going to pay for his sister's plight.

Chapter thirty-eight

"Can you tell us where you were between eleven o'clock and midnight on Friday the 11th of October?" said DCI Bradley.

"I was in the jamboree club until about half eleven then I went home with a mate."

"Did you go straight home or did you go anywhere else?"

"What do you mean anywhere else?"

"Just answer the question Mr Sullivan."

Tommy Sullivan was starting to sweat. DCI Bradley's face was just inches from his own. "Me and Dave Prescott left the jamboree about half eleven and called at Thompsons chippy. There were a few in. We got cod an' chips an' walked home."

"Was there anybody there that can confirm your story?"

"There were a young lad with his girlfriend, he let on to us. He'll confirm we were there."

"And you say this was about eleven thirty."

"Yeah give or take five minutes."

"Can you tell us what happened prior to your leaving the club?"

"What you mean the fight? That had nothing to do with me. Well not directly. I went to ask Sandie for a dance; next thing I know all hell breaks loose. Some bloke came over. He were drunk, took a swing at me an' started to pester the girl, wouldn't take no for an answer. Next thing I knew, he got thrown out, blood all over the place. Kicked the table over; drinks all over the place, right bloody mess."

"What was this bloke's name?" asked DCI Bradley.

"Joe, but I didn't catch his last name."

"And your friend Dave where did he go?"

"We went home together; we live in the same street a couple of doors away. I saw him go into his house."

"Thanks Mr Sullivan, you can go now but we might want to question you again." DCI Bradley closed his notebook and replaced his pen in the top pocket of his shabby suit.

"Looks like he might have a cast iron alibi," said DS Jackson.

"Looks that way sergeant; I think we should have a word with this Joe whoever he is."

"Betty Jackson. I think we should go and have a word with her first don't you; she seems to know who he is. She's no relation is she Jackson?" said Bradley smiling to his colleague.

"Not to my knowledge, Guv; not unless the old man had a bike," he laughed.

Betty Jackson had just put her feet up. The chores done and the Sunday joint was slowly roasting in the oven. A steaming hot cup of tea was sitting on the hearth along with two bacon sarnies. She was about to indulge her passion for the Sunday papers, and her weekly dose of scandal when there was a loud rapping on the front door. "Damn!" she said to herself. Who had the nerve to disturb her when Liz Taylor was getting married for the umpteenth time, or which young starlet was jumping into bed with which politician? Some people had no consideration. She answered the door in a huff.

"Mrs Jackson, DCI Bradley Thistlefield police," he said showing her his warrant card. "I wonder if we might have a word. We're investigating the death of a young woman Sandra Mason. We wondered if you could spare us a few minutes?"

"Oh Sandie, poor little soul, yeah come in." Her previous angst suddenly vanished as she let the two police officers in. I've just made a brew would you like one?"

"Don't mind if I do, milk and sugar for me," said DS Jackson ignoring the glare from his boss.

"Mrs Jackson you were in the jamboree club on Friday night. Can you tell us what happened?" said DCI Bradley.

"Well it was Sandra's eighteenth and a few of the girls had decided to have a bit of a do for her, you know her coming of age an' all. Lovely young lass, never did anything or anybody any harm, poor soul. They ought to string the bugger up that done that to her." She sniffed dabbing her eyes with a hanky. She went into the kitchen and picked up the large brown earthenware teapot, removing the multicoloured cosy that was covering it. "Was it one sugar constable?" she said to DS Jackson pouring tea into a large beaker. "Are you sure I can't pour you one inspector?"

"No not for me thanks. What can you tell us about the events of Friday night?" said DCI Bradley, eager to get some information, no matter how small or insignificant. "Was there anyone there that you hadn't seen before?"

"Mostly it was the girls from the factory. There were some lads as well but most of them work at Benson's. We knew most of them."

"Was there anyone there you didn't recognize?"

"The club was packed. There were bound to be people we didn't know."

"What about the group you were with, did you know all of them?"

"Yeah, I told you it was all the girls from the factory, well mostly out of the spinning room."

"And the lads you said you knew most of them."

"Yeah, they were mostly from the factory as far as I can remember. I'd say there were about ten or fifteen of them, but they were at the bar drinking."

"And you said that most of them were known to you. Were there any that you didn't know?"

"No I would say that I knew most of them, well by sight anyway, if not to talk to."

"At about what time did the fight start Mrs Jackson; do you remember?"

"It must have been early on. We'd only been in the club about an hour or so. I remember saying to Sandra that she was already a bit tipsy an' it was only about nine o'clock, something like that."

"That was when the fight broke out was it?" asked DCI Bradley.

"I think so. One of the young lads came over to ask Sandra for a dance, next thing I know all hell breaks loose."

"Who was it that started the fight? Was it the young lad?"

"No it were the older bloke. Drunk as a skunk he was. Made a grab for me round the throat but the young lad behind the bar threw him off. Kept pesterin' Sandra; wanted her to dance."

"Can you describe what this man looked like Mrs Jackson?"

"Don't need to describe him inspector it were Joe Warmsley," she said positively.

"Are you sure of that Mrs Jackson? The club was dark wasn't it? Can you describe him for us?"

"Joe, I'd say he were in his forties, dark greasy hair what there was of it, goin' a bit thin on top."

"Was he tall or short? What sort of build was he?"

"I'd say he was about six foot an' heavily built, you know muscular."

"And you definitely recognized him. It was Joe Warmsley?" said Bradley.

"Oh no doubt at all, it was definitely Joe."

The incident room was heavy with smoke. Several of the officers had lit up while DCI Bradley was outlining the case.

"The way I see it," said DCI Bradley. "Joe Warmsley would seem to have the perfect motive for killing the girl. She rejects him in front of a gang of people, and then he's thrown out of the club. He wouldn't be in the best of moods. He skulks off in a hissy fit, harbouring a grudge against the girl. Somewhere between the club and the canal bank, he waits for her, then beats her over the head with something heavy and rapes her."

"Sounds plausible Guv, but we've no evidence to back your theory up," said Jackson. "That's why we need to find him as soon as possible and bring him in for questioning. Are we any nearer to finding him yet?"

"Sorry Guv; we've knocked on doors where he lived, and spoken to his workmates but nobody seems to have seen him since Friday night."

"What about the lads in the club?"

"No joy either I'm afraid Guv. If anyone's seen him, they're not saying. By all accounts, he wasn't the most popular guy in the world. A bit of a bully boy from what I've gathered."

"So he had enemies then?"

"Would seem so," replied Jackson.

"Well he just can't disappear off the face of the earth, somebody must know something; Steve can you organize with uniform? Get them to check if he came home on Friday night. The rest of you I want you to question everyone that witnessed the fight in the club again." There was an audible groan from all around the incident room. "I know it's a ball breaking chore boys and girls." He said winking at the two attractive women DC's that made up the team. Although he was pushing fifty, Bradley had kept himself in good shape and had an eye for the ladies especially attractive ones. "It's imperative that we find Warmsley, and put this case to bed," he said.

Chapter thirty-nine

Charnley's mill had been a dilapidated wreck for many years. Standing just outside the town centre, it had been in steady decline thanks to the rapid import of cheap goods from abroad. Its tall chimney blackened by years of belching out smoke was already crumbling into decay. Unable to compete with the bigger group-owned mills in the area they had eventually gone to the wall. The factory gates had been padlocked years ago, but there were gaps in the perimeter fence where it was easy to squeeze through. Once through the fence it was easy to gain access to the premises themselves. All the security lighting had been smashed long since by the local kids using them as target practice and most of the glass in the windows had gone for a burton in the same way. There were a hundred and one places to hide once inside. It had become a popular haunt for the town's youth in pursuit of their favourite pastimes, drinking and sex.

Tracy Conroy giggled has she squeezed her ample bosom through the gap in the fence. "Come on slow coach," she said to her boyfriend Archie Daniels, as he struggled with half a dozen beer bottles in a brown paper carrier bag.

"Here grab hold of these while I squeeze through," he said thrusting the bag through the railings. She reached for the bag but let it slip with a crash onto the concrete floor. "Bloody hell, Tracy! Be careful somebody might hear us."

"It's ok I don't think there's anyone else here," she said peering into the bag, which was now dripping the contents of a broken beer bottle. "I think there's only one broken," she giggled hysterically.

"That's one less for you then, that lot cost me nearly ten bob."

"Come on let's get inside; I'm freezing my knickers off here."

"Make it easier for me then," he said trying to put his hand up her skirt.

"Naughty, naughty, you'll just have to wait you dirty bugger." She laughed slapping his hand away. They crept across the yard. It was almost completely dark except when the moon crept out from behind the clouds casting eerie silhouettes across the ground. The back of the factory had a large gate that led into one of the old dilapidated spinning sheds. The main gate was locked with a large rusty padlock, but there was a smaller door set in the middle of the larger gate that had worked loose over the years.

Archie pushed the creaking door open and clambered inside. "Come on," he said pulling Tracy through the narrow opening. "I can hardly wait."

He tried to push her to the cold concrete floor. "Not here it's bloody freezing, let's try a bit further in where it's a bit warmer."

Archie struck a match, the phosphorus light glimmered casting a luminous glow in the almost pitch dark room. "Over there through that door, it might be a bit warmer in there." He lit another match as they edged their way further into the shed. "This looks ok," he said as the match burned down to his fingers. "Over there." He pointed to a pile of cotton waste heaped in the corner. "There's plenty of stuff on the floor here that should stop your arse from freezing." He laughed pushing her down onto the soft cotton. "I hope you've brought a Johnnie."

She giggled making herself comfortable wriggling down in to the soft cotton waste. "Course I have stupid come on, I'm gasping for it." He pulled the foil wrapper out of his pocket, dropping his coat to the floor.

He unzipped his trousers and loosened the belt. "Brr it's bloody freezing in here," he said as his pants dropped round his ankles exposing his throbbing manhood. "Come on then lover-boy what are you waiting for." Her legs already spread in eager anticipation. She edged further onto the pile of waste spreading the cotton beneath her. Suddenly she recoiled; she had felt something cold and fleshy. She pushed it away in horror. "What's up?" Exclaimed Archie his ardour rapidly diminishing. "I felt something, it felt like a hand." She said shaking like a leaf.

Chapter forty

"The forensics team established that the body of Joe Warmsley had been in the mill for about twenty four hours. So that would put him there sometime between Friday night the 11th of October to Saturday the 12th," said DCI Bradley. "He had been hit over the head with something heavy. There was very little blood at the scene suggesting that he had been killed elsewhere and brought to the mill. If that was the case then whoever it was would have had to be pretty strong. Warmsley is a fairly big chap so I would suggest that it's a man we are looking for. Did we get a statement from the couple who reported finding him Steve?"

"Yeah they hadn't been in the mill long. They'd been drinking and were just about to you know..."

"Ok spare me the details, I get the picture. Did they see or hear anything?" said Bradley.

"Nothing Guv. They said they hadn't been in the mill long, and when the girl lay down on the waste she felt his hand. Nearly shit herself was what she said."

"If he had been killed elsewhere whoever did it must have had a vehicle."

"Or the killer had an accomplice Guv," Suggested DS Jackson.

"You could well be right Steve, but let's not complicate things too much at this stage. Let's just hope we are looking for one person."

"Do you think he was brought to the mill by car, Guv?" asked one of the Dc's. "It's entirely possible. I think it's a fair assumption he was taken there by a vehicle of some sort."

"Were there any tyre tracks at the scene Guv?"

"At the moment the forensic team are going to make another examination of the area, but we've nothing conclusive at this stage. For the time being, we are assuming he was brought there, but he could have been done on the premises. If that's the case, it would mean he was in the area at the time of death. The scuff marks on his shoes seem to suggest he was brought there from outside and dragged into the shed."

"Do you think there's a link between the two of them Guv?" asked DC Linda Francis. "The M.O. looks the same, but that's all we have to go on. Both had been hit over the head with a heavy blunt instrument, but that's where the similarity ends. Sandra Mason was brutally raped before she was killed. The forensics team found traces of hair and skin under her nails, which suggests she must have put up a hell of a fight before she was killed. Warmsley was battered about the head either on the premises or elsewhere but there are no other marks on his body to say he put up a fight. It looks as if whoever did him took him by surprise."

"Or he knew his killer Guv," said DS Jackson.

"It looks like the motive for Sandra was sexual, but what was the motive for Warmsley?" asked Linda Francis.

"Do you think it was robbery sir?" asked another of the DC's.

"That thought had crossed my mind; it could be. When he was found he still had his wallet on him, but there was no money in it. There was no loose change in his pants pocket either, so the motive could have been robbery."

DS Jackson sipped lukewarm tea from a cracked mug that had seen better days. "Is it possible that there might be two different killers out there Guv?" said Jackson. "If we look at the facts, Sandra Mason was murdered on her way home from the jamboree club sometime late on Friday night or early Saturday morning. Twenty-four hours later Joe Warmsley is found with his head bashed in, in a disused factory. He was heard having a right old go inside the club by Tommy Sullivan and Betty Jackson. He had a go at Sullivan and grabbed Mrs Jackson round the throat. The lad behind the bar broke it up apparently. "That was over the girl, wasn't it sir?" said DS Jackson. "The row I mean, that's what the fight was about, the girl Sandra Mason."

"Yes. I think we'd better have another chat with Jake Steeples don't you sergeant?"

Chapter forty-one

Brooke was in a bad mood; his latest conquest had given him the brush off. He thought he had done enough to woo her into bed. "Just watch the kids for half an hour, while I do my hair," she had said. He'd played with the little brats for nearly an hour. Jigsaw puzzles, stories, and rough and tumble on the rug with them. When what he really wanted was a tumble with the kids' mother. When she finally emerged from the bathroom she told him she'd gone off the idea, and could they go out for a drink instead.

"What about the kids? Who'd look after them?" he said.

"Don't worry about them. They'll be alright with their sister. She's looked after them before," she said, fluffing her hair up. Brooke made his excuses and decided to leave telling her he had a lot of business to attend to in the morning. Disgruntled he slammed the door on his way out.

He was sure that bloody rug was alive; he'd done nothing but itch since he left in an huff earlier! He ordered another drink from the bar but it was obvious that he had already had too much. "Are you going to serve me or not?" He snapped angrily, the alcohol giving him Dutch courage. Since the two recent murders' the jamboree had been packed with customers; all the gossip and idle chatter related to the killings. He nudged an elderly chap stood at the side of him. "Who's been murdered?" he slurred.

"Oh you've not heard then. A young lass and an old feller both had their 'eads bashed in," he said with relish eager to acquaint Brooke with the gruesome details. "Where've you been the last few days? There's been talk of nowt else this past week," said Bob passing him his drink.

"What happened?"

"Like Bert said somebody bashed the young lass over the 'ead and then the day after, they found this chap with 'is 'ead bashed in. Its' funny you've not 'eard about it. You were in 'ere the other Friday, the night it happened."

"I didn't stop; I had to go away on business the day after so I left early," he said sipping his drink, skulking behind the rim of the glass.

Suddenly, Bobs' eyes were drawn to the front door as he spotted DCI Bradley and his subordinate Jackson crossing the room. "I wonder what these two want."

Bradley approached the bar, brushing the rain from his Mac. It was damp at the shoulders from the steady drizzle that was falling outside. "We'd like a word with Jake Steeples if that's ok," said Bradley, still brushing the rain from his raincoat.

"Why what's he done?" asked Bob defensively.

"Is he here? We just want to ask him a few more questions, purely routine," said Jackson.

"He's out the back."

"If you wouldn't mind getting him for us," persisted DCI Bradley.

Jake came into the pub the crate of light ale no weight in his muscular arms. "What's up?" he said, lowering the crate behind the bar. His usual cheerful demeanour changed to one of wariness and caution.

"Mr Steeples, can you tell us where you where on Friday the tenth of October, between eleven thirty pm and one am on Saturday morning of last week?"

"I was here 'till we closed up and then we went home. Why what's this all about?"

"Mr Steeples do you know a Joe Warmsley?" said DCI Bradley.

"I know who he is but not personally like. Why what's up?"

"Mr Warmsley was found dead early on Sunday morning."

"What! And you think I had something to do with it? That bastard deserved everything he got," exclaimed Jake acidly.

"Mr Steeples we are not accusing you of anything, we are merely making enquiries into a suspicious death. You were heard threatening Mr Warmsley in the pub on Friday night. And I quote," said Bradley checking his notebook. "If you come near me again I'll kill you, you bastard." Unquote. "We have witnesses that heard you say it Mr Steeples, and we also found blood on his shirt which we have reason to believe came from you."

"Well there would be, he hit me so I hit him back. But it doesn't mean I killed him."

"But you don't deny that a fight between you and Mr Warmsley took place on Friday night."

"No there were a bit of a scuffle and we threw him out, he were pestering one of the lasses."

"And because he was pestering one of the lasses as you put it, you decided to beat him up," said Jackson.

"He started it. He hit me first. I was only defending myself."

"That's right, he smacked Jake in the face, thought he'd busted 'is nose, blood everywhere," said Bob. He were only protectin' 'imself. Anybody would 'ave done the same."

"Then what happened?" asked Bradley.

"There were a bit of a commotion; tables got knocked over lasses screamin' all over the place then me an' Jake threw 'im out."

"And which girl was the one that Mr Warmsley was pestering?" said Jackson.

"The one who was 'avin' the party," replied Bob.

"Sandra Mason."

"I didn't really catch her name but aye, I think that's who it was."

"And you said you were here until closing time at about one am. Is there anyone who can verify your story Mr Steeples?" said DCI Bradley.

"I were with him until we got home," said Bob warily.

"Is there anyone else that saw you after you left the club and made your way home?"

"There were some lads larking about in the street, but I doubt if they remember seeing us. They were off their heads," said Bob.

"What about when you arrived home. Was there anyone there that saw you?" asked Jackson.

"No, not really, mam were asleep; she's not been well lately and we didn't like to disturb her."

"No that's right. After we cashed up we made our way 'ome; didn't see another soul apart from the lads I mentioned but as I said they were too drunk to notice."

"And what time did you arrive home?"

"I would guess at about half one or thereabouts," said Bob.

"And there were no other witnesses who can verify your story," said Bradley.

"Only the lads who were larkin' about, but I wouldn't think they would remember much," added Bob with a shrug of his shoulders.

"Well, that seems to be all for the moment. We may need to question you again so please don't leave the district for the time being," said DCI Bradley turning on his heels and leaving the club. "Jackson see if you can round up any of the lads that were in the vicinity of the club on Friday night. One of them might just remember something."

"Where the bloody hell did you get to Jake? I didn't see hide nor hair of you after midnight," exclaimed Bob.

"I went to change my shirt. It was covered in Warmsley's blood. I went down the cellar, and got a clean one, and threw the dirty one behind some crates. Then I went for a walk to clear my head, uncle Bob, that's all."

Chapter forty-two

Joe Warmsley was one of seven kids the offspring of a brutal father and an alcoholic mother. He had five sisters and an older brother. His brother took great pleasure in dishing out unwarranted beatings on his younger sibling. Although he wasn't the youngest, four of his sisters and brother were older. His sisters would often belittle the young boy and humiliate him wherever possible. They would make him wash their dirty clothes in the old dolly tub, and when he had done his own, his elder brother and sisters would urinate all over them causing him to wash them again or go around stinking of piss. If he complained to his mother she would just dismiss him with the back of her hand, and his father would just use it as an excuse to beat the young lad with his belt. Joe's schooldays were no better. He was often the butt of jokes, and was always in trouble. Barely a day went by that he wasn't involved in some scuffle or other. By the time he was ten Joe had been in trouble most of his young life. He was brought before a young offenders court for setting fire to a neighbours washing and forcing excrement through a letterbox. Later he was found guilty of stealing sweets and money from the till of the local corner shop. He was also caught stealing money from the local poor box at the Catholic church. The kindly father took pity on the youngster and he let him off with a stern warning, telling him that next time he would go to the police. He also warned Joe that there was a higher authority watching him and if he stole from the church again he would go to hell! It seemed to have the desired effect in as much as he didn't steal from the church again. His father though wasn't as forgiving as the priest, and took great delight in meting out a severe beating with the buckle end of his belt, leaving Joe bruised and bloodied and barely able to stand. His mother had just sat and watched through an alcoholic haze, as her husband had practically flayed the skin off the young lads' backside.

Joe's teenage years were almost as bad. At thirteen he had spent six months in a young offender's institution for theft. When he was fifteen he served a further six months for assaulting a woman and stealing her handbag. As the years went by he was growing bigger and stronger, and soon his father found it more and more difficult to deal with his tear-away son. He was no longer able to dish out the beatings mainly because Joe was becoming too strong for him, but also the drink was having a telling effect on his health. He was also becoming more cunning waiting until his parents were out at the pub, or sleeping off their latest drunken binge. During this time, Joe had had years of taking his revenge on his sisters.

It was just after the New Year 1946. Mary Warmsley was nineteen, eleven years younger than her brother, and had already blossomed into a beautiful young woman. She was the envy of her sisters and of her friends. Her four sisters were pretty but none had the stunning looks of Mary. She attracted all the attention, and all the boys wanted to go out with her. At five feet six she was taller than most girls her age. She had a slim almost waif like figure, and a pale elfin face that accentuated her dark smouldering eyes and her glossy black hair. The glossy black hair cascaded over her shoulders and framed her silky smooth complexion. Mary knew that she was pretty and longed to have a boyfriend, but her father was a bully and woe betide any lad that tried it on with her!

Mary took great care of her appearance. She dreamed of the day that she would one day leave home, and become a model like in the glossy magazines that she was so fond of reading. It was on one such occasion that Mary was bathing in front of the fire in the kitchen. The Warmsley household was like many others in the area it had no bathroom. Joe came home to find that she was alone naked in front of the fire drying herself off. His lustful eyes greedily fixed on her young nubile body. Her full breasts protruding from her chest, and the dark thatch of hair sprouting from between her legs only served to inflame his desire. She quickly covered herself and ordered him out of the kitchen, but to no avail. She tried to scream but the house was empty. His meaty hand covered her mouth as he tore the towel from her. He was on her in an instant tearing at his trousers as he threw her to the floor. She tried to crawl away but he quickly pinned her to the floor. She fought with all her strength but she was no match for his inflamed passion. He brutally pushed his throbbing manhood into her thrusting and grunting until at last he was finished. Mary was left sobbing and threatened to tell her dad. Joe calmly went to the kitchen and took a knife from the drawer. He grabbed his sobbing sister by the throat his cruel lips drawn back over his sadistic mouth. He drew the knife just deep enough to cut the skin, but not penetrate too deeply, just leaving a faint line where the knife had been. The next time he told her he would cut her throat from ear to ear if she as much as breathed a word to anyone. The terrified girl just nodded in agreement.

At fifteen, Joe had left school with no qualifications. He was barely literate and could hardly read and write. He was however very strong and well built and soon got a job in a local slaughterhouse humping sides of beef around. This lasted only a few weeks, as he became the butt of some cruel jibes when he could scarcely sign his name for his wages. He was sacked on the spot, caught battering one of the lads with a mallet used to tenderize meat after the lad had ridiculed him in front of the rest of his workmates.

As he grew older, he could never hold down a steady relationship with any girl, due to his aggressive sexual demands. He flitted from one affair after another. He did however settle down with one woman. She was twenty-eight and lusted after him. At thirty-six Joe was eight years older, but it seemed his rough sexual appetites were just what she wanted. The rougher he was the better she liked it. One day she told him she was pregnant. She wanted them to get married but he didn't see it that way. He was a free spirit and refused to accept that he was responsible. He blamed her for not taking precautions, and disowned it. Her father however had other ideas. Joe was used to handling himself in tight corners, but this was a different kettle of fish. Her dad was just as rough and nasty as Joe, and twice as big. He had been a sergeant during the war and was used to handling men. He suggested to Joe that it was the right thing to do! He didn't want his daughter giving birth to his grandchild out of wedlock; even though Joe wasn't the catch he'd anticipated for his daughter, it wasn't as shameful as a bastard child. Joe reluctantly agreed to the marriage, but once she became too big to indulge in his sexual fantasies he began to stray. Once the baby was born, he disappeared. He finally resurfaced when the girls' dad tracked him down two years later, drinking in a pub on the other side of town. He almost beat him to within an inch of his life, and told him if he ever saw him, again he would kill him. He was divorced soon after on the grounds of cruelty and desertion.

Things deteriorated quickly after that. One night after a particularly heavy night of drinking in Hilldale, he tried to get a woman in the pub to go with him, but she refused. He waited until the she left the pub and followed her. He dragged her into a side alley where he tried to rape her. Luckily, a couple of late night drinkers were leaving the pub and heard the woman's screams. They quickly came to her aid. The two men overcame Joe's struggles until the police arrived. At Chelford crown court, he was sentenced to three years for attempted rape. On his release, he tried to get regular work, but his past record always caught up with him. He drifted from one dead end job to another. He worked at various building sites in and around Hilldale. It took him a while but he kept his head down. Some of the sites he worked at didn't ask too many questions, so long as you got your head down and could graft. After a few months doing general labouring, Joe got itchy feet. He wanted a more permanent job. He was sick of the poor money, irregular work, and bad conditions on most of the sites. A drinking pal got Joe a start at a local spinning mill in Hilldale. He knew Joe's history but was willing to give him a chance, as long as he was willing to keep his head down. For a couple of years Joe settled into the routine of factory life. He was good at his job and soon settled into his new life. However, the mill was full of young women, and it didn't take him long before he was up to his old tricks. He moved in with one gullible girl. She was naïve and was easily taken in by his persuasive manner. Within two years, she had two kids to look after and a wayward partner to put up with. Joe soon fell into his old ways. He was back drinking heavily and running around with a string of different women. Then she turned up at the factory one day with the children, demanding that he give her money to feed them. It was the last straw. He flew at her in a rage knocking the youngest child out of her arms. He was about to hit her when one of the managers' heard the commotion outside and went to investigate.

The girl was on the floor trying to pick up the screaming infant. "They should have kept you in jail where you belong. They should never have let you out," she sobbed wrapping the weeping child tightly in her arms. The manager called the police, and after spending the night in the cells, he was brought before the local magistrates. Because he had been of previous good character since his jail sentence, the magistrate bound him over for twelve months, ordering him to keep the peace and pay a fine. Things went from bad to worse between him and his girlfriend, and after suffering more abuse and beatings she left him and went back to her mother. His job didn't last very long after that, and he was subsequently sacked. With his job prospects all but gone, he left Hilldale and returned to Thistlefield. After several weeks just idling around, he came across an old mate he'd helped out of a tight corner in the past. He owed Joe a favour. He was a foreman at one of the mills in town. A few days later, he got a job at Bensons' mill.

Chapter forty-three

Brooke Steeples had always been fortunate. After being de-mobbed from the navy, he took up a position in the family business. His father William owned a successful engineering company in Thistlefield Park, where he became chief salesman, a job that took him all over the country. Although he was basically a bully, his good looks and easy charm found his way into many an unsuspecting girl's bed.

It was mid afternoon; the rain was still falling as he pulled his blue Austin Cambridge into the Royal Oak car park in Thistlefield. Satisfied that he had the Hemming's business in the bag, he pulled his mackintosh around his shoulders and ran into the pub. Another fat commission would soon be on its way into his already healthy bank account. Brooke was paid a healthy commission, as well as a generous salary on all orders he brought to the firm. Feeling good about himself, he settled at the bar and ordered a pint of bitter. The long drive from the midlands had left him with an empty stomach and a ravenous appetite.

"Not seen you in here before," said the barmaid smiling has she handed him his drink.

"I get in from time to time depends where I've been," he said draping the damp mackintosh over the seat next to him.

"And where have you been?"

"Why who wants to know?" he said giving the girl one of his most charming smiles.

The pretty blonde blue eyed barmaid went positively weak at the knees. "Georgina Laycock, but most of my friends call me Georgie."

"And what do you do for fun around here Georgie? I expect a pretty girl like you won't be short of boyfriends."

"No one special," she said coyly. He engaged her in polite conversation during his meal, totally captivating the young girl with his charm and allure.

"What are you doing later?"

"My, you don't let the grass grow under your feet do you."

"With a girl as pretty as you I can't afford to, somebody might come along and snatch you away from me and then where would I be. I'd have lost the prettiest girl in town," he said giving her his most captivating smile.

"I'll be finished in just over an hour. I only do lunchtimes during the week unless we get busy with a wedding or a funeral or something," she said looking at him from under her long eyelashes.

"What about tonight then? Would you like to go out somewhere?" he said.

"I hardly know you," she said rinsing some glasses in the bar sink.

"Well if you'd rather not go that's ok. I'm sure there are plenty of pretty girls out there who'd like a good time," he said pushing his empty glass towards her. He could see that she was weakening. "Well what do you say? Shall I pick you up about six o'clock? I promise I'll have you home before your mother knows you've gone. What's your address?" He gave her his most disarming smile.

"I don't know; my mum's warned me about going out with strange men," she said nervously.

"What's strange about me then? I'm just a poor rep that's on his way home from a business trip and I'm looking to have a bit of fun that's all," he said giving her his most engaging smile. "Anyway how old are you? You don't have to get your mother's permission to go out do you?"

"No of course I don't, I'll be nineteen soon," said Georgie indignantly.

"It's just that she doesn't like men coming to the house that's all."

"Well then we won't go to your house. How about if I meet you here at six, unless you don't want too? We could go to the pictures if you like, and then afterwards we could go for a meal." She was still very reticent, unsure of her feelings. She wanted to go but she wasn't sure. She'd never met him before. "I don't know; I hardly know you I don't even know your name," she said timidly.

"David Gregory, my friends call me Dave," He said. "You didn't seem nervous before when I first came in."

"I know I was just being friendly. We have to be friendly with all the customers."

"So you don't want to come out, you were just flirting with me," he smiled.

"Course not; I do want to come out with you," she said gazing at the bar top from under her long black eyelashes heavy with mascara. "Ok then it's a date. I'll pick you up here six o'clock."

"Alright I'll see you at six," she said, taking his empty glass and rinsing it under the sink. Brooke leant over the bar and kissed her lightly on the cheek.

"Until six then," he said, turned, and left the bar.

"How nice," she thought. "Seems like a real gentleman?"

Chapter forty-four

DS Jackson banged on the door of number eleven Crimea Street, loud enough to wake the dead.

"All right, all right I'm coming don't knock the bloody thing off its hinges," growled the voice from behind the door.

"Mathew Collins."

"Aye that's right. Who wants to know?"

"DS Jackson Thistlefield police. I wondered if we could have a few minutes of your time please sir," said Jackson flashing his warrant card.

"You'd best come in. Why what's up?" asked Collins rubbing the sleep from his eyes. Jackson and DC Linda Francis followed him into a grubby living room strewn with empty beer and spirit bottles. Collins clearly liked his booze.

"Were you drinking at the Jamboree club on Friday night, Saturday morning the tenth and eleventh of October?"

"Yeah I was with some mates and we ended up in there."

"Can you recall what happened during the evening?"

"How do you mean?"

"Can you remember the fight that happened earlier that night?"

"Yeah there was a scuffle. I heard glasses break and then some fella threatening the lad behind the bar. Then they threw him out."

"Who threw him out?"

"The young lad and the older fella."

"Then what happened?"

"I don't rightly recall. I'd had a skinful."

"What time did you leave the club?"

"About one ish."

"When you left the club where did you go?" said Jackson rubbing the bridge of his nose, the line of questioning clearly not telling him anything new.

"We made our way home."

"Your friends and yourself. Did you see anyone else that wasn't in your group? Please think very carefully it's very important," persisted Jackson.

"We were larking about you know, havin' a bit of a laugh. One of the lads threw a stone and busted a window, so we scarpered sharpish. Hey I hope you're not thinking of doin' us for that are you? It was an accident."

"No I don't think we'll be pressing charges," said Jackson with a sigh. "Can you think of anyone else you might have seen?"

Collins rubbed his stubbly chin. "Come to think of it, just after we'd busted the window, this bloke come running past almost knocked me over. We thought it might have been the bloke whose window we busted."

"Can you describe him? Did you get a good look at him?"

"I'd had a skinful, so I don't remember exactly."

"Was he tall, short, young, old or what?" asked Jackson hoping Collins might throw him a lifeline.

"I think he were fairly tall and well built. Not much fat on 'im the way he were running."

"When you say not much fat on him can you be more specific?"

"More what?" said Collin's.

"Can you describe him in more detail? Did you see his face? Was he wearing a cap or anything?"

"No he had a coat on I think, you know a Mac; it had been rainin' earlier on."

"What colour was it, can you remember?"

"It could have been navy or grey, it was dark out."

"Have you any idea if it was a young bloke or an elderly bloke?" said Jackson hopefully.

"Oh he weren't a youngish bloke. I'd say he were about fortyish. An old bloke couldn't run that fast. I'd say he were fairly fit looked like he might have been in the army or summat."

"Thanks," said Jackson. "Did any of your friends see this man run into you?"

"Aye Pete, that's Peter Davies, he helped pick me up when the bloke nearly knocked me flying."

"And where can we find Mr Davies?" asked Jackson.

"Spring Terrace, number 32, end of the road; turn right, second left. You'll have to knock loud he'll be in bed; we've been on nights, we work at the same place."

"Thanks for your help," said Jackson as he and DC Francis drove off down the street.

"Don't mention it." Grunted Collins as he slammed the door, eager to get back to bed.

Chapter forty-five

Georgina's face was black and blue. The split on her lips had formed a crust where the blood had started to dry around her mouth. She had rubbed her deep blue eyes red raw trying to stem the flow of tears that ran down her cheeks like a fountain. Underneath, her eyes were smudged almost black where the mascara had run into them. She cried uncontrollably as sobs wracked her bruised and battered body. She looked in the dressing table mirror at her torn and dishevelled clothes.

"Georgie love are you alright?" asked Mildred Laycock, worried to hear her daughter's anguished cries.

"I'm alright mum it's nothing to worry about," she said trying to stifle a cry.

"How could I have been so stupid?" she sniffed rubbing the tears from her eyes. "He was so nice. I should never have let him take me back to the hotel." She sobbed to herself. It had all started so well. They had gone to the pictures, then a nice meal, it was all going so perfect.

"I thought we might go to the Broadlands hotel, and then we could finish the night off in style, have a few late night drinks," he said in all innocence. She was a little wary at first, but he had been so nice and persuasive, even held the car door open for her while she got out, what was the harm. He had behaved like a perfect gentleman.

The hotel room was really nice; pale cream walls with heavy brocade curtains in pale green and cream to match. Through the bedroom door was the bathroom, tiled in two shades of blue. There was even a bidet. She had never been in a place as posh as this; much nicer than her bedroom at home. He had ordered room service, a bottle of champagne. He was a real gentleman; she had felt ever so grown-up and sophisticated, treated her like a real lady. The champagne was lovely; she'd never had champagne before, all those lovely bubbles tickling her nose. She'd started to feel a little giddy after the second glass but he told her this was completely normal, it was because she wasn't used to it.

"Why don't you come and sit on the bed? Lie down for a bit you'll feel better if you have a lie down." Her head sank back into the soft pillows as she felt herself drifting off to sleep. Her head was muzzy from the champagne and the room began to spin. She felt nauseous and tried to get up from the bed, but a firm hand held her down.

"What are you doing?" She cried trying to struggle free from his iron grip. "Shush, it's all right you've just had a little too much to drink and it's made you sleepy," he said holding his hand over her mouth to quieten her.

"Let me go. I want to go home." She shouted.

"Don't be silly I'm not going to hurt you. We've got the room booked until the morning. Why don't we just enjoy it?"

"I want to go home now please. Please take me home. I think I'd rather go home now if you don't mind," she said nervously.

"Well one little kiss, and I'll order a taxi," he said reassuringly brushing the hair back from her face.

"Just one kiss then I'm going home ok," she said pushing her lips towards his face. He held the back of her head with his hand as he bent forward to kiss her. His left hand rode up under her skirt pulling her flimsy panties around her ankles. "What are you doing? You said a kiss and then you'd take me home." She was sobbing loudly now, trying to push his hand away but he was to strong.

"Come on don't be a tease you know you want to." He was on top of her pulling at her skirt. The button popped and he ripped it off. He was struggling with his flies as she managed to hit him across the face, temporarily halting his progress. He fell off the bed with a thud. As Georgie tried to run for the door, he grabbed her ankle and brought her down with a crash. She lashed out with her foot trying to kick him in the groin, but he rolled to one side and the intended kick missed him by inches. The noise from the room must have been heard downstairs as Georgie fought to get away. She almost reached the door, when a blow sent her sprawling back into the room, her whole world went black. Brooke was incensed as he picked her up and threw her onto the bed. She moaned as she tried to regain her senses, but the blow had left her weakened and fragile. His passion inflamed he was in no mood to be denied again. He was on her in a moment tearing the rest of her clothes off her battered body. He stopped momentarily gazing at the young nubile body in front of him. She stirred shakily trying to get up off the bed, but she was too weak from the blow to fight anymore. He brutally spread her legs and forced himself into her broken body, spending himself in moments. Minutes later a knock on the door stopped Brooke in his tracks.

"Is everything all right in there?" enquired the hotel night manager suspicious of the noises he'd heard earlier. Brooke had to think fast.

"I'm sorry we've been celebrating my wife's birthday and we've had a bit too much to drink. She fell over but it's nothing to worry about, no bones broken, she's sleeping now."

"If you're sure. Can I get you a doctor or anything?"

"No that's quite alright, everything's fine thanks."

"Well if you're sure. Goodnight."

"Goodnight," said Brooke with a sigh of relief. He casually went to the sink and stared in the mirror. He was scratched where Georgie had raked her nails down his face. He washed the blood from his hands and face and quickly got dressed. He wanted to get as far away from here as possible. He waited an hour until he was sure the night manager had gone back to his office before sneaking out by the hotel's back entrance. If anyone questioned him about tonight, he would just say that she was up for it and things had got a bit rough.

Chapter forty-six

"Have we got any further on the chap seen running away late Friday, early Saturday morning yet?" asked DCI Bradley to the group of officers assembled in the squad room.

DS Jackson opened his notebook. "I took a statement off a Peter Davies. He reckoned he'd seen the bloke before. Says he might be a rep or something. He's seen him in the factory where he works; goes in the office now and then."

"Can he describe him?" said Bradley.

"According to Davies he's about late thirties early forties. Well built but not big, more athletic; well dressed, well spoken with a nice tan, says he could have been in the forces."

"Have we got a name for this mystery man, or an address?"

"Not yet Guv we're still working on it," said Jackson.

"Get uniform to go back to the club, see if they can jog anyone's memory and get somebody down to the factory where this Davies works, maybe someone there can give us a name. We need to track this fellow down see what he knows," said DCI Bradley.

"We've been back to the jamboree club again, Boss, and knocked on a few doors, including Betty Jackson's, and I think we might have turned up something interesting. It seems that Mrs Jackson was in the club that night, and she knew Joe Warmsley from his days at Taylors' mill. Turns out, he assaulted Lizzie Steeples. He raped her according to what she says; if it's right that is. But this is the important thing no charges were ever brought against him," said DS Jackson.

"And when was this."

"A few years ago; three or four from what I can gather."

"And what makes this significant now?"

"According to Mrs Jackson, she thinks that Jake might well have overheard her in the club."

"And did she know that Jake was related to Mrs Steeples at that time?"

"I don't know sir, but it's possible somebody in the group knew and told her," said Jackson.

"And if he did overhear her that would give him a motive for killing Warmsley."

"There's more sir. We interviewed Mrs Steeples about the rape, and she does confirm that there was an assault."

"Why didn't she press charges at the time?"

"She reckoned that it would have been his word against hers, and nobody would have believed her anyway."

"Hmm possible I suppose, anything else?" asked Bradley.

"Just one other thing, Sir; according to Mrs Steeples Warmsley might have raped the girl as well."

"Which girl, Sandra Mason?"

"No her daughter Lottie, Jake Steeple's sister."

"What!" said DCI Bradley incredulously." When was this?"

"A few months ago, but as yet it's not been substantiated."

"Why hasn't she come forward with this before?" said Bradley.

"It seems the young girl Lottie has been seeing this lad from work. They've been going out together for a few months. Well the girl got pregnant and obviously, Mrs Steeples assumed that the boyfriend was the father. Her daughter begged her not to say anything for fear of driving the young lad away, but after we pressed her, she broke down and told us that Warmsley had raped her daughter as well."

"Bloody hell it's a right mess. And did Jake know about his sister?" said Bradley rubbing his hand along his brow.

"Well we're not sure on that score sir. We're almost certain that he knew about his mother from what he heard in the club, but we're not sure about the girl."

"It would give him the perfect motive though, wouldn't it?" said Bradley.

"Revenge is a pretty strong incentive I would think, Sir."

"Have we anything else on the man they saw running away?"

"Only that he was late thirties, early forties, well built, athletic I think he was described as, though it beats me how anyone could tell that late at night probably because he was running," said Jackson somewhat sceptically.

"I take your point Steve," said Bradley using his colleague's first name. "It's not much to go on but I think we should re-double our efforts and see if we can't track this fellow down."

"There's not a lot to go on at the moment, but I think we should have another little chat with Mr Steeples don't you, and while you're at it get a warrant and search his house and the jamboree club."

Chapter forty-seven

Bob was busy re-stocking the bar ready for another busy night. He glanced up to see DCI Bradley and DS Jackson making their way over to him. What the bloody hell did they want? He went over to the cellar door where he could hear the rattling of crates and bottles being moved down below.

"Jake are you down there?" he barked, his gruff voice echoing down the cold stone steps.

"I'm just moving these crates and then I'm going to change a barrel," came the reply.

"Well can you leave it a minute and make yerself scarce. The bobbies are here again."

"Can't it wait? I'll be done in a minute," said Jake.

"Just nip out the back door and bugger off for a bit. I'll see what they want."

"Chief inspector what can I do for you?"

"We're just checking the whereabouts of your nephew, the night Sandra Mason was killed, is he about?" said Bradley.

"No, he's nipped out on an errand; he won't be back for a while. Anyway, I already told you we locked up about one am, an' then we went 'ome."

"A man was seen running away from the scene about that time," said Bradley.

"I told you Chief Inspector, we locked up an' went straight 'ome."

"And you didn't see anyone else? And no one saw you?"

"Like I said before, there were these lads larking about, but they were drunk. I doubt they can vouch for us."

"We know. One of the lads said he saw a bloke run past dressed in a Mac," said Jackson.

"Well that lets us off; we weren't wearin' Macs, neither of us. It had been rainin' but it wasn't a bad night so neither of us was wearing a Mac."

"The witness said the man was in his late thirties maybe early forties, tall athletic, with dark hair. Can I ask how old you are Mr Ashcroft?"

"I'm forty six. Why am I a suspect?

DCI Bradley looked at Bob; he could see he was well built, but only average height.

"No we are just checking everyone's alibi's for that night. How tall are you Mr Ashcroft?"

"Dunno exactly, about five foot five or six."

Bradley looked at Bob. He couldn't be described as being tall. His face was pale and he had a shock of blonde hair. He was in the right age bracket, but that was about all. If the witnesses were right they were looking for someone six feet tall, athletic and with dark hair. Bob was well built but hardly athletic.

"Well thank you for your help, we'll be in touch again."

Jake waited until he saw the unmarked police car leave the club before venturing back inside. "What were all that about?" asked Jake.

"They wanted to know where we were the night that young lass was killed."

"You didn't tell them anything did you Uncle Bob,"

"Course I didn't, but you went missin' for more than an 'our, an' I told 'em that you were here the whole time wi me, an' then we locked up an' went 'ome."

"Well so what? That doesn't mean I had owt to do with her death."

"But you went off in a right bloody huff if I remember. Where did you get to?"

"I went out I just needed to clear my head."

"Come on Jake, where did yer really go? Yer goin' ter 'ave ter tell me, otherwise I might tell coppers summat I shouldn't."

"That bastard raped me mam and he raped our Lottie as well," ranted Jake.

"You what? Which bastard?"

"Warmsley; it were Warmsley he did it."

"You mean the feller they've just found wi 'is head bashed in. Good God lad, tell me it weren't you."

"I overheard that woman, you know that Mrs Jackson. She were with that group that the young lass were with. You know them lot from Benson's. I heard her say she felt sorry for the woman at Taylor's that he raped. I couldn't believe it when I heard who it were. It were my mam, uncle Bob, that bastard raped my mam."

"Are yer sure you 'adn't miss 'eard 'er. It was yer mam she were talkin' about?"

"Course I'm sure. I asked her what woman at Taylor's an' she said Lizzie Steeples."

"That's why I went missing. I went looking for the bastard. I were going to kill him."

"Well it looks like somebody's saved you the trouble."

"I can't say I'm sorry Uncle Bob. As far as I'm concerned he got what he deserved, but it weren't me honest."

"I believe you Jake but will the coppers."

It was several days later before anything new turned up. Dalton's engineering company was a midsized business based on the outskirts of town; they made components for the mining and textile businesses, which were abundant around the area. DCI Bradley and DS Jackson pulled up outside the main offices and parked their Ford in the space reserved for visitors. Richard Miles shook hands with DCI Bradley and opened the door of his office. He invited him to sit in the dull but functional room. Bradley declined, preferring to stand.

"What can I do for you?" Asked Miles.

"We're looking into the deaths of two people. You've probably heard about it in the news lately," stated Bradley.

"Yes it's been in all the papers. How can I help you"?

"We are looking for a man, a rep, who we think might be able to help us with our enquiries."

"We are a fairly large organization officer; we deal with a great deal of reps from all over the place. Can you give me a little more information about this gentleman, a name perhaps?"

"Unfortunately sir we don't have a name but we have a description." Bradley described the man to Miles. "You might be better off talking to Peter. That's Peter Howard. You see I'm in the office most of the time and I don't really see the reps. Peter he's our chief buyer, if anyone can tell you, it'll be him." He pressed the button on his intercom.

"Marian could you get Peter and ask him to come to my office thanks."

Peter Howard was a slightly balding fifty something with a slight paunch around his middle, probably from too many years sitting behind a desk, or the wheel of a car, but his clear blue eyes and manner told you he was sharp and perceptive.

"I see many reps in the course of a week officer," he told Bradley.

"This one in particular sir, it's very important."

"There is one chap who comes in about once a month who might fit your description."

"Have you got a name or somewhere we might be able to contact him?" asked DCI Bradley.

"Just a moment." He went over to the filing cabinet. "Here we are," he said pulling a card out of the cabinet. "Brooke Steeples. He works for Anvil engineering in Trafford Park."

"Brooke Steeples. Thank you very much you've been very helpful," said DCI Bradley thoughtfully.

Chapter forty-eight

The door to door was beginning to bear fruit. The night that Sandra Mason was killed, several people recalled seeing a man in the vicinity. Bradley and Jackson decided that a visit to Anvil engineering might turn something up. Anvil engineering was situated about four miles from the centre of Thistlefield, on what was part of an old industrial estate. Although it did some light engineering work, it was mainly a supplier of components and cutting tools for general machine shop use. Bradley was told by the company secretary, a frosty old dear who looked older than the building and was about as welcoming as a dose of flu, that "yes," Brooke Steeples worked there, but he hadn't been seen for a couple of days, which wasn't unusual as his job took him all over the country. Bradley pressed on but old frosty told him that he could be expected to come back anytime, and now if there was nothing else she had work to do.

Back at the station, the house to house had borne fruit. The publicity surrounding the case had brought forward a number of new witnesses including Georgina Laycock.

"Miss Laycock could you tell us again what happened," said DC Francis.

"I'd heard about the young girl that was killed, and it started me thinking."

"It started you thinking. What about, Georgina? Take your time?" said DC Francis gently.

"I met this man in the pub where I work, and we got chatting.

We went out to the pictures and had a meal; he was really lovely." The tears began to flow freely down her cheeks.

"Here," said DC Francis handing her a handkerchief. She dabbed her eyes smudging her mascara.

"Then he said he'd got this hotel room booked and would I like to go back. I feel so stupid and ashamed, I should have known better, so I agreed. We had some champagne and then he was all over me, I couldn't get him off."

"When you say he was all over you what happened Georgina? Take your time you're doing really well," said DC Francis holding onto the distraught girls' hand.

"He raped me. I tried to fight him off but he was too strong. He punched me and I must have passed out. When I came round he'd gone," she sobbed uncontrollably.

"Do you know his name Georgina?" asked DC Francis.

"He said his name was David Gregory," she sobbed.

"And could you describe him for us?"

"He was tall, good looking with dark hair, sort of well built but not fat or anything."

"Athletic would you say," said DC Francis.

"Yes."

"Was there anything else you could tell us about him? Was he light or dark skinned?"

"Not dark skinned like he was black or anything, but he looked like he'd spent a long time in the sun."

"Was there anything else that you can remember, how old would you say he was?"

"He was a good bit older than me. I would say he was mid to late thirties, early forties something like that. I was flattered that he liked me," sniffed Georgina.

"Seems like this David Gregory could answer a lot of questions for us, the trouble is we have to find him first," said DCI Bradley to DS Jackson. "Meanwhile let's have another little chat with Jake Steeples; see if he can shed some more light on things."

Jake shifted uneasily the hard wooden chair digging into his back; they weren't designed for comfort. DCI Bradley sat across from Jake. DS Jackson sat at the end of the table.

"I don't know what else I can tell you," said Jake.

"Let's go back to the night of the fight in the club, shall we. You said Warmsley started to pester the girls and it got out of hand," said Bradley.

"That's right. I went over to see what the fuss were about; next thing he's throwing punches. I already told you all this."

"And the blood on Mr Warmsley's shirt, you say was when you hit him," said Bradley looking at his notes.

"Yeah, I've already told you."

"Can you tell us what the relationship is between you and Brooke Steeples?"

"Why what's that bastard got to do with anything?"

"You don't like him do you," said Bradley.

"Should I?"

"You tell us Jake."

"For what he's worth, he's my dad."

"And what's your relationship with your dad like Jake?"

"Can't stand the bastard."

"And why's that?" asked DCI Bradley.

"For what he did to Mam."

DCI Bradley left the interview room with Jackson. "What do you make of it Steve? Can we charge him or not?"

"Mrs Steeples was raped by Warmsley by her own admission. As far as we know, he did her daughter as well, from what she told us. We also know for sure that he knew that Warmsley raped his mother; not sure whether he knew about his sister or not, but he certainly had the motive and don't forget we found blood on his shirt that we found in the cellar of the club. It was the same as that found on Warmsley, and he was also heard issuing a threat in front of a police officer. "So help me I'll kill the bastard if I get my hands on him."

"And what about Sandra Mason can we pull him in for that one as well?" said Bradley.

"It's a real possibility. Could be that Jake fancied the lass for himself, went looking for her, and when she wouldn't give in, he hits her over the head," said Jackson.

"But what I can't understand is where Warmsley fits into this," said Bradley. "Maybe he came across the two of them and the lad belted him as well."

"Could be, Steve. What about Georgina Laycock's statement? Looks like this David Gregory or whatever he's calling himself, is in the frame for the assault on her if nothing else."

"We've not been able to trace him yet Guv; he seems to have gone to ground."

Well let's pull out all the stops on this one Steve, and get Miss Laycock back in. Let's see if she recognizes Jake Steeples. At least then, we'll know if we're looking for the same man or somebody completely different. I want this David Gregory found. Meanwhile I think we'll have another word with Tommy Sullivan and Dave Prescott. I want uniform to go and round up Mathew Collins and Peter Davies. They were there the night Warmsley kicked off. Looking at what we've got so far, I'm sure we have enough for the DPP to issue a warrant for Jake Steeples arrest on suspicion of the murder of Joe Warmsley at least," said Bradley.

DCI Bradley and DS Jackson pulled up outside Tommy Sullivan's Victorian terraced house on Glaston street. "Mr Sullivan we just wondered if we could have another word about the night of the fight at the jamboree club. Can you tell us what happened?" said Bradley flashing his warrant card.

"I've told you everythin' I know," shrugged Sullivan.

"If you would just indulge us once more," said Bradley with an insincere smile. Tommy went over the story for the umpteenth time. It was almost parrot fashion. "I understand that Joe Warmsley punched you. Is that correct?" said Bradley.

"Yeah he caught me one; punched me in the face."

"What did you do then?" asked Jackson. "Did you retaliate?"

"I was going to but then the lad grabbed his arm. He had his hands round the woman's throat."

"Which lad grabbed his arm? Who had their hands round the woman's throat?" said Bradley.

"The lad from behind the bar; Jake, I think his name was. He grabbed Warmsley's arm. He had 'is arm round her throat."

"Which woman do you mean?" said Jackson taking notes.

"The older woman; the one with the young lasses. Then all hell breaks loose. The lad an' another bloke pulled 'im off the woman. He was screamin' blue murder. Kicked the table over, next thing the lad threatens him. If he ever comes near 'im again he'll kill im."

"This was Jake Steeples. If you ever come near me again I'll kill you. You're quite sure of that?" said DCI Bradley.

"Quite sure," said Tommy Sullivan.

Chapter forty-nine

November 1957

Jake stood silently in the dock of the courtroom as the charges were read out. "You are hereby charged that you, Jake Michael Steeples, on or about the Tenth of October 1957 murdered Joseph Arthur Warmsley. How do you plead?" said the court usher.

"Not guilty," replied Jake his voice barely a whisper. The courtroom hushed as the crown prepared to call its first witness.

Leading the crown's case was Sir Henry Mortimer QC. Henry Mortimer was one of the leading prosecutors' of his day and was renowned for his forthright and direct courtroom manner. One of his most famous cases was in the successful prosecution of the notorious Hugo (Hughie) McPearson. McPearson had been a thorn in the authority's side for years. He ran the east end of London with an iron fist. Protection, prostitution and drug running were his main activities, and at least five people were dead because of him. He had been eventually brought to book when an innocent bystander's child had been paralyzed from the waist down, when a bullet from the gangster's gun went astray during a bank raid, and lodged in the child's back. The distraught father, an off-duty policeman who witnessed the raid, was adamant that nothing would stop him testifying against McPearson; even the threat of violence hadn't put him off. Sir Henry had gone after the gangland warlord with a ruthlessness that only matched his own, and eventually he secured the ultimate penalty for McPearson's brutal reign of terror, when he was sentenced to hang for his many crimes.

Jake's lawyer was up against a very formidable adversary. His QC, Donald Trigg, was himself no mean opponent, but had not the celebrity status of his distinguished rival. Donald Trigg was from the firm Latimer, Priestly and Trigg whose chambers where in London. Although a prestigious set, they had not the renown of Sir Henry Mortimer's Lincolns Inn London chambers. Donald Trigg took silk after a successful advocacy defending Sharp and Goodman, a firm of property developers. They had been accused of tax evasion, when the Inland Revenue had found discrepancies in their accounting. The case became known when it was discovered that they had put in a successful bid with the city council, for the opportunity to develop a prime plot of land for a shopping precinct and office block. The council became suspicious when their bid was many times less than their rivals. A deeper investigation into their affairs showed that the management of Sharp and Goodman had inside knowledge of their rivals' bids. It was also found, that certain taxes had been under-paid or not paid at all for several years. Donald Trigg argued that as his clients were abroad for a good part of the year pursuing other business, they could not reasonably be expected to oversee the running of the business here. Both Sharp and Goodman had hired the very best management team available at the time to run the business for them, argued Trigg, and they had no idea that the company had run into trouble with the Inland Revenue. It was found that senior managers hired by them, had been embezzling thousands of pounds into their own Swiss bank accounts for years. The management had since been prosecuted, and was now serving lengthy jail sentences for their parts in the fraud. Both Sharp and Goodman were exonerated of all blame, and as a reward for their endeavours, Donald Trigg's set were awarded all their future business.

Sir Henry Mortimer rose from the bench his right hand clutching his gown. He looked down at the sheaf of papers as he prepared to call his first witness. "M'lud, the crown calls Mrs Elizabeth Jackson to the stand."

Betty Jackson placed her hand on the bible. "Do you swear to tell the truth the whole truth and nothing but the truth, so help you God," said the court associate.

"I do." Replied Betty Jackson nervously.

"Mrs Jackson, I want to take you back to the night of Tenth of October of this year. In particular the events that took place in the..." Sir Henry stopped momentarily and glanced at his notes. "The events that took place in the Jamboree club," he said, pushing his glasses back onto the bridge of his nose. "In your own words can you describe the events of that evening?"

Betty coughed lightly behind her hand. "We were having a party for Sandra. It was for her eighteenth birthday."

"You were having a party for the deceased, Miss Sandra Mason."

"Yes sir."

"And how many were in the party?"

"About ten or twelve I'm not hundred percent sure. There could have been more I suppose, people were coming and going all the time."

"And could you describe the mood of the party Mrs Jackson?"

"How do you mean sir?" said Betty wringing her hands nervously.

"Would you say it was a happy occasion?"

"I would describe it as happy. Everyone was having a good time."

"You said everyone was having a good time. Was Sandra Mason having a good time, was she drunk?" said Sir Henry.

"Well she was a little tipsy. I wouldn't say drunk."

"So Miss Mason was a little tipsy but not drunk. Would you say that she had had quite a lot to drink, Mrs Jackson?"

"No, I wouldn't say she had an awful lot to drink."

"How many drinks would you say she had? Two, three, four," pressed Sir Henry.

"Probably two or three. We'd only been in there an hour or so."

"Miss Mason had had two or three drinks and was just tipsy. She didn't encourage Mr Warmsley in any way."

"No definitely not. She kept saying she wanted to dance, but she never encouraged him," said Betty Jackson.

"What happened next, Mrs Jackson?"

"There were a group of lads over by the bar, and one young lad came over, Tommy I think his name were, and asked Sandra if she wanted to dance."

"Please, go on."

"This other man came over and grabbed Sandra, and tried to drag her onto the dance floor."

"And this other man who was he?" said Sir Henry.

"It were Joe Warmsley."

"Go on Mrs Jackson; tell the court what happened next."

"The next thing I know, Joe, Mr Warmsley he's trying to drag Sandra onto the dance floor but she didn't want to go."

"Then what happened?"

"The next thing I know there's bottles and glasses all over the place. There was a lot of noise and the lads round the table were egging them on."

"When you say the lads round the table were egging them on. Who were they egging on Mrs Jackson?" said Sir Henry emphasizing the word 'egging' for the benefit of the jury and the less well educated in the gallery.

"The young lad, Jake Steeples, he'd come over to see what the commotion was about."

"And what happened next?"

"I didn't know who he was. I presumed they were his mates and they were egging Jake, Mr Steeples, to hit him."

"You thought they were goading Mr Steeples to hit Joe Warmsley?" said Sir Henry. "That's what it sounded like. They were shouting at him, yelling at him to hit him," said Betty.

"So Mr Steeples came over to the table, and his friends encouraged him to hit Mr Warmsley. Is that what you are telling the court?"

"Yes that's what it sounded like," said Betty.

"Mrs Jackson let me see if I have got this right. Mr Steeples came over to your table and encouraged by his friends, started a fight. With whom did he start the fight?" said Sir Henry turning to face the jury.

Donald Trigg was on his feet in a flash. "M'lud I must raise an objection. There is no evidence that my client went over to start a fight, he merely went over to see what the commotion was."

"Sir Henry, the prosecution will not jump to conclusions,." said Mr Justice Tremlow. "I'll re-phrase the question. Mrs Jackson when the fight started who threw the first punch?"

"Joe Warmsley. He were like a mad man. Jake, Mr Steeples, that is, did his best to break it up. The next thing I know, he had blood all over him. Mr Steeples tried to defend himself. I think he hit Joe, but he, Joe were getting the upper hand."

"Mrs Jackson only moments ago you told the court that Mr Steeples started the fight encouraged by his friends," said Sir Henry.

"There were a lot of noise and a hell of a commotion. It seemed like the young lad started it, but I'm not sure. I think Joe Warmsley started it," said Betty anxiously.

"But is it not true that Mr Steeple's uncle became involved, and between the two of them forcibly threw Mr Warmsley out of the club."

"But the lad was getting battered. Joe Warmsley was a big man and he was in a foul temper."

"Jake Steeples is quite a well built young man. Are you quite sure he needed the assistance of his uncle to deal with Mr Warmsley?" said Sir Henry pressing the point.

"Well it looked like the lad was coming off worse to me, and that's when his uncle got involved."

"So unable to deal with Mr Warmsley himself he enlisted the help of his uncle to throw Joe Warmsley out of the club."

"No it weren't like that. Jake was getting battered. That's when his uncle got involved. He only went to help him," said Betty almost in tears.

"Please answer the question Mrs Jackson, did Mr Steeples and his uncle throw Mr Warmsley out of the club?" Sir Henry had successfully turned Betty Jacksons' evidence round to make Jake look like the villain of the piece.

"Yes they did," said Betty Jackson.

"Mrs Jackson may I take you back to a remark you made after Mr Warmsley had been ejected from the club. You were heard to say, "it was that young woman at Taylors I feel sorry for, the one he tried to rape."

"Do you remember making that remark?"

"Vaguely, I'm not quite sure," she said.

"Do you remember Mr Steeples asking you who it was that he had tried to rape at Taylor's mill Mrs Jackson?"

"Yes," she said, her voice almost a whisper.

"Would you please tell the court who that person was, Mrs Jackson?"

"It was Lizzie Steeples." There was an audible gasp around the courtroom as the identity of Jake's mother was revealed.

"Elizabeth Steeples," said Sir Henry. "The defendant's mother, and would it also surprise you to know, that the police have evidence that Joe Warmsley also raped his younger sister Lottie Steeples." There was another audible gasp as Sir Henry's declaration echoed around the packed courtroom.

"I didn't know at the time that Mr Steeples and Lizzie Steeples were related. I only knew his name was Jake. I never knew his surname," said Betty Jackson.

"I put it to you M'lud, that after losing face in front of his friends, Mr Steeples went looking for Joe Warmsley. He had overheard a conversation that Mr Warmsley allegedly had raped both his mother and his sister. This was only hearsay in the club, and no proof that it had actually happened. Indeed, neither Mrs Steeples nor Lottie Steeples had reported either of the incidents to the police. On hearing that his mother had been raped, and that his sister had also been raped, Mr Steeples decided to take matters into his own hands. He then went looking for Joe

Warmsley, and in a fit of revenge, exacted retribution in the most brutal way and killed him." Sir Henry Mortimer had certainly forced his point across. Even if Jake hadn't killed him, the evidence against him was damning. The spectators in the public gallery and the jury now had reasonable cause to suspect that he had.

Chapter fifty

Donald Trigg rose to his feet. Where Sir Henry Mortimer was of short stature and somewhat portly, Donald Trigg was tall, over six feet and his build could best be described as spare. He looked over at Betty Jackson, his piercing blue eyes seeming to look straight through her. "Mrs Jackson we have heard from my learned friend that when the fight took place that Mr Warmsley was the one who instigated it. Is that true?"

"Yes he started it."

"Are you sure? You also said that Mr Warmsley he threw the first punch."

"Yes he hit Jake, I mean Mr Steeples first."

"So in actual fact when Mr Steeples hit Mr Warmsley he was merely defending himself."

"Yes he was."

"Then what happened?"

"Well, like I said before, Mr Steeples was getting the worst of it, and Mr Warmsley was ranting and raving all over the place, kicking and shouting; he was in a foul temper."

"He was in such a foul temper kicking and shouting that it took both my client and his uncle to restrain him."

"Yes sir, that's right. Like an animal he was," said Betty feeling more confident than a few moments ago.

"Mrs Jackson how long had you known Mr Warmsley?"

"Quite a few years."

"And what kind of man was he?"

"From my experience of him he was a bully."

"In what way was he a bully Mrs Jackson?"

"Well if he didn't get his own way especially with the lasses he gave them a hard time."

"When you say he gave them a hard time, how do you mean?"

Sir Henry Mortimer was on his feet in an instant. "I must raise an objection M'lud. I fail to see where this line of questioning is leading."

"Yes," said Mr Justice Tremlow. "Could you please get to the point Mr Trigg?"

"I'm merely trying to give an insight into Mr Warmsley's character, M'lud."

"Objection overruled, carry on Mr Trigg."

"If he didn't get his own way he gave them a hard time. In what way?"

"Well he put lasses on heavier jobs or he gave them dirty jobs like in the card room," said Betty.

"Can you tell the court what it was like, say, in the card room?"

"It was very dirty and heavy."

"It was very dirty and heavy, and for someone in Mrs Steeple's condition, someone who had been suffering from TB it was a considerably hazardous job."

"I would say that for a healthy person it was very hard work but for someone like Lizzie, Mrs Steeples, doubly so."

"M'lud I fail to see the significance of my learned friends' questioning," said Sir Henry forcefully.

"Yes Mr Trigg could you get to the point."

"I'm trying to establish my lord that Mr Warmsley could have made enemies, and that my client wasn't the only one who had a grudge against him."

"Very well carry on but do be brief," said judge Tremlow.

"Mrs Jackson could I take you back to the night of the party? How long had you known Miss Mason?"

"About two years, ever since she started at the factory."

"And in all that time Miss Mason had never been in any trouble. She wasn't promiscuous?"

"I don't know what you mean," said Betty looking perplexed.

"Miss Mason wasn't immoral, of easy virtue. She wouldn't have been looking for a sexual encounter."

"No sir. It was Sandie's first party for her eighteenth birthday. She'd been looking forward to it for ages. Talked about nothing else," said Betty dabbing her eyes that were now full of tears. Several members in the gallery of the courtroom, especially the women nodded in agreement with Betty Jackson's statement.

"So a quiet unassuming young girl who was looking forward to her eighteenth birthday party, who, by no fault of her own, was subjected to a terrifying assault and dragged onto the dance floor against her will by Joe Warmsley."

"Objection your honour; Miss Mason was not subjected to a terrifying assault and dragged onto the dance floor by Mr Warmsley. He merely wanted to dance with the girl," said Sir Henry forcefully.

"Mr Trigg, would you stick to the facts please? Did Mr Warmsley assault Miss Mason on the dance floor or not?" said Judge Tremlow.

"Your honour, Mr Warmsley was a known bully and tried to force Miss Mason onto the dance floor. Although there was no physical assault as such, he tried to drag her against her will onto the dance floor," said Donald Trigg. He went on. "The young girl, clearly from the evidence we have heard, was terrified of Mr Warmsley. He was a known bully, who preyed on people weaker than himself, and especially young girls. I also put it to the jury, M'lud, that the same thing happened to Mrs Steeples who was also in no fit state to resist him. I suggest that Mr Warmsley had more enemies than just Jake Steeples."

"Objection overruled," said Judge Tremlow. Donald Trigg seemed to have acquitted himself favourably with both the jury and the gallery who were nodding in agreement of his character assassination of Joe Warmsley.

Chapter fifty-one

The case against Jake was looking evermore fragile. The evidence against him was beginning to look overwhelming, and the prosecution's case led by Sir Henry Mortimer was damning. The jury looked like they had been swayed by Sir Henry's powerful opening argument. In his favour though, was Donald Trigg's damning evidence of the evil personality of Joe Warmsley.

The police still hadn't found David Gregory. The case against Jake looked solid enough, but they were still no nearer to finding the killer of Sandra Mason. Were the two murders linked? It looked as if Jake could have done the girl but they had little or no evidence to go on, other than the fact that Jake was there the same night. The only other thing in his favour was that Georgina Laycock was confident that it wasn't Jake that had attacked her.

They had to find David Gregory he was the key.

DCI Bradley was woken from a fitful sleep by a firm dig in the ribs. "Come on lazy bones rise and shine I've been up for ages," smiled DC Linda Francis, Bradley's current girl friend.

"Bloody hell. What time is it?" he said, his brain still foggy from the effects of too much alcohol the night before. "How long was I out for?" he asked, struggling over to the chair where his pants where draped.

"You mean you don't remember last night. Am I so forgettable?" she laughed. "You couldn't wait to get your hands on me if I remember rightly. We nearly got arrested in the pub car park for indecency. It was a good job it was one of the local lads otherwise I think we might have spent the night in the cells," she laughed.

DCI Bradley laughed. "Well if he had he would have been on traffic duty for the rest of his career," he joked. Phil Bradley was the wrong side of fifty, but was still considered quite a catch by many of his female colleagues down at the nick. Unlike a few of his contemporaries, he had kept in good shape with regular visits to the local gym. He was a shade over six feet, and his toned muscular body showed no signs of excess weight. His strong tanned features and dark brown eyes were highlighted by his thick shock of silver grey hair. Phil Bradley lived in the suburbs of Thistlefield in the same house he and his ex-wife used too share. He had bought her share out years ago, but he was still paying the mortgage. They had married when he was still a copper on the beat and the prospects of promotion hadn't been an issue. They had had two kids a boy and a girl who were now in their late twenties. Phil's son, the eldest by a year was working as an engineer in the newly blossoming nuclear energy industry, whilst his daughter was a primary school teacher. After five years he was still waiting for his first grandchild. He saw more of them now than in their formative years. He was always at work. Phil Bradley had set his sights on better things and worked his way doggedly through the ranks until he became a detective inspector at the expense of his marriage. Things had been going well until the cases he worked on became more and more involved. He had spent more of his time at work consumed by endless enquiries and paperwork than at home with his family. Consequently, he neglected his wife and children. She found solace in the arms of a lecturer from the local college. Luckily, the split had been amicable, and the two of them had remained friends, though it did rankle with Bradley that she had gone off with somebody ten years younger. DC Linda Francis had met him when they worked together on a child murder case, where she was the family's liaison officer. Linda was thirty-nine but looked ten years younger. She had shoulder length blonde hair and blue eyes, and due to some heavy workouts in the gym had managed to keep her svelte like figure. She had just broken up with her current boyfriend, also on the force, when she met Phil Bradley. It had been somewhat on the rebound. The case had been traumatic, and consequently she had suffered stress. It had upset Linda more than she had let on. Even her police training couldn't hide the fact that the trauma of seeing children's mutilated bodies had been more than she could cope with. Phil had taken her under his wing and helped her through it. Added to the fact that she was just getting over a relationship this drew her closer to her boss. At first, it was just a casual friendship, a few drinks in the pub, a coffee in the canteen, but as time went on his feelings for her grew, so much so that he had asked her to move in on a permanent basis. They had been together for the last two years and had settled into some kind of domestic harmony albeit as much as the job would allow.

"I've made a pot of tea do you want one?" she shouted from the untidy kitchen. Neither of them had mastered the art of domesticity, and the tiny kitchen resembled a war zone with dirty pans and crockery vying for space on the cluttered worktops. She found two cups and rinsed them in the sink. "Tea?" she said again.

"Milk and one sugar," he shouted from the equally untidy bathroom, as he finished pulling a dull razor through a two-day growth of beard. "Damn!" he shouted as the blunt razor nicked his skin drawing blood onto his only clean shirt.

"What's up?" said Linda.

"Just cut myself with this bloody razor and now I've got blood on my only clean shirt."

"Let's have a look. It's bugger all, I'll soon have that off." She said attacking it with a damp cloth. "There you are good as new, the stains' almost invisible," she said kissing him on the cheek. "Do you want anything to eat? I can do you some bacon and eggs if you like."

He pulled her towards him nuzzling her neck and biting her ear. "I'll have you if that's alright," he said with a smile gripping the cheeks of her backside as she felt the hardness grow as he pushed himself into her groin.

"Down boy, remember we've got a case to solve and it won't get solved if we play silly buggers now will it." She laughed smacking his hands playfully away.

"But I like playing silly buggers, it's the only pleasure I get these days," he said mischievously.

"Right," she said, throwing the damp cloth in his face.

"Seriously though Linda," he said, throwing the cloth into the sink."There's something about this case. I've just got that gut feeling that we're missing something."

Back at Thistlefield central, DCI Bradley was going over the events of the tenth of October. The publicity campaign still hadn't brought the whereabouts of David Gregory. Bradley was more convinced than ever that he was at the heart of the case. Hard evidence was what brought most criminals to justice but Bradley's gut feelings were never far out, and he had a gut feeling about this case. All the evidence pointed to Jake Steeples being responsible for Warmsley's death, but there was nothing concrete to tie him to the death of Sandra Mason. The blood found on his shirt matched the blood on Warmsley's. He had threatened to kill Warmsley in front of witnesses including a police officer, for the attempted rape of his mother and the rape of his sister, and he was there in the vicinity around the same time. Apart from that, there was nothing to implicate that he had anything to do with the death of Sandra Mason.

DS Jackson put the phone to his ear and scribbled on the notepad in front of him. "That was Hilldale nick on the phone Guv. It seems that Warmsley had form there. It would appear that our friend served two years in Medway jail for attempted rape. But here's the interesting bit, Guv, when he got out, he left Hilldale where he'd been living and he moved back to Thistlefield, and somehow got a job at Bensons Mill."

"Isn't that where Sandra Mason worked?" said Bradley.

"Yes, so it's possible that Warmsley knew the girl, Guv," said Jackson.

Chapter fifty-two

The Dog and Partridge was just off Grasmere Road in Langford just north of Thistlefield. It was noted for putting on good club acts on a regular basis and filling the place. If they went down well here you could guarantee they would go down well anywhere, the pub's punters were a tough crowd. Bob was here to see a couple of singers he'd heard were appearing with a view to booking them for the Jamboree. The pub was fairly large; the main room had a sizeable expanse of floor space with a raised podium that acted as a stage. He stood at the bar facing the stage in order to get a better view of the acts. The Dog and Partridge was crowded and all the tables were full with punter's trying to get a better view. The MC, a dumpy individual with a considerable girth, in an ill-fitting dinner suit and a white shirt that looked like another spin in the washer wouldn't go amiss, called for order as he was about to introduce the first turn. The noise in the place seemed to get louder as the MC tried valiantly to get the punters to be quiet. The first act up was a skinny lad with one too many spots and a ducks-arse haircut. He introduced himself as Johnny de Voss and he absolutely crucified the Elvis Presley number Jailhouse Rock. The crowd booed the poor lad off the stage and waited noisily for the next act. Sweating profusely the MC tapped his mike and asked for order for the very lovely Denise Silverton. The girl was slightly built and her blonde bouffant hair had been teased around her pretty face. The MC passed her the mike and she uttered the title of the song she was going to perform.

"Speak up lass we can 'ardly bloody 'ear you," snorted one reveller, obviously the worse for wear.

"I'm going to sing 'Tenderly,' by Rosemary Clooney. It's a melodic ballad. I hope you like it," she said, her voice barely a whisper. Bob felt sorry for the girl she was certainly pleasing on the eye, but he doubted these hard arsed bastards would give her a chance. The band gave her an introduction and the music started. She fairly belted out the number and soon had the audience clapping and tapping their feet along with her. Her next song was 'All My Love,' by Patti Page. It was another pulsating ballad, and she had them dancing in between the tables and in front of the stage. Her last song, 'Secret love,' by Doris Day, absolutely knocked them dead. Her frame defied the powerful voice as it soared to a crescendo at the end of the song. Now the entire pub was on its feet shouting for more as she handed the mike back to the MC. Bob shoved his way over to the backstage to see the girl.

As he pushed past a group of drinkers, out of the corner of his eye he spotted Brooke. He was sitting near a couple of women in the corner, but he hadn't seen him. What was he doing in this neck of the woods? he thought to himself. He could see the two women were arguing. One of them was obviously drunk; and was shaking her finger in the direction of her mate's face.

Bob pushed his way to the bar and ordered another pint. "I think you might have a bit of a problem over there," he said, pointing in the direction of the two women who now appeared to be arguing vehemently.

"Oh don't worry, that's only mad Mary Warmsley, she's been like that for years. Goes off on one if she can't get a drink. Don't worry Brenda will look after her. They work together in the same office in town when she's sober," said the landlord.

"Why what happened?"

"Rumour has it that years ago, she was raped. It was never proved but they recon it was her brother Joe. He was a right bastard, in and out of jail for all sorts. He got two years for the attempted rape of a woman. When he got out, he disappeared over Hilldale way. Poor lass never really got over it. Brenda sort of took her under her wing and looked after her. She was only a girl about eighteen or nineteen at the time, though you wouldn't think to look at her now," said the landlord.

Bob looked over at the woman. Her face wore the ravages of excess. She had dark bags under her eyes, and the skin on her cheeks sagged a little. It was obvious that at one time, she had been a good-looking woman, but too much drink hadn't done her any favours. However, they weren't Bobs' problem he was here to book acts for the club. He turned his attention back to the stage where the last of the acts were getting ready to perform.

Brooke left his seat in the corner and went over to join the two women. He took his drink over to where they were sitting. "Can I help? You seem to be having a bit of trouble."

"We're alright thank you," said Mary's friend. "She gets a bit upset at times, but I'm going to take her home now. Come on pet are you ready?"

"I don't want to go home, Brenda, I want another drink," she grunted.

"Do you live far?" asked Brooke.

"Not really, it's only a few minutes on the bus."

"I've got the car outside I can run you both if you like."

She pulled Mary to her feet but she slipped and almost fell onto the floor. Brooke quickly caught the woman and helped her to her feet. He guessed her age to be late twenties early thirties. He could see that she had once been quite a good-looking girl before she had succumbed to alcohol.

"Thanks," said the woman. "She can be a bit of a handful at times."

"It's no bother really." He said eyeing the attractive brunette up and down.

"Come on, it'll be better than the bus especially with your friend in that condition," he said nodding in the direction of the inebriated girl.

"If you're sure we don't want to be any bother do we pet?"

"Don't worry it's no bother," he said helping Mary to her feet and guiding her towards the door. Ten minutes later, he pulled up outside a rundown terraced house. "Is this it?" he asked pleasantly.

"Yes thanks. I'll get her inside. Thanks for the lift."

"Here let me help you, she looks heavy," said Brooke holding the car door open.

"It's ok, I can manage, I should be used to it by now."

"I insist; can't have a pretty girl like you humping her upstairs all by yourself."

"If you're sure, she is a bit of a weight."

With a bit of manhandling they managed to get the woman upstairs and into bed. She started to come round and tried to sit up in bed.

"Oh who's your friend?" she slurred looking Brooke up and down through an inebriated fog.

"He's just someone I met in the pub, Mary. He's helped me get you home love. Lie down you'll be all right in the morning when you've had a sleep. I'm sorry I never even asked your name," said Brenda.

"David... Dave Gregory," said Brooke with a smile.

"Well Dave, thanks for your help I don't know how I would have managed on my own."

"That's ok. Why don't I take you for a drink? I'm sure your friend will be ok now that she's tucked up in bed."

"Oh I don't know. I really should be getting back home."

Just then Mary stirred in bed and propped herself up on the pillows. "Oh he's gorgeous," she tittered to herself staring at Brooke.

"Mary I thought you were asleep," said Brenda.

"I am. Oh he's lovely," she whimpered again.

"Are you going to be alright? I have to be getting home." Before she could answer, Mary's head slumped back on the pillows dead to the world. She wouldn't wake up again for hours.

"What about that drink? We might just catch the last orders if we hurry, then I can drop you off at home."

"Well I don't suppose one will hurt, will it?" she said getting into the car.

Chapter fifty-three

"How long ago was it that Warmsley was done for the attempted rape in Hilldale?" asked DCI Bradley

"Must be about three or four years. According to Hilldale Nick, he assaulted some woman, but was caught when some passersby saw him and gave the local cops his description," said Jackson. "There's more. He'd just started work and he almost killed one of his workmates with a mallet because, he couldn't write his name to pick up his wages."

"Where was this?"

"In Thistlefield; it was in one of the slaughterhouses. He was only a lad about sixteen, I think," said Jackson.

"So he had quite a reputation for violence."

"And not only that," continued Jackson. "It's rumoured he raped his sister. She was only eighteen or nineteen at the time; he was about thirty but nothing was ever proved. No charges were ever brought against him. It looks as if he's had a history of violence all his life"

"And what happened to the sister, do we know?"

"She disappeared off the radar. Last anyone heard of her she was on the game and drinking herself to death," said Jackson.

"There must be a lot of people out there who had a grudge against him. I'd like to find his sister and see if she can shed any more light on this. Steve, get back onto uniform see if we can find where she might be."

The November air was decidedly chilly as Tom Howard walked into the local nick in Thistlefield and rang the bell on the counter.

A burly sergeant in a uniform that seemed to be at pains to keep his ample girth under control ambled to the front desk. "Yes sir how can I help you?"

"I want to report a missing person."

"And who might that be?" asked the stocky sergeant.

"My daughter."

"When did she go missing?"

"Wednesday."

"Last Wednesday that would be the 25th of October sir," said the sergeant making notes on his pad.

"No yesterday."

"Wednesday, yesterday the 1st of November. But that's less than twenty-four hours sir. Do you not think she might just be staying with friends?"

"She's never missed coming home before," said Tom.

"What's her name?"

"Brenda Howard."

"And how old is your daughter sir?"

"Thirty-two; but she's never done anything like this before. She always comes home."

"Is your daughter married?"

"No she lives at home. She's a good girl she would never stay out and not tell us. My wife's not in the best of health and Brenda helps me look after her."

"Does your daughter have a boyfriend sir?"

"I don't know, she might have, I'm not sure."

"What about girl friends. Could she have gone out with one of them?"

"I suppose so, but it's not like her to not come home."

"When did you last see your daughter?"

"About six o'clock last night. She said she was going out and she would be back about eleven or eleven thirty, she usually get's the last bus."

"Any idea where she was going, or who she was going with?" said the sergeant making more notes on his pad.

"No, she often went out on Wednesday. She had a friend out of town that she saw on a regular basis, but she was always back before midnight. She works in an office in town, and is a meticulous timekeeper she would never be late for work."

"Can you describe your daughter?"

"Brenda's thirty-two. She's got shoulder length light brown hair and brown eyes."

"How tall is she?"

"I would say medium height about 5 foot 4 inches."

"Has your daughter got any distinguishing marks, you know like a birth mark or a mole or anything like that?" asked the sergeant.

"She has a small scar on her left knee. She fell off her bike when she was a kid and the cut was quite deep, needed a stitch, it's hardly noticeable, but you can just about see it," he went on.

"What was she wearing when you last saw her?"

"She had a blue coat with a bit of black fur round the collar; said it was a bit chilly. We bought it for her birthday," he added nervously.

"What else?" Said the sergeant, matter of factly.

"She had a beige two piece suit with two buttons on the jacket and she was wearing light brown shoes, well more like tan, with a small heel."

"Thank you sir; I'll inform the duty officer and we'll ask our patrols to keep a lookout for her. In the meantime I wouldn't worry too much. I'm sure she'll turn up very soon."

"But she's never done anything like this before, she's always come home, can't you do anything?"

"I'm afraid until she's been missing for forty-eight hours she's not classed as a missing person. I should go home sir and try not to worry, I'm sure she'll turn up soon."

Chapter fifty-four

Thursday night was clear and the moon was casting shadows over the Brookdale golf course. A footpath ran along the south side of the course only yards away from a small river that ran through the middle of the course. It was a popular walk for courting couples taking the night air. Colin Jones and his girlfriend were out walking their Jack Russell 'Scamp.' The moon had just gone behind a cloud as Colin threw Scamp's ball into the thicket. "Go on, go and find it boy," said Colin urging his pal on.

"He'll never find it in there," said Colin's girlfriend Julie. "We'd better go and help him."

Suddenly scamp barked.

"Come on then lad, have you found it?" said Colin brushing away the thick growth of bushes. "Bloody hell!" he exclaimed. "We'd better call the police."

"What have you got for us doc?" said DCI Bradley. He pulled his coat tighter round his muscular frame. The chilly November air was blowing across the deserted golf course threatening to freeze his gonads.

"Young woman I'd say in her late twenties early thirties."

"How long has she been dead?" said Bradley.

"Hard to say, a day, two days maybe, I'll know more when I get the poor girl back to the mortuary." He said matter of factly.

DCI Bradley waited patiently as pathologist Dr Paul Grantley performed the post-mortem on the girl lying on the gurney.

"How old would you say she was?" asked Bradley knowing full well that the girl lying in front of him was almost certainly Brenda Howard. She had shoulder length brown hair, and light brown eyes. He also noticed the small scar on her left knee. He would hardly have noticed it under normal circumstances, but he knew what he was looking for.

"My guess would be in her late twenties early thirties, twenty nine, thirty, I would say," said Grantley expertly probing the girl's stomach and extracting what looked very much like one of the girl's kidneys. DCI Bradley looked away as the pathologist dropped the dripping organ into a kidney shaped tray.

"What was the cause of death doctor?"

"Severe trauma to the cranium. If you look here," he said turning the girl's head to one side so that Bradley could get a better look. He pulled back the hair from one side to reveal extensive bruising to the back of her head, and a deep indentation just below the crown.

"So she was hit with a blunt instrument. Was she killed at the scene?" asked Bradley.

"Something heavy, and with a great deal of force judging by the wound on her head; I would say she was killed elsewhere and dumped," said Grantley.

"How long would you say she's been dead doctor?"

"My guess would be twenty four hours at the most, but I'll know more when I've completed the post mortem. There are also signs of sexual activity."

"You mean she was raped?" said Bradley.

"There is a considerable amount of bruising around her inner thighs. I would suggest that intercourse took place, but not with her consent I would hasten to say."

"Hmm, It seems to me that it's the same bloke that did the other one. Was there anything else on her that might identify her doc?" said Bradley.

"Nothing with a name or address; her clothes are over there in a tray, they might tell you something," said Grantley.

DCI Bradley examined the dead girls clothing. Beige two piece with black buttons, brown shoes with low heel, blue top coat with black fur collar, the same outfit described by Tom Howard as to what his daughter was wearing when he last saw her. He was convinced that the latest victim on the coroner's slab was Brenda Howard.

"Jackson, best get onto Tom Howard, we need to get a positive identification. I'm pretty certain that that's his daughter lying in there," he said turning his head in the direction of the mortuary.

Chapter fifty-five

Bradley looked pensive as he pored over the mass of paperwork on his desk. "We have to be looking for two different killers Steve. Jake Steeples is already on trial for the Sandra Mason murder, so it can't be him for this one, even though it's the same m.o."

"Or we've got the wrong man in the dock and the real killer is out there," said Jackson. "I've had an uneasy feeling about this case for a while. I'm back in court tomorrow and I can't help feeling we've got the wrong man. I know the evidence points to Steeples and he certainly had a motive. He finds out that Warmsley raped his mother and sister and he has a fight with him in the club over Sandra Mason. Yet he doesn't strike me as murderer. I'm going to issue a photo fit of the guy running away from the gang of lads the night that Sandra Mason was killed, it might just jog someone's memory."

The Dog and Partridge pub in Langford was a fair distance from his usual haunts in Thistlefield. Brooke had been here before and no one had bothered him. He knew he had to find Brenda's mate. He felt comfortable that he was less likely to be known around here. The radio in the corner was switched on to the local news. The crackly set was reporting the death of a young woman believed to be Brenda Howard. She had been killed some days earlier by a blunt instrument. The police were asking that anyone who had last seen Brenda Howard should come forward. They also had a photo-fit picture of a man they wanted to interview, which would be in all the local newspapers. It would also be posted around town. They urged that all young women should keep their doors locked and only go out if it was really necessary; at least preferably with someone else until this man was caught. Brooke listened to the broadcast, finishing the last dregs from his glass.

"Bad do that," said the barman passing Brooke another pint of bitter, whisky chaser and a ploughman's. "Not safe for young women to go out anymore."

Brooke nodded in agreement. "No," he said as he took his order back to the booth in the corner. He bit into the thick crusty bread unaware of how hungry he was. From the corner of his eye, he could see the woman looking over in his direction. He nodded to her and she sidled over to join him in the corner booth away from prying eyes. He thought he recognized her but he couldn't be sure. Her face was familiar, and he could see that she had once been quite a good-looking woman. She looked to be in her mid to late thirties, but the ravages of time and alcohol had taken its toll.

"I hope they get the bastard who did that," she said pointing to the news on the radio. "Like to buy me a drink?" she slurred pawing his knee with a grubby hand.

"I don't think so love." Suddenly he realized who she was. He pushed her hand away from his leg.

"We could have a bit of fun later if you like." She winked suggestively pushing her hand further up his groin. "Oh I see you like me already," she said feeling his hardness grow under his trouser leg. Brooke was becoming aroused. She wasn't the usual type that he went for, but underneath the thick makeup, she wasn't that bad.

"Ok why don't I buy you a drink and then we could go somewhere a bit more private," he suggested. "What would you like? I don't even know your name."

"Mary," she said. "And I don't even know yours."

"Dave," he said.

"I'll have a gin and tonic, Dave, a large one," she giggled.

Mary rummaged through her handbag for her keys. She could barely keep her hand steady has she inserted it into the front door of the scruffy terraced house. Inside wasn't much better. There were clothes and papers all over the floor, and the kitchen sink was overflowing with pots and pans that hadn't been washed for a week at least.

"Do you live here on your own?" asked Brooke. "Why are you worried my husband might come home and catch you?" she laughed.

"Well it might be embarrassing if he suddenly burst through the door."

"Don't worry love, I'm not married," she said waving her left hand to show him that there was no wedding ring there. "Gave up on men years ago."

"Why bother with me then?" said Brooke puzzled.

"You looked nice and friendly, and I like a bit of company now and then if you know what I mean," she winked. "Do you want a beer? I think there's some in here," she said rummaging through the ancient fridge. She passed him a bottle and he took a healthy swig of the contents. "Now what's say we get comfortable?" she said grabbing his hand and pulling him up the stairs. "Pull the curtains to love; we don't want all the world to see us, do we?" She stripped off her clothes down to her underwear.

Brooke could see that she had been a stunner in her time. Her face might have stood the ravages of time, but her body was slim firm and voluptuous. Her hips had just a hint of thickening, but her waist was still fairly slender accentuating her ample breasts. Her legs were slender and perfectly shaped. He could feel himself growing harder as he gazed at her shapely body. She slipped between the covers and Brooke was on her in a moment.

"Take your time love there's no rush we've all night." Suddenly his ardour wilted and he could feel his passion waning. "What's up love? Can't you get it up? We'll soon put that right," she said bending her head towards his wilting cock. "Leave me alone," he snarled. "Don't bloody touch me you fucking bitch."

"Ok, keep your hair on. It's not my fault if you can't get it up, too much beer if you ask me."

"Shut your mouth you fucking slag," he raged at her. Mary got out from under the covers the fear was etched into her face. Now she remembered where she had seen him before. The night Brenda had brought her home drunk. She had to get away. "I think you'd better go," she said reaching for her dress that was hanging over the back of the chair.

"I'm not going anywhere," he snarled. He grabbed her and threw her down on the bed. She screamed but he put his hand over her mouth stifling the noise. She bit his hand and tore at his face, her nails gouging huge scratches on his cheeks. For a split second, he lost his grip. "You fucking bitch," he yelled. She made it to the bedroom door but he was on her before she could make it down the stairs. He dragged her back into the room and threw her down onto the floor her head cracking against the iron bedstead. She was momentarily dazed. Brooke leapt on her battering at her face with his fists. Mary was a fighter and wasn't easily subdued. She lashed out with her foot catching him in the groin making him yell in pain. Brooke doubled over as she made another effort to get to the door. He reached into his coat pocket and pulled out the metal pipe he had hidden there. She was almost through the door when the first blow stunned her, knocking her senseless. She stumbled and fell against the doorjamb. He grabbed her and threw her back onto the bed; he could feel his ardour returning. He stripped her naked and parted her legs. The sight of the dark thatch of hair and her naked body only inflamed his desire. Mary groaned as she tried to regain her senses and get off the bed, but another savage blow to the head knocked her unconscious. He savagely thrust his engorged member into her comatose body. Groaning and shouting brutally it was only seconds before he emptied his seed into her. The noise had alerted the neighbours and a heavy banging on the door told Brooke that he had to get out of there fast. He pulled on his trousers and coat and ran down the rickety stairs almost falling in his rush to get away. He tugged open the back door and ran down the back alley falling over some dustbins that were partially hidden in the darkness.

The neighbours kicked the front door in and rushed up the stairs. Mary was still alive but blood was pouring from the wound in her head. "Somebody call an ambulance and get the police as well."

Chapter fifty-six

The trial was in its fourth day and things were looking progressively worse for Jake. Sir Henry Mortimer was about to call his next witness, DCI Bradley.

"Detective Chief Inspector Bradley; when did you become involved with the investigation into the death of Joseph Warmsley?"

"It was Friday the Tenth of October this year. We were informed that a fight had broken out at the Jamboree club, and later that evening the body of Mr Warmsley was found by the canal by a young couple."

"And this fight, who did it involve Chief Inspector?"

"As I understood it sir there were quite a few people involved."

"But who specifically did it involve?" pressed Sir Henry.

"Witness statements say the two principals were Jake Steeples and Joe Warmsley."

"Jake Steeples and Joe Warmsley. When you questioned Mr Steeples what was his reaction?"

"He was adamant that it was self-defence. He said that Joe Warmsley was pestering the girl, and that when he went to enquire what was going on, he attacked him. This was also substantiated by several other witnesses that said that Joe Warmsley started the fight."

"Were there any other people involved in the fight Chief Inspector, or was it just Mr Steeples and Mr Warmsley?"

"It was just the two of them at first, and then Mr Steeple's uncle helped to throw him out. There was a lot of shouting and screaming, people urging them on, according to witness reports."

"Mr Steeples and his uncle eventually ejected Mr Warmsley from the club. Is that correct?"

"Yes sir. Although Mr Steeples was trying to separate Mr Warmsley and Miss Mason, he was coming off the worst, and his uncle and he eventually ejected him from the club."

"When the deceased's body was found there was blood on his shirt was there not?"

"Yes there was."

"Whose blood was on the shirt?"

"Forensic evidence proved that the blood came from Joe Warmsley and Jake Steeples."

"On a search of the premises, what else did you find chief inspector?"

"We found a shirt belonging to Jake Steeples."

"Where did you find this shirt inspector?"

"It was found in the basement of the club."

Sir Henry could feel the tide turning against Jake and he ruthlessly pressed home his advantage. "You say the shirt was found in the cellar of the Jamboree club. Where exactly was it found Chief Inspector?"

"Behind some boxes in the corner."

"In other words the shirt had been hidden from view, would that be correct?"

Bradley looked uneasy as he answered. "Come Chief Inspector, was the shirt hidden from view?"

"It looked that way but it could have easily have just been thrown there."

"You said moments ago that forensic evidence proved that the blood on Mr Warmsley's shirt also came from Mr Steeples," said Sir Henry.

"Joe Warmsley had blood on his shirt that we believed came from Jake Steeples, yes."

"And when you searched the Jamboree club you found a shirt belonging to Jake Steeples that also had blood on it, that a forensic examination proved was the same blood as Joe Warmsley?"

"Yes that's correct." The jury had made its mind up that Jake was guilty. Several members along with members in the public gallery were nodding in agreement with Sir Henry. From this damning piece of evidence, Jake sat in the dock ashen faced convinced that he was going to face the hangman's rope.

"So to sum up, Chief Inspector, a fight took place in the Jamboree Club on Friday evening the Tenth of October around nine pm. Jake Steeples in a fit of rage decided to take matters into his own hands. We have already heard from Mrs Jackson, that Mr Steeples had overheard that Joe Warmsley had raped his mother and sister, and I suggest in an act of retribution set out to exact his own brutal justice on Mr Warmsley, no further questions M'lud." Satisfied that he had just sentenced Jake to the hangman's rope Sir Henry Mortimer took his seat.

Donald Trigg looked across at his client and nodded. He mouthed silently for Jake not to worry, but Jake's pale young face had aged ten years by the overwhelming evidence given by the prosecution. In the gallery Lizzie wept as she heard Sir Henry's forceful argument, it had surely condemned Jake to the gallows.

Donald Trigg looked at his notes. "Chief Inspector Bradley, did you say that the shirt my client had been wearing appeared to have been hidden. Was it out of sight where no one could see it?"

"Well no, it was on some boxes."

"But you have just told my learned friend that it was behind some boxes. Was it behind the boxes or on the boxes chief inspector?"

"Objection My Lord, where is this line of questioning going?" said Sir Henry.

"Yes said Judge Tremlow, I'm at pains to know myself, Mr Trigg."

"My Lord, I'm trying to establish if the shirt was deliberately hidden or merely placed there."

"To what purpose Mr Trigg?"

"If my client had hidden it there, then surely he would not just have thrown it behind the boxes. He would have made sure that it was out of sight, and therefore not easily found. I suggest my lord that the shirt was put there in order that my client could change into a fresh one, and not to hide any damning evidence."

"Objection overruled, but do get on Mr Trigg."

"I put it to you again Chief Inspector, could the shirt have just been thrown there haphazardly in order that my client may have changed into a clean one?"

DCI Bradley looked distinctly uncomfortable as Donald Trigg pressed home his point. "Yes my lord it is entirely possible that could be the case."

It was a clever ploy by Trigg, he just hoped that the jury would be swayed.

Chapter fifty-seven

A large crowd had gathered outside the terrace where the assault had taken place. "What's happened?" asked one perplexed neighbour.

"Somebody's been attacked, a woman I think."

"That's Mary's place," said a thin faced woman. "Is she ok?"

"Please let us through," said the ambulance man wielding the heavy stretcher through the throng of onlookers.

Only the bandaged head on the stretcher was visible, but the thin faced woman recognized her. "My God!" she exclaimed, "Its Mary."

"Do you know this woman?" asked the fresh faced constable taking his notebook out of his pocket. "Yes it's Mary Warmsley, lived here a few years now."

Mary groaned on the stretcher, the young fresh faced officer bent over her. "Mary can you hear me?" he said. "Who did this to you?"

Mary was drifting in and out of consciousness. "D... Dave," she mumbled.

"Dave who?" asked the officer again.

"D... Dave and J... Joe," she stammered. "My b... brother Joe he raped me as well," she said before lapsing into unconsciousness.

"Your brother raped you as well. When was this Mary?"

"I'm sorry officer but she's in no fit state to answer any questions," said the paramedic as he pressed the oxygen mask over Mary's face.

"How is she doctor? When will we be able to question her?" asked DCI Bradley. This could be the break they had been waiting for.

"Not for some time yet. She's in a critical condition; she might not even pull through," said the doctor.

"Mary Warmsley, that rings a bell, Steve. Wasn't she Joe Warmsley's sister? I wonder if it's the same girl he raped when she was younger," said Bradley.

"Doc could you give us an idea of the woman's age?" said Bradley

"I would say that she's about early to mid thirties. But that's as close as I can get," said the doctor.

"The time frame fits, Guv. She's about the right age. Warmsley raped his sister when she was about nineteen according to form. What are you thinking? That she might be the one that's done Joe?"

"She certainly had a motive."

"How would she have moved the body though? Even if she did kill him I'm pretty certain that she would have needed help to shift him."

"Your right, but we have to look at all possibilities. We're not even certain that it is his sister yet," said Bradley.

The publicity campaign was starting to bear fruit. There had been several calls to say that they knew Mary Warmsley, and that she had had a brother that had lived in Hilldale, and moved back into Thistlefield some years later.

DCI Bradley was spooning sugar into his tea he needed the energy, this case was proving to be a real headache. "I think we should have another word with Georgina Laycock. She seems to be the last person to have positively identified Brooke Steeples," said Bradley.

Bob was pulling a pint when the thought hit him. Not long after he'd seen Brooke in the Dog and Partridge another woman is attacked. The night of the fight in the pub, Sandra mason is found dead. The police publicity campaign had turned up Georgina Laycock also with head injuries similar to the murdered girl, and now another, Mary Warmsley had been found with her head bashed in and Brooke had been in the same pub the same night. It couldn't just be coincidence. He had to find Brooke and find out what was going on.

Chapter fifty-eight

Sir Henry Mortimer was ready to call his next witness. The trial had reached the end of the week and it wasn't looking any better for Jake. All the evidence was damning and he could feel the noose tightening around his neck as each day passed.

"M'lud, the prosecution calls Thomas Sullivan," said Sir Henry looking impassively down at his notes.

Tommy raised his right hand. "Would you please read the words on the card," said the usher.

"The evidence I shall give will be the truth, the whole truth, and nothing but the truth," he said adjusting his tie as he handed back the card. He was dressed smartly in his best suit for his court appearance. His mother had pressed it freshly for the occasion. He wore a crisp white shirt no doubt neatly ironed by his mother, along with a dark maroon tie. She didn't want her boy to let himself down because of his shoddy appearance, not if she had anything to do with it.

"My Tommy's evidence could be vital to this case," she said to the woman sitting on her right.

"Silence in court," said the court usher looking sternly up into the gallery to where Mrs Sullivan was sitting.

"Mr Sullivan, were you at the jamboree club on the night of Tenth of October this year?" asked Sir Henry.

"Yeah, I was," said Tommy feeling important.

"Can you tell the court what happened, in your own words."

"Well we were drinking, me and the lads, havin' a bit of a laugh."

"Then what happened?"

"I don't know what you mean," said Tommy running his fingers round his shirt collar. "Did you approach Miss Mason and ask her to dance?"

"Well I wasn't going to but the lads were egging me on. You know it was like a dare."

"So you were encouraged..." He paused for effect. "You were egged on by your friends to go over to where Miss Mason was sitting, and ask her to dance."

"That's right."

"Then what happened?"

"The lads started cheering and shouting. I don't think they thought I would go through with it."

"How many were in your party Mr Sullivan?"

"You mean altogether or just the lads?" asked Tommy puzzled by the question.

"No just the youths in your group," said Sir Henry.

"I'm not sure exactly," said Tommy uneasily.

"Well could you say approximately?"

"About eight or nine altogether I would think, but there were a couple of lads at the bar, so I would guess there was about six or seven of us round the table."

"So you asked Miss Mason to dance, encouraged by your friends around the table. Did she seem keen or reluctant to dance with you?"

"I thought that she seemed keen, until Joe Warmsley stuck 'is oar in an' started draggin' Sandra onto the dance floor."

"Can you describe what happened next?" said Sir Henry.

Donald Trigg was on his feet in seconds. "M'lud surely it has already been well established what happened in earlier testimony. Surely we needn't go over it again." Trigg was keen not to let the jury think that his client had been the possible cause of the brawl.

"Yes, Sir Henry. I think the court is well aware of what happened on the night in question, could you get to the point, please," said his worship.

"I'm trying to establish, M'lud, if Mr Warmsley was provoked in anyway by the accused. We have heard that a group of boisterous youths were out for a good time, and in the process of their exuberance, encouraged their friend Mr Sullivan, to dare to go and ask Miss Mason to dance. I am merely trying to establish if Mr Warmsley was simply asking the young lady to dance, and in the process was caught up in a brawl that he had not instigated and was simply trying to defend himself."

"You may answer the question Mr Sullivan," said judge Tremlow.

"He wasn't trying to defend himself, he just pushed in and tried to get Sandra to dance with 'im, an' when she wouldn't, he grabbed her an' tried to drag her onto the floor. Mrs Jackson she tried to stop 'im but he just grabbed 'er round the throat, that's when Jake tried to get 'im, Mr Warmsley, I mean, off 'er."

"Are you are telling the court that Mr Warmsley simply pushed his way through a gang of seven or eight noisy unruly youths who had been drinking all night, in order to get to Miss Mason to dance with him," said Sir Henry.

"No it weren't like that. Jake tried to get 'im off Mrs Jackson, she was trying to stop Joe Warmsley from draggin' Sandra onto the dance floor. That's when Joe 'it 'im. Jake just tried to defend 'imself that's all," said Tommy.

"Could you tell the court what happened next?"

"He punched me in the face."

"Who punched you in the face?"

"Joe Warmsley, caught me a right one."

"Did you retaliate?"

"Sorry beg your pardon sir, did I what?"

"Did you hit him back?"

"I was going to but then Mr Steeples, he steps in an' tries to break it up before I could get to him."

"Did Mr Steeples warn Mr Warmsley before getting involved in the affray?"

"How do you mean sir warn him?" said Tommy perplexed.

"Did he ask him to stop?"

"He shouted somethin' like what's goin' on 'ere, but there were such a commotion goin' on, I couldn't really be sure what he said, to be honest."

"Mr Steeples didn't issue a warning, he simply waded in regardless of the consequences and along with his uncle forcibly ejected Mr Warmsley from the club.

"At which point Mr Steeples was heard to say, by several witnesses, 'If he ever comes near me again, I'll kill him.' No more questions M'lud," said Sir Henry.

Donald Trigg rose from the bench. "Mr Sullivan may I just take you back a few moments, you said that you were going to ask Miss Mason to dance. You were encouraged by your friends. Is that true?"

"Yes sir."

"You went over to her table and asked her to dance. What was her reaction?"

"I think she wanted to."

"You think she wanted to. What gave you that impression? What made you think she wanted to dance with you?"

"She was just getting up out of 'er seat when Joe Warmsley pushed in," said Tommy.

"Was Mr Warmsley one of your group of friends?"

"No we didn't know 'im from Adam."

"Mr Warmsley, whom you say you didn't know and was not one of your friends, simply pushed his way into your group and grabbed Miss Mason and tried to drag her onto the dance floor."

"That's right, that's just what happened."

"Did Miss Mason go willingly, or did she protest?" said Trigg.

"She was screaming for 'im to let 'er go but he wouldn't. That's when Mrs Jackson tried to stop 'im."

"Thank you no more questions M'lud." Donald Trigg hoped that he had painted Warmsley as the bully he had been, but that would be up to the jury to decide, at the very least it had given them food for thought.

"I think now would be a good time to adjourn," said Judge Tremlow removing his glasses and massaging the bridge of his nose. The court is adjourned, and will reconvene on the Monday the 9th of November at 10:00am. May I remind the jury to disregard anything they might see in the newspapers or hear on the radio or television?" said judge Tremlow.

Chapter fifty-nine

Lizzie was making yet another pot of tea. She didn't want it but she had to, try to keep her mind off Jake rotting away in some jail cell. Bob heaped sugar into the mug and stirred aimlessly. Jake was a good lad and he could no doubt handle himself, he'd proved that more than once in the club on many a rowdy weekend, but he was no killer, of that he was certain. Bob kept thinking back to the night in the Jamboree. Brooke had been there. He had also been at the Dog and Partridge; he was almost certain it was him. The young woman, Brenda Howard, was found dead on Brookdale golf course about the same time. Georgina Laycock had escaped with head injuries and the latest victim Mary Warmsley had been rushed to hospital with severe head injuries. All had one thing in common, Brooke Steeples. Somehow Bob had to try and find the connection.

"Lizzie I know it's painful for you lass but why didn't you go to the police when Brooke and Joe raped you?"

The shock was etched on Lizzie's face. She turned from her brother. "I don't know what you mean. Who told you that?"

"Jake told me. It's no wonder he wanted to kill that bastard Warmsley."

"When was it?"

"Nothing happened, just leave it, Bob," she cried, tears flowing in torrents down her cheeks.

"But you want to help Jake, don't you. If Jake did kill Warmsley, at least he had good reason. Don't you think it would help his case if the jury knew why he'd done it?"

"Who do you think would believe me anyway? You know what folk are like round here, they would just say I egged him on."

"Who would they say you egged on?"

"Brooke."

"Why would they say that if it's not true?"

"Because it's not really true," she sobbed wiping her eyes on her hanky.

"What do you mean it's not really true? Did Brooke rape you or not. Come on lass you've got to tell me."

"Brooke wanted to go to bed with me. I was broke and he offered me ten bob and I told him where he could shove it. Next thing he offers me another pound. I snatched at the money. I tripped and fell into his arms, he took that as a come on. I shouted at him that I wasn't interested but the next thing I know he drags me upstairs. There were nothing I could do so I just let him have his way."

"You didn't agree, so that's rape Lizzie."

"I didn't exactly push him away either."

"How could you in your condition? You've had TB, for God's sake. Anyway where does Warmsley fit into all this?"

"That were at Taylors' mill, about five years ago it was now. Do you remember I got the sack? I couldn't tell dad for ages and then when he found out he went mad. I'd just found out I'd got TB and I asked for a lighter job. Joe Warmsley promised me one if I would sleep with him. Anyway I told him to bugger off. Well one day I'm outside the waste shed having a smoke and he caught me. Well cut a long story short, he drags me into the waste shed and tries to have his way with me. I managed to fight him off but dropped a fag end into the waste. It caught fire and I got the blame, ended up with the sack," sobbed Lizzie.

"Bloody hell lass I didn't know all this," exclaimed Bob. Lizzie had come this far she decided to tell Bob everything. "That's not all."

"Why what else is there?" He asked.

"There's Lottie."

"What about Lottie?"

"Joe Warmsley raped her."

"Christ almighty! No wonder Jake wanted to kill the bastard. I'd a' done it myself if I'd got there first. When was this?"

"That were at Benson's. A few months ago. Same as me, promised her a light job if she slept with him. She refused and he raped her in the cotton shed."

"How's Lottie now? Is she alright?"

"As right as any young girl can be carrying a baby she doesn't really want."

"Can't she get rid of it?"

"It's not that easy getting rid of something that's growing inside of you, even though it's not what you wanted."

"What about young Frank? What's he said about all this?"

"At first I thought it was his, but to be fair to the lad he's willing to stick by her. A lot of lads' would have just buggered off."

"Christ it's a bloody mess, no wonder Jake wanted to do that bastard in."

"What are you going to do Bob?" Cried Lizzie.

"I can't do much about Warmsley, he's dead, but I'm going to find that ex-'usband of yours and get the truth out of 'im."

Chapter sixty

DCI Bradley's car pulled up outside the home of Georgina Laycock, accompanied by DC Linda Francis. Bradley rapped on the front door of the neat semi-detached house. From the corner of his eye, he saw a flicker of movement from behind the curtains. "Mrs Laycock, do you think we could have another word with Georgina please?" said DCI Bradley. He heard the lock click, and the safety chain slide to one side.

"She's still in bed. All this has upset her no end," said Mrs Laycock sharply.

"It won't take more than a few minutes. It's very important," said Bradley trying his best to be sympathetic.

"You'd better come in then," said Mildred Laycock slipping the safety chain and opening the front door.

Georgina had heard the door and came down the stairs. "What's up mum?" she asked wiping the sleep from her eyes.

"Georgina," said DC Francis gently. "On the night that you were attacked could you describe the man again for us?"

"I've told you all this once," she sobbed pulling the pink quilted dressing gown tightly around her shaking body.

"Is all this really necessary? You can see how upset she is."

"Mrs Laycock, there was another woman attacked and killed last week, and another was attacked a few days later. Luckily, she's still alive but she's in a critical state in intensive care. The man we are looking for, attacked all three women in the same way. He used a blunt instrument to overcome them before he assaulted them. Can you remember what happened when he attacked you?" said DC Francis.

Georgina was sobbing uncontrollably as the memories of that night came flooding back.

"I'm sorry we have to put you through all this again Georgina, but we have to stop this man before he strikes again. You are the only person who can positively identify him for us. Please take your time. Can you remember what he was wearing?" said DCI Bradley.

Georgina blew into her handkerchief and dabbed her eyes.

Mildred put a comforting arm around her distraught daughters' shoulders. "Come on love it'll be alright."

"He was well dressed. He was wearing a suit."

"What colour was it, do you remember?" asked DC Francis scribbling in her notebook.

"It was dark, black or navy blue. I don't really remember," said Georgina.

"Can you remember what colour his shirt was or his tie?"

"It's so long ago, I can hardly remember. I think it was a white shirt and a dark tie. I think the tie was maroon with a silver or grey stripe, but I couldn't swear to it."

"You're doing fine Georgina," said DC Francis. "Is there anything else that you remember that you can tell us? I know you've told us all this before but can you tell us how old he was?"

"I think he was about 35 to 40. He was a lot older than me. I feel so stupid I should never have gone with him."

"You say he was about 35 to 40 and he was well dressed. Is there anything else that you might have forgotten that you can remember now? Was there anything distinctive about him, or anything he was wearing?" coaxed DCI Bradley.

"I don't think so; that's all I can think of," she said, an involuntary shudder sending a shiver down her spine. "Oh there was one other thing I nearly forgot. When he came into the pub, he was wearing a dark Mac. It had been raining now I come to think of it, and when he put it over the back of the chair next to him, I noticed he was wearing a signet ring with a big black stone in it if that's any help."

Bradley looked at Linda Francis; the man seen running away from the gang of lads the night of Sandra Mason's murder was wearing a dark overcoat or Mac. "Just one last question Georgina, and then we'll be on our way. What did you say the name of the man was who attacked you?"

"He said his name was Dave... David Gregory."

"Well that will be all for now," said Bradley. "We'll be in touch if there are any further developments. Thanks, you've been very helpful." As they left the house, Bradley turned to Linda. "Get on to uniform and put a patrol on the street, discreetly mind. I don't want to scare Miss Laycock or her mother. She's the only one who can identify David Gregory."

Chapter sixty-one

The trial was about to enter its second week. Things weren't looking to good for Jake; the evidence against him seemed to be overwhelming. Donald Trigg had made a valiant attempt to sway the jury in Jake's favour with his account of Joe Warmsley's bullying ways. Nevertheless it was up to the jury what they believed. Donald Trigg may have painted Joe Warmsley as a bullying oppressive womanizer, but all the evidence pointed to Jake having the motive and the opportunity to kill him. Unless something turned up soon, he feared for his client.

DCI Bradley waited impatiently outside of the intensive care unit at St Mary's hospital. "Where are these bloody doctors when you need them?" he grumbled sharply to DS Jackson.

"The sister said he was on his rounds, sir. I'm sure he'll be here soon," replied Jackson.

"What did the sister say about Mary Warmsley? Is she likely to come round anytime soon?"

"I don't know sir. Oh, here's the doctor now, maybe he can tell us."

"DCI Bradley of the Thistlefield police. I wonder if you could tell us if Mrs Warmsley is likely to come round soon?"

"It's Miss Warmsley. According to a neighbour who came in with her, Miss Warmsley never married. I'm afraid I can't offer you much hope of her coming round in the near future, she suffered severe trauma to the head. She's lucky to be alive," said the doctor routinely glancing at his notes.

"But she will pull through though, won't she doctor?" said Bradley.

"It's hard to say with an injury like that."

"Can you give us any idea when she might come round? It's vitally important that we question her," said Bradley.

"Afraid not, Chief Inspector. She has severe bruising on the brain, and until the swelling goes down, I really can't say. She's in a coma, and she could be unconscious for weeks with an injury like that, month's maybe. Sorry I can't be more positive than that."

"Was there any sexual activity?" asked Bradley already guessing the answer.

"We found bruising on her inner thighs and traces of what looked like semen. I would say there had been sexual activity," said the doctor.

"So you think she had been raped?" said Bradley.

"I would say so. It looks very much like rape to me," replied the doctor.

"Thanks," said Bradley.

"What now boss?" said Jackson.

"I want a twenty four hour watch on Miss Warmsley. Have we still got patrols watching Georgina Laycock?"

"Yeah, they're watching her night and day," said DS Jackson.

"Good. I don't think we've heard the last from Mr Gregory."

The radio crackled with the news that the police were hunting for a David Gregory in connection with the assaults on two women in the Thistlefield area on the eighth and ninth of November. He was described as between 35 and 40 years old, and well dressed. He was about six feet tall with a tanned complexion. He was last seen in the Hilldale area north of Thistlefield possibly driving an Austin Cambridge. Anyone with any information should contact the incident room on Thistlefield 739153 or any police officer. It warned that all young women should not go out at night alone, and if possible only go out with a friend or in a group until this man is apprehended. The bulletin stressed that this man was extremely dangerous and must not be approached under any circumstances.

Brooke slumped deeper into the corner of the vault of the Hare and Hounds pub in Langford; an involuntary smile creased his lips.

"Extremely dangerous," said the newsreader. The pub was quiet with only the odd drinker propping up the bar, it suited him, and he needed time to think.

"Steve did Georgina Laycock mention if David Gregory had a car?" said DCI Bradley. "Come to think of it I don't remember her saying so."

"Let's get back round there, it could be important," said Bradley.

Chapter sixty-two

Bob listened to the Saturday evening newscast on the radio. They had just described Brooke to a tee. Brooke was 42 years old, tall, well dressed with a tan. It couldn't just be a coincidence. Bob was certain that Brooke was behind the murders of Brenda Howard and possibly Sandra Mason. He was also pretty sure that he had something to do with the assaults on Mary Warmsley and Georgina Laycock. He had to find him, if he didn't young Jake would hang for a murder he was certain he hadn't done. Time was running out.

Brooke parked his car a couple of streets away from St Mary's. There was a steady drizzle of rain falling. It suited him, he was less likely to be spotted with his coat collar pulled up tight around his neck. He unfurled his umbrella and made his way to the hospital. He cautiously approached the entrance, and looked around but he didn't see anything untoward. He entered the main entrance, and shook the rain off his umbrella. He glanced round to see if he was being observed, before calmly walking down the corridor. The passageway was busy with people visiting their loved ones, too busy to notice him. He was just another visitor going to see a sick relative. He had no idea where he was going, or what he was going to do when he got there, he just knew he had to do something. He was almost at the end of the corridor when he spotted that it opened out into a wider thoroughfare. Situated to the left was a café. There were a number of people waiting to be served; he cautiously approached hunching his shoulders deeper into his coat. As he got closer to the counter, he overheard two women talking.

"I think it's a disgrace; my mum in the same ward as that poor woman that was attacked," said the woman indignantly. "You'd think they'd have a special ward for cases like that wouldn't you. It's off-putting when you see the police outside the door," she went on, stirring more sugar into her tea.

"What ward is that then dear?" asked her friend completely unfazed.

"St Hilda's. Disgrace that's what it is," she said heatedly. Brooke looked up at the sign pointing to the various wards. St Hilda's straight on. He made his way along the corridor, halfway down another sign said St Hilda's pointing to the right. As he turned right into the ward, he could see a police officer sat outside the side ward door. He quickly stepped back. At least now, he knew where she was. He waited a few minutes before looking down the corridor again. He saw the officer look at his watch. Guard duty was so boring!

The next moment he was startled. "Can I help you?" asked the young orderly, pushing a trolley overflowing with cleaning materials.

"Oh yes. I know I shouldn't but I'm dying for a fag and I wondered if there was anywhere I could go. It's pouring down outside."

"No you shouldn't, its' bad for you," she laughed. "Visiting a relative are you? Does get a bit much trying to find something to talk about especially when they're not well," she said. "When we want a quick drag we go into the storeroom. Come on I'll show you. It's down here round the corner just before you get to St Hilda's ward," she said pushing the trolley ahead of her. "If you just go out that door there," she said, pointing to the door just before St

Hilda's, out of sight of the police guard. "If you just nip out there you can get in the back way, nobody will see you."

"Thanks," he said to the girl.

"Don't tell anyone I told you or you'll get me the sack," she laughed.

"Don't worry I won't," he said. After what seemed an age Brooke looked at his watch. It read 8:30 he must have been in the storeroom for about half an hour. He poked his head around the door it was all clear, most of the visitors had gone home. He slowly poked his head out from the storeroom door and looked towards the ICU. The intensive care unit was in a side ward, a little way off the main ward and was only manned by one or two nurses at the most, unless there was a change in the patient's condition. The only other person present was the constable who was guarding her. He peered round the corner. He could still see the officer sitting outside the ICU. He couldn't see anyone else. He would have to act quickly before somebody noticed him. Suddenly a nurse approached the ICU. The police officer got to his feet and indicated that he needed to go to the toilet. The nurse pointed him down the corridor to where the toilets where situated. The officer made his way towards the toilets probably thankful for a few minutes respite from a boring duty! Brooke guessed the officer would take the opportunity to skive for a few minutes before returning to his guard duties, he didn't have long. He crept along the ward until he was outside the ICU. He looked around and slipped unseen into the room. The nurse had her back to him and didn't hear him come up behind her. He slid the heavy metal bar from his coat pocket and in one swift movement hit the unsuspecting nurse on the back of the head. Brooke put his arm under her shoulder as she immediately slumped unconscious to the floor. He went to the door. Good! He hadn't been seen. Mary didn't move as he quickly pushed the pillow over the unconscious woman's head. She gave an involuntary groan as Brooke pressed the pillow down harder, he was sweating profusely he didn't have much time. Moments later, he lifted the pillow from her face. He leaned over to see if she was breathing and felt for her pulse. There were no signs of life; he had to get out of there fast.

"My word you're in a hurry," said the young ward orderly as he brushed passed her. "Did somebody catch you in the storeroom then?" Brooke didn't answer as he rushed past her; he had to get out of there as fast as he could.

Chapter sixty-three

St Mary's was swarming with police. Roadblocks had been set up all around the area.

"Who was supposed to be on duty?" raged DCI Bradley.

"PC Dobson sir," said DS Jackson.

"Get him in here now!" shouted Bradley. Jackson ushered the distraught constable into the matron's office.

"Well what happened?" snapped Bradley.

"I just needed to answer a call of nature sir. I was only gone two or three minutes, and there was a nurse in the room with Miss Warmsley when I went," he said miserably.

"And in those two or three minutes Constable, we have one nurse with severe head injuries and Miss Warmsley is dead. Did you see or hear anything?"

"Nothing sir. Everything was quiet; there had been nobody about all night except for the nurses."

"And you didn't see anything unusual or anything suspicious?"

"Not that I can remember sir, only a young orderly talking to a chap but he disappeared. He had his head turned away from me so I didn't get a good look at him."

"What time was this?"

"I don't know for certain sir."

"Well, try, man, it could be vital!" snarled Bradley at the distressed officer.

"I think it was about 8:30 sir. Yes it was 8:30 because I remember looking at my watch and thinking it wouldn't be long before my shift ended."

"Did you get a look at this man as he went past you?"

"I'm sorry sir he didn't come this far down. The orderly, she was pointing down the corridor. I thought he was asking for directions. I didn't really see him after that, he just disappeared."

"Jackson, see if you can round up the girl who was on duty about 8:30 tonight, we'll see if she can shed a bit more light on it. You can go, Constable, but I'll want to speak to you again."

"Yes sir," said PC Dobson sheepishly.

"This is Doreen Metcalf sir; she was on duty earlier tonight," said Jackson

"Come in Miss Metcalf have a seat," said DCI Bradley indicating the stark wooden chair in matrons' office.

"You can call me Doreen," said the distraught girl dabbing her eyes with a crumpled hanky.

"Doreen what can you tell me about earlier this evening?"

"I'd just finished cleaning the corridor and I was on my way to clean the toilets on St Hilda's ward, when this chap asked me if there was anywhere he could have a smoke. I told him when we wanted a smoke we used the storeroom when it was raining. We're not supposed to. You won't tell anyone, will you sir? I could get the sack."

"Of course not," said Bradley smiling. Then what happened?"

"I showed him where it was, and we walked down the corridor towards the storeroom. We was chatting all the way down, you know about smoking being bad for you and that. I told him he could nip out the back way, just before you got to St Hilda's, nobody would see him. Then I left him."

"Can you describe him for me?" said Bradley.

"He was fairly tall, good looking, a bit of a tan."

"How old would you say he was Doreen?"

"I'm not too good with ages, but I'd say he was getting on a bit."

"Could you be a little more precise?"

"I would guess at about 40 or thereabouts."

God, thought Bradley, if she thought 40 was getting on a bit, what must she think of him in his 50's? "Doreen, can you remember what he was wearing?"

"He was smart; he was wearing a suit and tie."

"Anything else?"

"He had a dark overcoat or a Mac." Bradley looked at Jackson. It certainly looked as if it was the same man.

"Well thank you Doreen you've been very helpful. We might need to speak to you again so if you could just leave your address with the constable," said DCI Bradley indicating that the interview was over.

"Will they be alright?"

"The nurse will recover, but I'm afraid Miss Warmsley is dead"

Brooke had seen the police block but he had managed to get away before they had cordoned off the roads near him. He had to lie low for a while and think of a plan to get as far away as possible. He drove to a pub about fifteen miles away. He ordered a pint from the bar and tried to think what to do next. The police would be all over the place by now. His description would be all over the papers by morning.

Chapter sixty-four

Monday morning. Jakes trial had entered its third week. Bob had decided not to go to court with Lizzie. If he was to save Jake from the hangman's noose, he had to find Brooke. He was more convinced than ever that Brooke was the killer. The police had issued the name of the man they wanted to interview along with a description. Bob was convinced that David Gregory was Brooke Steeples. Lizzie was beside herself with worry. "Bob what if they find Jake guilty," she cried.

"They won't. Everythin's gonna be alright, you'll see," said Bob, not really convinced. "Lizzie where do you think Brooke might go to?"

"I don't know. I don't think he'll go back to his own place; the police they'll be watching won't they?"

"You could be right, but he's gonna need money an' a change o' clothes."

"He might go to his dads', he still has a room there," said Lizzie.

"It's worth a try I'll drive over there. See if 'is dads' seen 'im."

Bob pulled up outside the imposing detached house on the outskirts of Thistlefield. It was a far cry from the back-to-back terraces he was used to. He rapped the ornate knocker on the front door.

"Bob, what are you doing here? Come in lad come in," said a surprised William Steeples. "What brings you here?" Bob related the recent events of the last few days to William.

"I thought the police were looking for someone called David Gregory," said William, flabbergasted.

"I think that David Gregory an' Brooke are the same man."

"No it can't be true not Brooke. We've given him everything why would he want to kill anybody?"

"What's going on? Why is he here?" said Anne Steeples, looking at Bob in disgust as if he was something the dog had done and brought in on the bottom of his shoe.

"It's nothing Anne, go back inside while I have a word with Bob."

"Get him out of my house now. I always said that family was no good. I told Brooke at the time not to marry that... that tart," she shouted.

"Be quiet Anne. Go and make us a pot of tea will you love," he said, gently ushering her from the hallway. "What makes you so sure that its' Brooke?" whispered William as his wife went into the kitchen.

"You've heard about the lass who was killed recently, Brenda Howard," said Bob. "She was in the Dog and Partridge pub, an' I'm almost certain Brooke was in there as well."

"What makes you so sure that it had anything to do with Brooke?" said William. "The police description fits Brooke to a tee," said Bob.

"But there must be dozens of men that fit the same description; it doesn't mean it's our Brooke."

"A few days ago a woman was attacked in her home, again by a man matching Brooke's description. The same woman ended up in hospital where she was murdered. Witnesses gave the same description, they all fit Brooke," said Bob.

"It still doesn't mean he had anything to do with it."

"No I admit it's not much to go on," said Bob. "Do you remember a few months back, early June? A young lass was murdered on her way 'ome from the jamboree club."

"I remember, but they never caught her killer."

"That's right. The same night Brooke was in the club, another coincidence," said Bob.

"I thought that they had got Jake for that," said William.

"They got your grandson for the murder of Joe Warmsley not the girl. I 'ave to admit it looks' bad for the lad, but I'm convinced he 'ad nowt t' do wi it."

"But from what we've read in the papers and heard on the news, everything points to him being guilty," said William. Jake's grandparents had distanced themselves from the trial from the start. Anne especially didn't want anything to do with it.

"I know everythin' points to 'im bein' guilty of killin' Joe Warmsley. I admit Jake might be a bit 'ot 'eaded, but I'm still not convinced that he's a killer," said Bob.

"I can't believe our Brooke could be mixed up in anything like this, not again," said William shaking his head. Anne was sobbing uncontrollably. She had overheard the conversation from the kitchen.

"William make him to leave now," she said, through tear stained eyes.

Bobs' ears pricked up. "What do you mean not agen?"

"I think it might be better if you left," William said ushering Bob towards the front door.

"I'm not goin' anywhere until you tell me what's goin' on. What do yer mean not agen?" snapped Bob sharply.

"It's nothing, now would you please go and leave us alone," wailed William dejectedly.

"I'm goin' nowhere, 'til you tell me what you meant." William could see that Bob was determined to find out what was going on. He took Bob through to the drawing room followed by Anne.

"Will you leave us alone a few minutes love?" he said to his distraught wife. She left the room dabbing her eyes.

"Our Brooke got himself into a bit of trouble when he was a lad," said William.

"What sort o' trouble?" asked Bob.

"He was at grammar school. He was only a lad about fourteen or fifteen. There was this young girl; she was a few years older than Brooke. Well, they said that Brooke molested her. She came from a good home. Her parents' owned a high-class jeweller's shop in town and so both families got together, and it was all hushed up. They didn't want their daughter's name dragged through the mud anymore than we wanted Brooke's."

"Yer mean 'e raped 'er?"

"According to Brooke she encouraged him, egged him on."

"Oh I bet she did," exclaimed Bob.

"Anyway she lost the baby."

"Bloody hell, he got 'er pregnant?"

"William shrugged his shoulders. "The girl lost it, best thing all round in the circumstances, although I was sorry for the lass."

"An' what 'appened after that?"

"Brooke finished school worked in the family business for a year or two, and eventually joined the navy. Best thing he ever did."

"So he's got an 'istory of violence?"

"Violence was never proved. He got the lass pregnant and we managed to keep it quiet. You didn't go airing your dirty washing in public, not in those days."

"I'll bet the police don't know all this," said Bob.

"There was no need to involve the police in it. It could still be anyone. There's no proof that it's Brooke," said William not really believing it himself.

"Georgina Laycock; the girl that was attacked, she gave a description to the police of a man who attacked her. The description fits Brooke to a tee," said Bob.

Chapter sixty-five

Twenty-four hours had passed since the death of Mary Warmsley. It had prompted the police to put a twenty-four hour guard on Georgina Laycock. She was the only person who could positively identify her attacker; they weren't going to be caught out a second time. The press had had a field day with the inadequacies of the police to protect the public from a mass murderer!

Brooke watched from the old Ford. He had decided to swap it. The Austin Cambridge was too conspicuous. The police had issued a description of the man they wanted to interview and the car. There was a police car parked right outside Georgina Laycock's house; there was no chance that Brooke could get to her now. This was the second day he had driven past her house; he would have to think of something; she was the only person who could positively point the finger at him.

Inside DCI Bradley was going over the plan he hoped would smoke the killer out, but he needed Georgina's co-operation. "Georgina I'll understand if you don't want to go through with it," said DCI Bradley. "I know it's a risk, but I think it might be our best chance of catching this man."

"I don't know," said Georgina nervously.

"I promise there will be someone with you all the time. You won't be out of our sight for more than few seconds," insisted Bradley.

"What exactly is it you want me to do again?" she said fearfully.

"We would like you to return to work at the Royal Oak as normal. There will be a plain clothes officer behind the bar with you all the time, as well as plain clothes officers in the bar as well."

"How can you be sure that the maniac won't get our Georgina again?" said Mildred Laycock.

"At the first sign of trouble we'll be in there. All we want is for you, Georgina, to go to work as normal and point out to DC Francis if you see this man come into the pub. Leave the rest up to us."

"Yes, if you see him come in the bar just give me the nod," said DC Linda Francis.

"I doubt he'll ever come near here again. Won't he know that you'll be watching the place?" said Georgina.

"That's a chance we'll have to take," said DS Jackson. What we are hoping is that he's desperate enough to try and get to you again. He knows that you are the only one who can identify him."

The thought of it sent a shiver down Georgina's spine. What if they couldn't get to me in time? She thought.

"We'll understand if you feel you can't go through with it, Georgina, no-one will think any less of you," said DC Francis.

"If you want to say 'no' that's quite alright, but we do think it might be our best chance to smoke him out, before he has time to kill again," said DCI Bradley. The words to 'kill again' sent another involuntary shiver down Georgina's spine.

"Ok I'll do it," she said.

"Good girl," said DC Francis.

Chapter sixty-six

The sun shone brightly which was unusual for November. The last thing Lizzie was feeling, was bright. Today, Tuesday the 10th was the day that the jury brought in the verdict against Jake. All the evidence pointed to him killing Joe Warmsley.

Sir Henry Mortimer rose from the bench and turned towards the jury. He polished his glasses with a handkerchief and returned them to the bridge of his nose. His ruddy face glowed with a pinkish hue as if he had enjoyed a glass or two of claret over the weekend. He shuffled some papers into a neat pile as he addressed the court. "Ladies and gentlemen of the jury, in my final summation in the case against the accused, I will try to reveal the true nature of the defendant Jake Michael Steeples, who stands before you accused of the most wicked crime; that of the wilful murder of Joseph Arthur Warmsley. I will try to point out, that here was a young man so infuriated by the knowledge of the rape of his mother and sister, that he took it upon himself to exact revenge in his own way. Whilst the court has every sympathy with the alleged offences against his mother and sister, we cannot allow individuals to take the law into their own hands. Otherwise we would have anarchy." Sir Henry paused to let the impact of his statement sink in to the jury. "We have heard over the length of this trial the overwhelming evidence against Jake Michael Steeples. We have heard how on the night of the 6th June of this year a fight broke out in the Jamboree Club. Some say that it was instigated by Mr Warmsley. Indeed Mr Warmsley did try to dance with Miss Mason, and I concede that he was perhaps a little rough. What we must remember ladies and gentlemen is that Mr Warmsley was not an educated man. He was not a man accomplished in the art of seduction. His approach was at worst should we say a little overzealous. At no time did he strike Miss Mason during the fracas. I repeat again. At no time was he seen to strike Miss Mason."

The jury listened intently as Sir Henry painted a figure of an ill-educated lout who was lacking in the social graces, but was not a killer. Sir Henry went on. "When the fracas broke out in the Jamboree Club it was because there were several people involved, and not Joe Warmsley alone. Several of the crowd there were urging both Mr Warmsley and Tommy Sullivan to dance with the girl. In fact, it became a dare for most of the revellers, to see which of the pair would end up with Miss Mason. If it had been him alone, I don't think we would be in this courtroom now. We have heard from Mrs Jackson that Sandra Mason wanted to dance, and that she was a little tipsy. It was after all her eighteenth birthday and she had already consumed two or three drinks; two or three drinks that she wasn't used to drinking." Again Sir Henry paused. He wanted the jury to think that Sandra Mason might in some way have been partly responsible for Joe Warmsley's advances towards her.

He went on. "Mr Warmsley who had also been drinking heard Miss Mason say she wanted to dance. He decided he would try his luck with Miss Mason. When she resisted, he foolishly grabbed her arm and tried to pull her onto the dance floor. In the resulting confusion, the table was knocked over and a fight broke out. Mr Steeples came over to see what the fracas was about, and soon became involved in the fight. When Joe Warmsley appeared to be getting the upper hand, Mr Steeples' uncle became involved, and between the two of them ejected him from the premises. Two days later the body of Joseph Warmsley was found in Charnley's Mill with head wounds, and the blood of Jake Steeples on his shirt. We have also heard that the same night that the fight took place Jake Steeples found out that Mr Warmsley had raped his mother, Elizabeth Steeples. We also later heard that Jake Steeples found out that Joseph Warmsley raped his sister, but we have no evidence to prove that was the case.

"If I can just take you back to the night of the fight in the Jamboree Club; Jake Steeples was heard by several witnesses to say and I quote. 'If you come near me again you bastard I'll kill you.' Meaning he would kill Joseph Warmsley. I put it to the jury that he took it upon himself to exact revenge for the alleged assaults on his mother and sister; assaults that were never brought to the attention of the police. I suggest to you that Jake Steeples exacted his own revenge in the only way he knew, and brutally killed Joseph Warmsley.

"I put it to you ladies and gentlemen of the jury that the only possible verdict is guilty." Sir Henry Mortimer sat down, satisfied he had just condemned Jake to the gallows.

Chapter sixty-seven

Bob pulled away from William's house, convinced more than ever that Brooke was responsible for the deaths of Mary Warmsley, Brenda Howard and Sandra Mason. He was also convinced that he had attacked Gerorgina Laycock, but fortunately she was still alive, but for how long? Bob knew that if she was the only witness that could identify Brooke, her life was in danger.

Brooke watched as Bob's car drove away from his parent's house. He needed to get in, get a change of clothes and some money. His eyes scanned up and down the tree-lined road. The pale morning sun cast wispy shadows from the trees, which were bare, except for a few evergreen pines dotted here and there. That meant there wouldn't be much cover; he would have to be quick. There was no sign of the police just yet, but he knew it would only be a matter of time before they were watching the house. He pulled the Ford round by the back entrance of the house, and using his key, crept in through the back door. He could hear his parents talking in the drawing room, the sound echoing along the corridor. He could hear their animated arguing, and his mother crying. 'What had they done wrong?' 'Why had he turned out like this?' 'What was going to happen to him?' At that moment Brooke had no concern for their feelings, all he needed was to get some things and some money, and get as far away from there as possible. He crept up the stairs trying his best to stay silent. He reached the top of the stairs and turned to go to his room. It was situated at the far end of the landing. As he turned he tripped over his mother's walking stick. He went flying knocking over a vase perched on a pedestal table. The noise echoed down the landing. In the drawing room, William had heard the crash.

"What was that?" cried Anne.

"Stay here; I'll go and have a look," said William picking up his own walking stick and brandishing it like a club. "Who's there?" he shouted. Brooke tried to blend into a recess in the wall, but his father had already seen him. "Brooke! What the bloody hell are you playing at, creeping about like a bloody burglar for God's sake?"

"Dad, I didn't want to disturb you and mother. I just need to get a few things and some money."

"Why, where are you going?"

"I'm meeting this bloke from down south. He's promised me a big order for the firm, so I need a change of clothes and some cash for a few days that's all."

"And which company's this then?"

"They're based in London, Dad. If I can land this order it'll keep us going for years."

"What's the name of the company, Brooke? I'm sure if it's an order so big I would know about it."

"Dad, I just need some money and some clothes that's all."

"There is no company in London is there. You're in trouble son. What have you done? You're the one the police are after for the murders of those young women. Bob was right." William's eyes were filling with tears.

"Dad it's not true I had nothing to do with it," he wailed.

"If you've nothing to do with it, stay here and tell the police, me and your mother will help you."

"Dad I've got to go. I've not much time." He pushed passed William into his room and started throwing clothes into a suitcase. "I need some money dad, give me the key to the safe."

"Give yourself up Brooke. You won't get away with it. You're only making things worse for yourself," said William blocking his path down the stairs.

Brooke swung the case at his father and knocked him flying, almost catapulting him down the stairway.

The commotion brought his mother up the stairs. "Brooke darling what's going on? Whatever's the matter?" she said a look of shock on her face as she saw William struggle to his feet.

"I need some money, Mother; I have to get away for a few days; that's all."

"Go where? Why are you going away?"

"Call the police Anne," said William as he stumbled towards his son. Brooke grabbed his father savagely and pulled the heavy cosh from his coat pocket.

"I wouldn't do that if I were you, Mother," he snarled savagely. "Just go to the safe and get me whatever is in there."

"Don't do it Anne, he won't hurt me, call the police," he said as he struggled with his son. Brooke viciously brought the heavy cosh down on his father's shoulder sending waves of excruciating pain down his arm. William collapsed in a heap at his son's feet unable to get up.

"I mean it, Mother. If you don't get me the cash straight away, I'll kill him," he said thrusting the heavy bar in his fathers' face.

"Please don't hurt him I'll get you the money." Anne went to the safe in the office and bundled a wad of notes into an envelope, and handed them to her son. He snatched the money from her and stuffed it into his coat pocket.

"Just so you don't get any funny ideas about calling the police." He ripped the phone line out of the wall. "You're coming with me." He dragged his father who was barely conscious out towards the little Ford aided by his mother. He bungled them both in the back seat. His father was still numb from the blow to his shoulder and was groaning from the pain. The light was beginning to fade as the clouds covered the fading morning sun. He pulled the car into the disused Charnley's factory yard. He forced them out of the car and across the yard. There was a small gate just in front of them. He pushed them roughly through it, and into a small dark room at the back of the building. William could barely stand; Anne had to prop him up in order for him to make it into the tiny dimly lit space.

"Get in and keep quiet. It's no use trying to shout for help, nobody will hear you in here. This place has been empty for years," said Brooke savagely.

Anne was crying, she was heartbroken. She tried to ease the pain in William's shoulder, but he winced every time she went near it. She feared it was broken. "Where are you going Brooke? What are you going to do?" she cried.

"Don't worry about me I'll be ok."

"But, what about your father? He needs a doctor; I think his shoulder might be broken."

"When I get myself sorted out, I'll let somebody know where you are," he said leaving his distraught parents shaking in the tiny room. On his way out, he found an old brush handle. He pushed it through the door latch locking the door from the outside. That would hold them long enough for him to get miles away from there.

Chapter sixty-eight

"All rise," said the court official, as the court reconvened after a short break for lunch.

Donald Trigg rose from the bench and looked down at his notes. The crown had presented a redoubtable case against his client. He would have to be at his most persuasive if he were to put a doubt into the minds of the jury.

He began. "My learned friend has presented what appears to be a watertight case against my client.

"If I could take you back to the night of the party for Sandra Mason; Mrs Betty Jackson told you she had known Joseph Warmsley for a number of years, and that he was a vicious bully. She also told you that if Mr Warmsley didn't get his own way i.e. sexual favours from the women, then he put them on heavier dirtier jobs; one such case being the mother of Jake Steeples. Mrs Steeples had not long been recovering from TB, when she was put into the cardroom. The cardroom is one of the dirtiest and dustiest jobs in any cotton factory, and a particularly heavy job for a fit person, let alone a woman of Mrs Steeple's condition who had been suffering from TB.

"We have also heard that on the night in question, it was Joe Warmsley who started the fight. He started it because Miss Mason wouldn't dance with him. That was how the blood came to be on Jake Steeples shirt. When Joseph Warmsley started the fight, Jake Steeples only intention was to see what the ruckus was about. Having gone over to see what was happening, he sustained a heavy blow to the face. Jake Steeples did what anyone else would do in that same situation, and that was to defend himself."

Donald Trigg stopped momentarily and observed members of the jury nodding in agreement to his statement. He continued. "Further evidence has shown that the deceased was found with severe head injuries; injuries consistent with a blow, or blows from a heavy blunt instrument. No such instrument was ever found on the accused. In fact, to this day the weapon has still not been recovered. The only evidence against the accused is that his blood was on Mr Warmsley's shirt; blood which was spilled when he was attacked by the deceased."

Donald Trigg was in full flow, and he was confident of winning the jury over as he continued. "He has admitted that a fight took place in which he and the accused came to blows. Blows, which I must emphasise to the jury, were in the defendant's case, in self-defence. Jake Steeples was defending himself from a known bully."

Donald Trigg was warming to the task of placing doubt into the minds of the jury; "but the evidence against him was pretty damning, and he certainly had a motive. At this point, I would like to take the jury back for a few moments if I may to assess the character of Joseph Warmsley during childhood. At the age of eleven, he was sent to a young offender's institution, for setting fire to his neighbours washing, and forcing excrement through their letterboxes." Again members of the jury looked shocked at Trigg's revelation. "Six months later, he was caught stealing money from the poor box of the local catholic church. It was only on the intervention of the local priest that he was not sent to borstal for another term of confinement. Several years later, he was found guilty of the attempted rape and indecent assault on a young woman, after he had spent the night drinking."

Trigg could feel the tide turning in his favour, as he continued to paint a repulsive picture of Joe Warmsley's character. He went on. "He was sentenced to two years in Medway jail for those offences. Joseph Warmsley was a know bully with a history of violence. He was also guilty of the rape of his own sister although he was never prosecuted for it."

Some members of the jury were visibly shocked by Trigg's latest revelation. "I put it to the members of the jury, that Joseph Warmsley was a violent man, with a history of vicious assaults, especially on women. In the light of the evidence against the accused where it can only be said with any degree of certainty, that he defended himself against the assault of a vicious known criminal, I therefore urge the jury to find the accused not guilty."

Donald Trigg took his seat hoping he had done enough to spare Jake the rope.

Chapter sixty-nine

Georgina stood behind the bar of the Royal Oak pub looking pensively around every time a strange man entered the bar. She brushed her hair to one side out of her eyes, and straightened her black pencil skirt nervously. Alongside her, looking stunningly attractive, was DC Linda Francis. Linda was dressed in a tight fitting clingy top that accentuated her pert breasts, and a pair of tight slacks that showed off her long shapely legs. Her long blond hair was tied up in a ponytail highlighting her deep blue eyes.

"Are you ok?" asked Linda.

"Yeah, I'm fine, just a bit nervous, that's all," said Georgina forcing a smile.

"Don't worry. See those two lads over there," said Linda pointing to the two burly young men in the corner of the pub. "They're policemen. If there's the slightest hint of trouble, we'll have you out of here in a flash. We've got an unmarked car parked round the back, so don't worry." Georgina relaxed, a little more confident that she wouldn't be in any danger.

Brooke parked the car in a side street just off an industrial estate. He had managed to change his clothes, and dumped his old ones' in a waste bin. He was feeling hungry, it was past six, and he hadn't eaten since lunchtime. He could risk going into a pub. The police were looking for David Gregory not him, but they had David Gregory's description, it was too dangerous. He drove round for a while, his stomach growling with hunger. He found himself nearing the Royal Oak. He pulled up a short distance away in a side street and waited. He wondered if the police would be watching the place. After about twenty minutes, he decided it all seemed quiet. He couldn't see any patrol cars. Brooke pulled the Mac close around his shoulders and pulled the collar up hiding most of his face. The pub had a large car park, which was fenced in on three sides. There were also several vehicles parked there. It would provide some cover as he stealthily crept towards the pub.

In the bar, Georgina was busy serving a group of businessmen. She took them their drinks and asked them if they wanted anything else. They asked her if they served food. She told them that they did and would bring over a menu. The men gave Georgina their orders and she told them that it would be about fifteen minutes before they were ready.

Brooke crept nearer the pubs' back entrance it was near the kitchen. He could hear voices from inside. He sneaked unseen past the kitchen area, and stopped outside the gents' toilet. He could hear a woman's voice coming out of the pub. He was sure he'd heard it before, a young woman's voice.

"I'll just go and see if your food is ready," said Georgina to the group of men.

Brooke nipped quickly into the gents and hid behind the door. He opened the door a crack; he had a clear view all the way down the corridor. Georgina left the bar and made her way to the kitchen. Brooke opened the toilet door another crack. He couldn't believe his luck. He hadn't expected to see her again, especially back at work so soon. He took a large handkerchief out of his coat pocket and rolled it into a ball. As Georgina passed the gents' on her way to the kitchen, Brooke was out like a flash. Before she knew what was happening, he had clamped his hand with the handkerchief over her mouth making it impossible for her to scream out. She struggled but he was too strong for her. She kicked and scratched his face, but he managed to bundle her out of the back door and across the car park unseen. He dragged her to the car parked in the next street and bundled her into the back. She spat out the handkerchief and was just about to scream out when he punched her in the face knocking her out. He forced the key into the ignition and tried to start the engine. The car wouldn't start; he turned off the engine for a few seconds and pulled out the choke a little. He tried again this time with a splutter the engine burst into life. With a screech of rubber, he scorched away from the pub.

Back in the pub, the group of men were becoming impatient waiting for their food. "Any chance we might eat tonight?" said one of the men patting his stomach.

"I'll just go and see what the holdup is," said Linda making her way through to the kitchen area.

"Lenny are the orders ready?" said Linda to the chef. "Where's Georgina?"

"No idea. She came in about fifteen minutes ago but I've not seen her since; maybe she's in the ladies."

Linda concerned for Georgina's safety did a quick search of the toilets, she wasn't there. She quickly raised the alarm to her two colleagues in the bar, but there was no sign of her on the premises. Linda radioed through to police headquarters. She explained that Georgina had gone missing maybe in the last ten minutes, and to put an immediate blockade on all the roads leading from the pub. If David Gregory had got her, she was in grave danger.

Chapter seventy

Bob turned into the busy road where he'd been at least twice in the last hour or so. As he did, he noticed that further along, two police cars blocked the road. He slowed down as a police constable flagged him down and indicated that he should pull over. Bob brought the car to a stop by the kerb and wound the window down. "What's up officer?" he asked the constable.

"Would you mind getting out of the vehicle please sir?" said the young copper. Bob got out of the car. The PC shone his torch into the back of the car letting the bright beam of the torch light up the back seat.

"Nothing here," he said to his colleague. "Would you open the boot please, sir?" he said to Bob, pointing to the cars' boot.

"What's up?" asked Bob, again inserting the key into the car's boot.

"Just open the boot if you don't mind," said the other PC sternly.

"I've a right to know why you're searching my car. I haven't done owt."

The police constable rummaged among a pile of junk in Bobs' car. A wheel jack, some jump leads and an old battery was all he could find. He looked Bob up and down, and shook his head. "Can I see your driving licence and insurance papers?" Bob took the relevant documents out of his wallet and handed them to the officer. The officer scanned the documents. "They seem to be in order, sir. I don't think he's the one we're looking for," said the older of the two PC's handing Bob his documents back.

"Who are you looking for? What's going on?" said Bob.

"You can go now sir. Thank you for your co-operation," said the younger PC. Bob drove away convinced that it had something to do with Brooke. He drove around for about ten minutes, but everywhere he went there were roadblocks. Down the road he was driving along, he spotted a pub. He pulled into the car park. There was a police car parked across the entrance. He went into the bar.

"What can I get you squire?" said the ruddy faced barman.

"A pint. What's all the excitement about?" He said to the barman.

"A young woman's been kidnapped from a pub a mile or so from here. Somebody said they think it's the same chap that's been doing all them murders," said the barman with relish.

"When were this?" asked Bob.

"Earlier this evening, not too long ago by all accounts, that's why all the roads are blocked off," he volunteered.

"Did they say who's been kidnapped?" asked Bob.

"No, radio said it were just a girl that worked in the Royal Oak," said the barman.

"Who did they say they were lookin' for?" asked Bob who was sure he knew the answer.

"No idea mate. They just said they were looking for a tallish man about forty. Said his name was David Gregory."

"Bloody hell!" exclaimed Bob rushing out of the pub.

"What about your drink?" said the startled barman.

"No time," said Bob. "And ring the police, tell them that the man they're looking for is not David Gregory, but a man called Brooke Steeples."

Chapter seventy-one

Brooke drove around, aware that the police would be watching all the roads. He had to get away before they had time to catch him. Georgina stirred in the back of the car. He had to think fast. He couldn't finish her off here it was too busy. She was starting to come round; he had to get off the main roads. He drove to the end of the road and turned into a disused railway repair yard. The place hadn't been used for years, nobody ever came down there. He would be safe for the time being. He switched the little Ford's lights off, and bumped and banged his way over the rough potholed yard, eventually stopping near an old railway shed. He drove the car into the shed and switched the lights on for a moment illuminating the inside of the shed. It was empty except for a rusting hulk of an ancient A3 class locomotive LNER 462, that probably hadn't seen action since before the war. He stopped the car and switched off the engine. The silence inside the building was eerily quiet. The moon cast ghostly shadows from the holes in the dilapidated roof. Georgina groaned in the back of the car. Brooke opened the back door and dragged her roughly out of the car. As he pulled her, she caught her head on the doorframe causing her to shout out in pain.

"Who's that?" came a rasping voice from somewhere inside the shed.

"Help me," cried Georgina. Brooke shoved Georgina back into the ford. An old tramp appeared from nowhere. He was holding a bottle of something in a brown paper bag; he was obviously drunk, but Brooke was in no mood to wait to find out. Georgina cried out again. This time Brooke turned and punched her full in the face knocking her senseless, she slumped back into the seat. The tramp stumbled towards the moving vehicle. Brooke drove straight at him, but at the last minute, he hit a pothole causing the little car to veer to the left and avoid hitting the tramp head on, which would surely have killed him. He screeched out of the rail yard and back onto the main road. He was desperate to get away but all the main roads were blocked. He drove round the back streets. There were no police here, all the extra manpower was watching the main roads, but he needed to get away. The railway station wasn't very far away. There were goods trains coming and going all the time, some of them ran slowly through the station to pick up water. If he could make it, he might be able to jump on one of them and get away. He drove for another few minutes eventually pulling up a few streets from the railway station. He grabbed the bag of clothes he'd got from his parents' house and checked the stash of money in his wallet. Georgina began to stir again. It was still too public to do anything here. He had to deal with her somewhere quieter. He dragged her from the car and pushed her in front of him. "Get moving and don't try anything funny or I'll let you have it here," he said savagely.

"Please don't hurt me. I'll do anything you want. Just let me go. I won't tell the police anything I promise," she pleaded.

The old tramp staggered out of the railway yard still clutching his bottle. He staggered into the street just as a Panda car on a routine patrol spotted him.

"Hello what have we got here?" said the driver. The Panda pulled over. "Now then what do you think you're doing at this time of night, granddad?" said the drivers' mate.

"Bloody idiot could a' killed me," he said tipping the bottle to his lips. "Who could have killed you granddad?" said the pc.

"Bloody idiot in the car. Mindin' me own business I was, next thing I know bloody fool nearly runs me down."

"What fool nearly ran you down? When was this?" said the officer.

"Not long since. 'Im an' a young lass looked like they'd been arguin'. He shoved 'er in the car an' drove off like a bloody maniac, that's when he nearly run me down," said the old tramp.

"Can you be more specific? What did the man look like?" The older of the two could see he wasn't going to get much sense out of the tramp.

"Put him in the back. I'll radio headquarters; it could be the man we're looking for," said the constable.

Frustrated Bob didn't know where to turn next. A steady drizzle was pitter-pattering on the car windscreen. The ancient Vanguard's heater was barely keeping the chilly night air at bay as he let the car's engine idle. He'd driven around for about half an hour since he'd been stopped by the police, but as he had expected all the main roads had been blocked off. If all the main roads were closed off, then Brooke would have to use the back roads and side streets. It was worth a shot he thought, as he gunned the cars' engine and pulled away from the kerb.

Brooke stopped the car. He decided it was too much of a risk to keep driving around. He didn't want to risk being pulled over. He wasn't sure where he was, but he was sure he wasn't very far from the mill where he had taken his parents. The street they were in was poorly lit with alleyways leading to the ginnels at the back. There were only a few of the streetlights still working, making it even more difficult to see where they were going. He pushed Georgina in front of him. She stumbled tripping over the rough uneven road. She fell heavily spraining her ankle.

"Get up," he shouted angrily at her.

"I can't walk. I think I've sprained my ankle, I think it might be broken," she cried. Brooke went over to her, he grabbed her arm and dragged her to her feet.

She cried out in pain. "I can't move my ankle its agony," she moaned.

"You'd better get moving if you know what's good for you. Now get moving," he said cruelly. Georgina terrified, stumbled unsteadily to her feet, her high heels making it hard to walk over the uneven surface; the pain in her ankle shooting like hot knives up her leg. The rain started to fall heavily, making it even more difficult to negotiate the pot-holed street. Just then, a light appeared at the top of the road. Georgina's heart raced maybe someone would rescue her at last.

"Quick in there," said Brooke quickly shoving her into an alleyway along the dilapidated terraced street. He placed his hand over her mouth preventing her from crying out. She tried in vain to struggle free but he was to strong, and the pain in her leg was agonizing. The motor bike drove past squelching water onto the pavement only feet away from where they were hiding. Georgina sobbed from the pain in her ankle terrified that she was never going to get away from this maniac.

Bob looked at his watch. Daylight was just beginning to fade as it approached tea time. Tomorrow, Tuesday the jury was due to bring in its verdict on young Jake. He couldn't give up, not if he had any chance of saving Jake from the hangman's noose. He tried to think. Where would Brooke try and hide away? He knew he couldn't go back to his parent's house; he would have to keep to the back streets. He drove around until he eventually came across another police roadblock. The police stopped the car and asked him to get out. Another fruitless search revealed nothing. "Who's in charge of this case?" said Bob to the officer.

"Why the interest sir?" said the officer suspiciously.

"I might have some information that might help catch the killer," said Bob.

"And you are Bob Ashcroft," said the officer looking down at Bob's driving license. "Yeah. I'm Jake Steeples uncle. The lad that's on trial for a murder I'm convinced he didn't do. The man calling himself David Gregory is Brooke Steeples, Jake Steeples dad."

Chapter seventy-two

DCI Bradley listened intently as Bob related what he knew to the Chief Inspector. "Let me see if I understand you correctly. You say on the night of Sandra Mason's murder, Brooke Steeples was in the Jamboree Club."

"Yeah, up to about 11 or 11:30 about the same time as the lass," said Bob.

"And what was Mr Steeples doing? Was he involved in the fight with Joe Warmsley?" said DCI Bradley.

"He was drinking at the bar, but he weren't involved in the fight," said Bob.

"Miss Mason left between 11:00 to 11:30 you say. What about Mr Warmsley?"

"I think he must 'ave left about the same time. I didn't see 'im after that."

"And Mr Steeples, what time did he leave the club?"

"I would think it were about the same time, I didn't see either of them after that."

"And where was your nephew at this time?" asked Bradley.

"Jake disappeared for a while. He told me he went 'ome to change 'is shirt, because there were blood on it from the fight with Warmsley."

"How long was he gone?"

"I don't remember exactly. I would guess about half an hour, as near as I can remember, but he did come back because we locked the club up about 1:00 to 1:30am. It were over a month ago."

"Time enough to kill Joe Warmsley, and possibly the girl as well," said DCI Bradley.

"Can I now take you back to the night you say you were in the Dog and Partridge public house in Langford? You said that Mr Brooke Steeples was present the same night."

"Yeah I'd gone to watch a couple of acts that I thought might go down well at the club, and he was there."

"Did you definitely see him? What was he doing?"

"I didn't want 'im to see me so I kept out of sight."

"How can you be sure it was him? I know that pub, it gets pretty crowded and it's pretty dimly lit at the best of times," said Bradley.

"I know it was 'im. He was up to 'is usual tricks."

"Up to his usual tricks. What do you mean?"

"Chatting up a couple of women."

"Could you describe the women he was chatting up?"

"There were two of 'em. One was a bit rough lookin' look like she'd bin round the block a bit if yer know what I mean."

"And what about the other girl, can you describe her?" said DCI Bradley beginning to put a picture together in his head. "Well like I said it were dark."

"Well do your best. It's very important."

"I would say she were late twenties, 28 or 29; somethin' like that."

"Do you remember her hair colour?" said Bradley.

"Mousy I think; you know light brown, not dark."

"What was she wearing?"

"They were sat down in the corner so I didn't get a really close look."

"Try Mr Ashcroft it's very important," stressed DCI Bradley.

"The older woman had a dark coat on, and I think she had a 'ead scarf on as well, but she took it off later, I couldn't be sure."

"What about the other woman."

"She had a blue top coat on."

"Do you remember anything else about it?"

"How do you mean?" said Bob perplexed.

"Can you remember anything distinctive about the coat?"

"Not really. It were just a blue coat with a bit of black fur round the collar," said Bob innocently. DCI Bradley looked across to DS Jackson. Bob wasn't aware of the significance of his last statement. DCI Bradley was sure Brooke Steeples was the same man they were looking for.

"Can you remember anything else she was wearing, what she had on under her top coat?" asked Bradley.

"She were sat down most of the time, and I didn't want Brooke to see me, but I think she had a light coloured suit underneath, it could 'ave bin cream or beige I'm not sure," said Bob.

"Thank you for your help Mr Ashcroft. You can leave the rest to us," said DCI Bradley ushering Bob from the interview room.

"If what he says is true it all fits into place," said DS Jackson to his boss. "Brenda Howard was found dead on the golf course; the day after she was seen in the Dog and Partridge," said Bradley to DS Jackson.

"And it couldn't be the lad Jake Steeples. He's been in custody before Brenda Howard was killed, and Joe Warmsley's dead," said DS Jackson. "Then there's Georgina Laycock. She's still missing, and that bastard is still out there. We should have kept a closer eye on her. If anything happens to her, I'll never forgive myself. The press will have a bloody field day if this gets out," said DCI Bradley.

"I want every available man we have on this, Jackson. Get them out of bed, bring them in from holiday if you have to, but I want this maniac caught," said DCI Bradley.

Bob left the police station and drove home. Something in the back of his mind told him to drive round the derelict industrial estate one last time. He drove down Ironcastle Road, over the old disused railway lines. He used to come and play down here when he was a kid. There were loads of places to hide. There were old railway sidings and old mills all over the place. It was once the industrial heartland of Thistlefield. The cotton mills and engineering factories had sprung up after the first world war, at one time employing more than three or four thousand people before its' fall into steady decline. You could hide someone in here and they wouldn't be discovered for ages, if ever. He remembered Charnley's mill was one of the biggest in the town employing over two thousand people in its heyday. Today it was just a rundown shell. It was just a hunch, but it was there that they had found the body of Joe Warmsley. Could it be that Brooke would take his victims here to finish them off? He drove up the deserted road and stopped his car outside the abandoned building. The streets were derelict and the houses unoccupied. He searched them more in hope than actual chance of finding Brooke. There were dozens of empty houses in one street alone, he could be anywhere. He rummaged around for a few more minutes then decided to give up. It was like looking for a needle in a haystack. He got back in the car and drove to the end of the road. At the end, he could see the outline of the old cotton mills in the distance. Bob wound down the window of the car and poked his head out of the door. The rain was still falling but not as heavily as earlier. He could see a group of what looked like kids further down the street. He pulled the car along side of them. "Have you lads seen anybody come along 'ere lately?" he said to the rough looking bunch.

"Who's askin'? You the fuzz?" said one particularly scruffy individual dressed in a dirty leather jacket and dirty jeans that looked like they'd never seen the inside of a washing machine. "No I'm not the fuzz. I just wondered if you'd seen anybody around 'ere lately," said Bob.

"What's it worth?" said the scruffy youth in the dirty jeans.

"I'll give you a packet of fags and ten bob."

"It'll cost you more than ten bob," sneered the yob who was obviously the gangs' leader. "Have you seen anybody?" persisted Bob.

"What's so important anyway?" sneered the yob.

Bob was trying to think of something plausible to tell the gang. "My sister, she should 'ave come 'ome ages since, an' 'er kids are cryin' their eyes out wonderin' where their mam's got to," he said, hoping it would do the trick.

"There was a fella."

"Shut up you stupid bitch," said the yob to the blonde haired girl. "How much is it worth mister?"

"I've got a fiver and twenty fags. Now have you seen anybody?"

"Tell him Billy," said the blonde haired girl.

"Will you shut your fucking mouth you stupid cow. Let's see the money and the fags first."

Bob took a packet of cigarettes from the glove compartment and handed the yob his last fiver from his wallet. "Well have you seen anybody?" said Bob beginning to lose his patience.

"We've been here all night and all we've seen is some bloke and a bird. She looked like she was limpin'. They went down Corporation Street."

"When was that?" asked Bob.

"Dunno about an hour ago or so, I should think," said the yob pocketing the five-pound note and shaking a cigarette from the packet. "Which is Corporation Street?"

"Straight on over the waste land you can't miss it. Charnley's mill is right in front of you."

"Thanks," said Bob thinking he would really like to punch the scruffy shit's lights out.

"If you hurry up you might just catch them havin' it off," sniggered the shabby youth.

Chapter seventy-three

"Please can we stop for a minute?" said Georgina dropping to the wet pavement. "My ankle's really hurting me," she cried.

"Stop your moaning and get a move on, we're nearly there," snapped Brooke.

"Where are you taking me?" sobbed Georgina.

Since he had abandoned the car, it had taken Brooke nearly an hour to walk the mile or so distance to Charnley's mill. The route over the rough strewn streets was made even more difficult having to stop every few minutes with Georgina's swollen ankle. It wasn't much further; he could see the outline of the Victorian mill in the distance just over a slight incline. It would be quiet there, and then he would be able to deal with her.

"Come on," he said savagely pulling the distraught girl to her feet. She whimpered in pain and fear, sure, she was never going to get out of this alive. It was only a few hundred yards to the entrance of the mill over some railway tracks. It wouldn't be long now, he was nearly there.

Bob stopped the car at the end of the road. In front of him was waste ground, and some railway tracks. There were several railway carriages and freight wagons along the sidings. He couldn't take the car any further; he would have to go on foot. He scrambled up a slight incline losing his footing on the loose gravel and slipped back down the slope. He got to his feet and scrambled back up the bank. He heard a cry. He stopped and listened again fearing his hearing was playing tricks on him. No, there it was again, definitely a cry, a girls' cry. As he reached the top of the slope, he heard it again. "Please, I can't go on," pleaded Georgina.

"Get moving or I'll not be responsible for my actions now get going," snarled Brooke savagely pulling the terrified girl to her feet. Bob thought he recognized the voice, he was sure it was Brooke. As he peered over the incline, he could see movement ahead. From where he was at the top of the bank, he could see the outline of a man and woman. It was hard to see them; they were some distance away and kept disappearing behind the carriages, but from the look of the man, he was almost certain it was Brooke. He thought about calling out but that would only alert him. He had to think of something to get the girl away from him, God knows what he might do to her if he discovered him. He kept a short distance behind them, dodging behind the wagons every few seconds to avoid being seen. About a hundred yards away there was a fence; on the other side of it was Charnley's mill. It looked like that was where they were heading. Bob crept a little closer making sure he was out of Brookes' sight. He saw him grab the girls arm and drag her towards the fence. She stumbled over the railway line and fell onto the hard gravel, grazing her knees. She cried out in pain, pleading with Brooke to stop a minute. Bob took advantage of the girls stumble and crept a little closer. He could make out the man's features more clearly now in the moonlight. There was no doubt it was Brooke. Georgina was struggling to get to her feet when out of the corner of her eye she saw Bob. She was just about to shout out when Bob put his hand to his mouth to indicate to the terrified girl to keep quiet. She shuddered involuntarily and kept her mouth shut. They reached the fence and squeezed through a gap in the railings. Brooke shoved Georgina roughly through the fence, tearing her skirt and stockings on the rusting railings as he scurried in after her. He looked around to make sure they were alone. He pushed Georgina in front of him.

"Over there," he said sharply, pushing her in front of him.

"Where?" she cried.

"There." He snapped, indicating a door with a brush handle through the latch. She hobbled to the door, Brooke was only inches behind her. He started to pull the brush from the door handle.

"Who's there?" came the cry from inside.

"My god. Who else have you got locked up in there?" cried Georgina.

"Just shut up and get in," he said, viciously shoving her towards the door. Bob had slipped through the railings and into the yard. He could see the door about fifty yards away. Georgina was petrified and started crying again.

"Help. Help us please," croaked William from behind the door. Bob slipped through the door, and slid along the wall in the shadow obscuring Brooke's view. Brooke had his cosh out. He was standing over Georgina who had slipped to the floor. She was curled up, knees drawn up tightly to her chest, waiting for the deadly blows to arrive. Bob could see the door was still wedged shut with the broom handle. Georgina was slumped at the bottom of the door. Bob was frantically trying to catch the stricken girls' attention. If he could get her to pull the broom handle free it would give Brooke something else to think about, and buy him precious seconds. Georgina spotted Bob making gestures to pull the broom handle from the door. Brooke raised the heavy bar above his head ready to finish her off. In a split second Bob kicked a heavy can that had been lying by the side of the door. The noise distracted Brooke just long enough for Georgina to pull the broom handle from the door. Bob leapt from the shadow of the wall, and crashed into Brooke sending the two of them sprawling onto the floor. Brooke was agile for such a big man and was on his feet in seconds.

"You," he screamed at Bob as he swung the bar viciously at his head. Bob was much smaller than Brooke. He was giving away both height and weight, but what he lacked in size he made up for in agility. He ducked as the heavy club just missed his head by inches. He swung a vicious blow to Brooke's solar plexus knocking the wind out of him. Brooke slumped to the floor.

"Run for it," he shouted to Georgina.

"I can't I think my ankle is broken," she sobbed. The door creaked open.

"William," exclaimed Bob. There was no time for explanations he had to get them away from this maniac as quick as possible.

"Take the girl and get out as fast as you can. Get to the main road; there's police all over the place lookin' for 'im." Brooke got to his feet and swung the cosh at Bob catching him a heavy blow on the shoulder. He went down on one knee, the pain shooting through his body incapacitating him temporarily. It was all Brooke needed to get away. He darted past Bob and into the dilapidated factory. Bob staggered to his feet.

"Which way did 'e go?"

"He went through that door," said William pointing in the direction of the disused factory. Bob cautiously opened the door and looked around; there was no sign of him. The shed was dark the only light coming from the holes in the damaged roof. He crept inside his eyes trying to focus in the dim light. He stopped to listen, but it was deadly quiet, like a graveyard. Suddenly from nowhere Brooke was on him again. He was like a man possessed. He punched Bob in the face knocking him to the floor. In a moment, he was on him. He dropped the heavy cosh, as his powerful hands started choking the life out of him. He could feel his lungs bursting as he gasped for air. Out of the corner of his eye, he could see where Brooke had dropped the heavy iron bar. He clawed his fingers towards it. Brooke dug his fingers deeper into his throat threatening to strangle the life out of him. Bob grabbed the bar and with his remaining strength swung it at his head. The blow drew blood from his forehead, but stunned him long enough for him to push Brooke out of the way and slowly get his breath back. Brooke rolled over and staggered to his feet snatching the blood stained cosh back out of Bobs grip. He stumbled through the dark passageway deeper into the factory. Bob followed him but he was gasping for breath before he had gone fifty yards. The place had been empty for years and dust and cobwebs covered every inch of the building. Empty bobbins, old cans, and all manner of litter made walking painful and slow. Bob stopped to get his breath; he couldn't see or hear anything. He carried on for a few more steps, brushing the myriad of cobwebs that were intent on suffocating him before he had gone ten feet. Suddenly there was a crash from up ahead. Brooke had stumbled across some empty cans that had been used in the old card room for storing the cotton. The crash reverberated along the passageway sending echo's bouncing off the empty factory walls. Bob cautiously made his way towards the sound. Brooke cursed his luck as the heavy cans rolled around the floor. He was sure Bob would have heard them. He moved further into the mill until he came to a set of stairs. At the side of the stairway was an old lift that had long since been out of use. He climbed the stairs until he reached the second level. He waited for a few seconds until he was sure he hadn't been followed.

Bob crept along the passageway feeling his way in the dark. He stopped where the cans littered the floor, but he couldn't see anything. He looked ahead but saw nothing in the gloom. He bent to get his breath, if he hadn't, in the dim light, he wouldn't have noticed the footprint in the dust. It was fresh nobody had been here in years, it must be Brooke. He slowly crept up the stairs feeling his way along the damp walls. He reached the top and inched his way into the old spinning room. He slid along the wall; he could feel his heart pounding through his thick coat. Without warning, Brooke rushed Bob knocking him off his feet. The two of them staggered towards the stairs.

Chapter seventy-four

Georgina hobbled, an arm around each of Brooke's parents as they made their way out of the old mill. Anne sobbed, she couldn't believe the enormity of what her beloved son had done. They made their way over the waste ground and back onto the main road. In the distance, they could hear the police sirens and made their way towards them.

Georgina was taken to St Hilda's hospital where they set her broken ankle.

William and Anne were also treated for shock. They had been locked up for nearly twenty-four hours without food or water. A bigger shock was the fact that their son was a murderer. DCI Bradley was at the hospital waiting for news of the victims.

"When can I speak to them?" said DCI Bradley to the doctor. "You can have five minutes no more; they have had a terrible shock."

DC Linda Francis knocked on the side-ward door where Georgina Laycock was lying on the bed, her right ankle plastered to the knee.

"Alright if I come in?" said DC Francis.

"Don't keep her to long will you; she's had a nasty shock," said the nurse.

"Hi Georgina; how are you doing?" said DC Francis as cheerfully as she could.

"I thought he was going to kill me," she cried. Linda put her arms around her as she sobbed uncontrollably.

"I'm sorry we should have kept a better eye on you. You were only gone for a few minutes when we noticed you hadn't come back," said Linda.

"It was horrible. He just grabbed me and shoved me in his car. It all happened so quickly."

"Is it the same man who attacked you before?" asked DC Francis.

"Yes it's definitely him."

"Well at least now we know who we are looking for," said DC Francis.

Anne Steeples sobbed incessantly. "What have we done to deserve this?" she cried. Her eyes were red raw from the tears streaming down her cheeks.

"It's not your fault. We're both to blame I suppose. We never checked him when he was a lad. We gave him everything," said William doing his best to console his distraught wife.

DCI Bradley approached William whispering quietly in his ear, "Could I have a word outside if you don't mind sir?" aware of what pain his wife was going through.

"As you may be aware, we are looking for a man who fits your sons' description, and we wondered if you could tell us tell us what happened during the last twenty four hours?" said Bradley, as gently as he could.

"He came home, said he needed money and a change of clothes. He said he was going to meet a client down south or somewhere, some new business or other. I knew he was lying. I know most of our contacts and as far as I know, we didn't have any business going on down there. I told him he wasn't getting a penny, that's when he hit me and he took me and his mother to that old mill. He told his mother that if she didn't open the safe he would kill me." Old William shook his head in disbelief the years lying heavily on his strained face.

"What was he wearing when you last saw him?" said DCI Bradley.

"He had a dark overcoat over the top of his suit, but he took a change of clothes, so I'm not really sure what he'll be wearing now," said William.

"Not to worry sir, I'm sure we'll have him soon. All the main roads are closed off, he won't get very far."

Chapter seventy-five

Bob and Brooke headed towards the top of the stairs. Brooke was like a man possessed, he couldn't believe how strong he was. It was strength borne out of desperation. Bob managed to struggle to his feet and swung his fist at Brooke's head, he ducked and the intended blow just whipped by into fresh air. Brooke's foot lashed out catching Bob squarely in the groin causing him to double up in pain. He grunted in agony as the blow sent waves of pain into his vitals. He tried to get to his feet but Brooke was on him in a flash. He caught him another vicious blow in the stomach with the cosh sending him tumbling down the stairs. Severely winded, Bob lay at the bottom of the stairs trying to catch his breath. He lay there for several seconds wondering when the next blow would come. The blow never came Brooke was halfway down the narrow passageway looking to make his escape. Bob staggered to his feet he wasn't sure which way Brooke had gone. He couldn't remember if he had gone past him or not. He crawled back up the stairs, he looked up and down the gloomy corridor but he couldn't see anything. He looked out of one of the mill's broken windows hoping to see where Brooke had gone, but all he could see was empty ground surrounded by the railway yard. He searched the passageway up and down but Brooke wasn't there; he must have got away. Bob cursed to himself. He went back down the stairs but there was no sign of him.

Brooke had managed to find a way out at the back of the spinning room. At the end was an iron fire escape. The rusting hinges creaked as he opened the door that lead onto it. He looked all around as he crept down the groaning steps, aware that there would be police looking for him everywhere. At the bottom of the steps, it opened out into a yard. There wasn't much cover; he would have to be careful. The yard was walled in on all sides except for a large wooden gate at one end. It looked to Brooke that that was his only way out. He slipped into the shadows and pressing himself against the ageing brickwork made his way along the wall to the gate. He reached the gate but to his anger and frustration, the small inner gate was locked. He rattled the ancient rusted brass padlock but it wasn't going to give. Although it was old, it was still too strong to break. He still had the heavy metal bar in his hand. He gave it a couple of hefty smacks, but it held firm. He gave it a couple more, he was sure it had come loose. He hit it again. The lock was loosening.

Bob's ears pricked up. He heard the banging reverberating down the corridor. He had recovered a little and raced as fast as his aching legs would carry him towards the noise. From the top of the fire escape, he saw Brooke battering away at the lock unaware that he was there. He crept down the stairway hoping that Brooke would be too busy with the lock to see him. The stairs creaked with each step that Bob took, but luckily, the noise was veiled by the constant hammering at the lock. He reached the bottom and hugged the wall trying to keep out of Brooke's sight. Inch by painful inch he crept slowly towards Brooke grimacing with each step, as the pain from the blows to his shoulder and groin shot through his body like hot irons. His only chance was to take him by surprise. If he didn't get him this time, he would be a dead man for sure. Brooke grunted as he continued to hammer at the lock. It was loosening a couple more blows and it would be off. Bob was only feet away, he could see Brooke's face contorted with the effort of trying to break the lock. Bob was sweating, he wasn't sure whether it was from his exertions or from fear; he suspected it was a bit of both. He knew he would only get one chance to take Brooke down. He looked around for something he could use as a weapon but he couldn't see anything in the gloom. Suddenly the lock snapped. Brooke tore at the broken lock and ripped it from the door. Still clutching the iron bar he scrambled through the door. This was the chance Bob had been waiting for. He rushed from the shadows of the wall and leapt onto Brooke grabbing at the heavy cosh at the same time trying to avoid another vicious blow.

Brooke was taken by surprise as Bob clambered onto his back. However, he was strong; he slammed Bob heavily to the floor and swung the heavy bar at Bob's head missing it by inches, and scooted out of the door. Winded Bob got to his feet and scrambled through the door, he could see Brooke just ahead of him running up the street towards the railway line. If he made it to the rail yard, he would lose him for sure. Brooke scuttled up the bank his fingers digging into the loose gravel to gain momentum up the steep incline. He looked behind; Bob was still doggedly pursuing him. He reached the top of the bank stopping momentarily to catch his breath. If he could reach the yard there were a hundred places he could hide while he thought of what to do. He started to cross the tracks; he looked behind to see where Bob was. As he stepped across the tracks, his foot caught in between one of the track switch rails. His foot was jammed he couldn't move he was trapped. He struggled but the more he tried the harder his foot remained fast. Bob reached the top of the bank. He looked up and down the line but in the dim light, he couldn't see any sign of Brooke. He made his way along the bank and towards the railway line. He could see nothing only a heavy movement in the distance. It was one of the yards Shunters making its way slowly towards him. Brooke could see it too. It was on the same line that he was trapped in and was headed straight for him. He screamed out in panic battering at the railway line with the iron bar. He waved his arms frantically, trying to catch the engine drivers attention, but the driver couldn't see him. If he didn't get out the train would cut him in half. Bob heard Brooke's screams and ran towards the noise. He could see what was about to happen. He could leave him there and let the bastard get his just deserts or he could try and save him and clear Jake's name. He rushed towards the Shunter shouting to the driver, but he couldn't make himself heard. The train was less than four hundred yards away now, if he didn't do something fast Brooke was a dead man. He ran down the track still trying to get the drivers attention when he spotted a point switch, if he could get to it there was a chance he could switch the Shunter to another track. The train was getting closer as Bob raced down the track.

Brooke was frantic. He tore at his foot hysterical with fear as the heavy train bore down on him, still trying frantically to free himself by wedging the bar between the railway line; but to no avail. He felt a sharp snap as his ankle broke in an effort to break free, and the agonizing pain shot like a lightning bolt up his leg. The train was only two hundred yards away as Bob raced for the switch. He was gasping for breath as he reached the switch. He barely had the strength to push the lever over as the Shunter approached. Maybe it was weakness, or the switch hadn't been used for some time, but it wouldn't budge. He had only seconds to save Brooke. With his last remaining drop of strength, he put all his weight against the switch; the lever moved sending the Shunter safely onto the other track only yards away from Brooke. He collapsed sobbing at the side of the line inches away from certain death. Bob got him to his feet and made his way towards the railway yards' main gates. Through the gates, the street was swarming with police.

Chapter seventy-six

It was Tuesday the tenth of November, and the jury was about to deliver its verdict on Jake. The evidence against Jake killing Joe Warmsley was overwhelming. The jury had been out most of Monday and hadn't been able to reach a verdict. It was the second day of deliberations, but a unanimous decision was proving hard to get. Some members of the jury believed that Jake was guilty of premeditated murder; sighting the blood found on his shirt and also on Joe Warmsley's'. They also pointed out that he threatened to kill Warmsley because he had raped his mother and sister, and was overheard threatening to kill him by a police officer. Other members of the jury were not as convinced that it was premeditated, and that Jake had acted on impulse, and in the circumstances although he was guilty of murder it was not premeditated.

DCI Bradley came into the interview room with DS Jackson. Georgina Laycock was wringing her hands nervously.

DC Linda Francis was with her. "It's all right Georgina nothing to worry about," said Linda trying her best to put the young woman at ease.

"Miss Laycock, there's nothing to be afraid of or worry about. We have got some people lined up in the next room. Don't worry they can't see or hear you so you are quite safe. All we want you to do is just look along the line and pick out anyone you recognize. Do you think you can do that for us?" said DCI Bradley in an almost fatherly way. He led Georgina through into the next room. There was a large pane of glass, and a group of six men stood facing her. "Don't worry they can't see or hear you," said Bradley gently nudging Georgina towards the window. All the men were of similar height and build. They were all wearing dark overcoats. Brooke was stood next to the end of the line, hands crossed in front of him. "Just take your time," said DCI Bradley. Just point at anyone you recognize."

Georgina looked up and down the line. Eventually she stopped at Brooke and pointed to him. "The one next to the end," she said. "That's him."

"Yes," exclaimed DS Jackson punching his balled fist into his hand.

"Are you sure? Take your time have a good look," said Bradley.

"Yes I'm quite sure. That's Dave Gregory," she said, quickly turning away and running out of the room.

"Well we've got a positive identification but not much else," said DCI Bradley to DS Jackson. "Unless we can find something that places him at the scene we'll have to let him go," said Bradley.

"But we know it's him Guv," said DS Jackson. "Everything points to it being him."

"What we need is proof. We know he was in the Jamboree Club the night that Sandra Mason was killed. He admitted that much."

"What I can't understand is where Joe Warmsley comes into this."

"No. It looks very much like the lad's in the frame for that one," said Bradley. "The young lass has identified him as the one who attacked her. Can't we do him for that?"

"At best we could only do him for GBH, and that would only put him away for six months at the most," sighed Bradley.

"What about the parents. The bastard kidnapped and locked his own mother and father in a dilapidated mill. God knows what he would have done if Bob Ashcroft hadn't caught up with him," said Jackson.

"The problem is they won't press charges against their precious son, so there's not much we can do about it," said Bradley.

"Bob Ashcroft saw him in the Dog and Partridge the same night that Brenda Howard went missing. Twenty-four hours later, she turns up dead with her head bashed in. It's the same m.o. Guv."

"We've still no proof. There were no prints on the weapon. Forensics didn't find any fibres, hair, or anything that would tie him to the crimes. The bastard has been clever enough to wipe the prints off the weapon, or he wore gloves," said Bradley.

"What about fibres from when he attacked Bob Ashcroft? Was there nothing on it then?"

"Not really. He caught him mainly on the shoulder, the only other blood we found was his own where Bob had caught him one on the head during the fight at the mill."

"Where does Mary Warmsley fit into the picture Guv?"

"That's another puzzler Steve. I don't know."

"She was killed in the same way as the other three including Warmsley," said Jackson.

"Whoever it was shut her up because she obviously knew something," said Bradley.

Chapter seventy-seven

The jury had deliberated long and hard. It had been a most difficult case. They had had to make the right decision. They foreman of the jury had asked Judge Tremlow for more time to deliver their verdict. Judge Tremlow agreed, and sent them back to their hotel for the night, and told them to return in the morning. Most of the evidence pointed to Jake's guilt, but there was also some doubt that he hadn't planned to kill Joe Warmsley. If that was the case he wasn't guilty of premeditated murder, and the charge would be reduced to manslaughter. Another of the arguments they had to consider was that he had threatened Joe in front of witnesses, and was also heard to say that he would kill Joe if he ever came near him again, in front of a police witness. The jury also had to decide if Jake was guilty of a revenge killing. He knew that Joe had raped his mother, and that he had also raped his sister, pointing further to his guilt. Coupled together with the blood found on Jake's shirt, the evidence looked overwhelming. Several of the jury members agreed that although Joe Warmsley was no angel they had to try the case on the evidence presented to them, and that evidence was pretty damning. The foreman had asked for a show of hands. Nine of the jurors were sure Jake was guilty of first-degree murder. Three only wanted to convict him of manslaughter. Their argument being that the extenuating circumstances had driven the young man kill in order to appease his mother's and sister's shame. They argued that in similar circumstances, any one of them might have acted in the same way. The jury foreman argued that whilst that was true, they had to act within the law, and as such they had to agree to a charge of first-degree murder. After much argument and heated debate, they made their way back into the packed courtroom. The tension in the chamber was intense as the crowd hunched forward to hear the verdict. The court official rose from his seat and approached the jury foreman. You could hear a pin drop as the assembled horde waited with baited breath for the verdict.

"Ladies and gentlemen of the jury have you reached a verdict that you are all agreed upon?" asked the court official.

"We have said the foreman of the jury."

"And what is your verdict?"

Chapter seventy-eight

It wasn't looking good. If they couldn't find any physical evidence then Brooke Steeples was going to walk away from a multiple murder charge. At best, he would get six months for GBH.

DCI Bradley was determined he wasn't going to get off scot-free. "Steve have we got anything else from forensics that we could use; anything at all?"

"Nothing we can pin the bastard down with," said Jackson. "I'll get back onto them. Maybe they've missed something." He said hopefully.

Bradley went through his case notes with a fine toothcomb hoping there was something there he might have missed. He was just about to start on his second cup of tea when he looked down at his notes. What's this? He thought to himself. He read and re-read the notes. All victims had signs of Pediculus Capitis. "Steve have you got a minute?"

"What's up Guv, you found something?"

"Pediculus Capitis. All victims had Pediculus Capitis."

"What the bloody hell is Pedi... whatever that is when it's at home?" Said Jackson bemused.

"I don't know Steve but it might just be what we're looking for. How come we've not picked up on this before?"

"No idea Guv."

"Never mind that; get back onto forensics, and find out what it is. Quick as you can Steve this could be important; it might be the break we're looking for."

Thirty minutes later Jackson had the information in his hands. "Pediculus Capitis. You'll never guess in a million years Guv."

"Stop pissing about Steve and tell me what you've got."

"Nits Guv."

"Nits. What you on about man?"

"Nits Guv. Head lice. Pediculus Capitis are head lice. Moreover, all the victims had them. Sandra Mason, Brenda Howard, and Mary Warmsley. In addition, guess what? Joe Warmsley had them as well, and they were also found on Georgina Laycock."

"Bloody hell. When laddo was brought in did we do a full body search?"

"I think so Guv. Stripped down the lot, with him being a murder suspect."

"Did they do his hair?" Said Bradley.

"I can find out. I'll get onto the duty sergeant."

"If not do one now before it's too late."

"I had a word with the duty doctor. He had been to hospital before he came here, broke his ankle on the railway line. They cleaned him up, set his ankle and then we got him. And bingo, we did the works, his hair the lot. And guess what?" said DS Jackson holding the cellophane bag like a trophy. "These little buggers are head lice. He was full of them," he said gleefully.

"So can we tie him in to all the murders then?" asked Bradley.

"Well according to what forensics say these are common head lice."

"But I thought it was only kids that got nits," said Bradley.

"Normally that's true, but it's not exclusive to kids, adults can get them too."

"How so?"

"Well it's usually from contact. According to the lab boys, these little buggers are about the size of a sesame seed. That's about a sixteenth of an inch to an eighth of an inch long. The female lays her eggs called nits in the head, and they feed on blood from the scalp."

"Urg! Quite an expert on these little monsters hey Jackson."

"There's more Guv. The young take about a week to hatch and they live for about thirty days then they die off."

"So what's the time frame on the victims?" said Bradley.

"The time frame fits, Guv. The first victim was Sandra Mason, on or about the 11th or12th of October, and the last one was Mary Warmsley on the 5th of November."

"How long have we had Jake Steeples in custody?" said DCI Bradley.

"We took him in on the 14th October."

"So he couldn't have done any of the others. He could only be in the frame for Warmsley, and possibly Sandra Mason," said Bradley.

"It's possible Guv, but if you ask me I don't think he was responsible for any of them."

"When he was brought in was he searched like Brooke Steeples?"

"Yes standard procedure Guv."

"Did they find any of those bugs on him?"

"None were reported as far as I know."

"Check, will you, Steve. We overlooked that once, maybe we did it again," said Bradley.

Twenty minutes later DS Jackson reported back. "He was clean Guv; not a thing, not a nit in sight. As far as I can tell he was nowhere near Joe Warmsley when he was killed," said DS Jackson.

Chapter seventy-nine

"How do you find the accused guilty or not guilty?" said the court official.

"Guilty," said the foreman of the jury. A gasp went around the courtroom as the verdict was announced.

"No." cried Lizzie from the gallery. "No, he's innocent." She sobbed. Others gasped in dismay at the jury's verdict. Several members of the public crossed themselves and muttered for mercy under their breath.

"And that is the verdict of you all?" asked the court official.

"Yes," replied the jury foreman as members of the public shouted in uproar at the verdict.

Judge Tremlow banged his gavel on his bench repeatedly, trying to restore order to his courtroom. "Silence in court," he shouted above the uproar. "Silence in court," he bellowed. "I will not have disorderly behaviour in my courtroom. If there is another outburst like that again I will have the courtroom cleared." The chamber went quiet as order was restored. The court official stood behind judge Tremlow and placed the black cap over his head. That could only mean one thing; the death penalty. "Jake Michael Steeples having been tried and found guilty of the wilful murder of Joseph Arthur Warmsley, I hereby sentence you to be taken from here, to a place where you are to be hanged by the neck until you are dead, and may God have mercy on your soul. Take him down."

"The jury's just brought in its verdict. The lad's been found guilty. He's got the death penalty," said DS Jackson.

"Bloody hell!" said Bradley. "Let's get back and have another word with Mr Steeples otherwise his son's going to swing."

Lizzie paced up and down the kitchen. She frantically cleaned everything in sight. Pots, pans, work surfaces anything to take her mind off the horror of the judge's words. "Hanged by the neck until dead." It wasn't real, they couldn't hang her baby. "Bob what am I going to do? They can't hang him he's not done anything," she cried pitifully.

"Somethin' will turn up. They've got Brooke. Surely they know Jake's the wrong man," said Bob trying to be positive.

"But the jury found him guilty of killing Joe. They'll believe Jake had good reason when he found out what Joe had done to me and Lottie."

"I know. It looks bad, but all the evidence points to Jake doin' it. I know he's not guilty Lizzie," said Bob.

"I'm goin' down to the police station. I'll beg Brooke if I have to. I won't let them hang Jake."

"They won't listen. They'll just turn you away," said Bob.

"I have to do something, I'm not just going to sit here and let them hang my son."

Chapter eighty

The burly sergeant brought Brooke into the interview room. He was looking a little weary. His once smart suit was crumpled, and his tie and shoelaces had been removed. The cockiness had gone from his face since he had been in the cells. He sat at the sparse table simply staring into space. The burly sergeant stood behind him on the back wall. He sat there wondering. He knew he was guilty, but they had no proof. He had worn gloves and he had made sure he always cleaned the cosh afterwards. No he needn't worry they didn't have anything concrete they could pin on him. At worst, he might get a few months for assault on the young girl from the pub, but with a good solicitor, he would be out in no time. The interview room door opened and in walked DCI Bradley followed by DS Jackson. Bradley and Jackson sat opposite Brooke. DCI Bradley shuffled the files in front of him, and looked Brooke directly in the eyes. "Mr Steeples we would like to give us an account of your whereabouts on the night of 11th and 12th of October this year," said DCI Bradley.

"I've already told you," said Brooke vehemently.

"You were in the Jamboree Club. What time did you leave?"

"I told you about ten to ten thirty."

"And then where did you go?"

"I went home."

"Yes, but there was no one to verify you were there."

"I've told you already, my mother had been ill, and I didn't want to disturb her."

DCI Bradley looked down at his notes again. "Can you tell us where you where on the night of the 28th of October this year?"

"I can't remember."

"Well try," said DCI Bradley.

"I'd been away on business."

"Whereabouts had you been on business?" said Bradley.

"The Midlands. I think somewhere around Birmingham."

"And on your way back you called at the Royal Oak pub in Thistlefield."

"I might have done. I call in at a lot of places in my job," said Brooke cagily. "On this occasion, you met a young woman. A Miss Georgina Laycock, a barmaid at the Royal Oak."

"I've already told you I meet a lot of people in my line of work. It's part of the job."

"Is it part of your job to assault them as well?" said Jackson leaning forward and pointing to Brookes face. "The scratches, I couldn't help noticing them, you've got some very nice scratches down your cheeks Mr Steeples. Where did you get them?"

Brooke was flustered he pawed nervously at the weals on his cheeks. "I don't know what you're talking about. I've not assaulted anyone."

"The scratches; where did you get the scratches?" said Jackson, persisting with the question.

"They... They must have been when I was out. Yes, I remember, I was playing with a customer's cat. It was in the office. I bent down to stroke the bugger and it suddenly went for me. Nearly took my eye out," he said unconvincingly. Bradley looked across to Jackson neither men believed a word he had said. "Can we go back to the night in the Broadlands hotel? Miss Laycock has already identified you as the man who attacked her that same night," said DCI Bradley.

Brooke shifted uneasily in his chair. He threw his hands up in the air. "Alright, I admit things might have got a little bit out of hand."

"A little bit out of hand. You almost caved her head in with an iron bar," snapped DS Jackson angrily.

"Ok we had a little set to. Things started to get a little... how can I put it... heated. There was a bit of a scuffle, and she fell and hit her head on the dressing room table."

"Why didn't you call a doctor, when you knew she was injured?" asked Bradley. "I suppose I just panicked. I wasn't thinking straight. We'd both had quite a bit to drink."

"So you just left her there to possibly bleed to death," said Jackson.

"I told you I panicked. I just wanted to get away. I didn't intend to do the girl any harm. I just wanted keep her quiet."

"So you decided the best way was to bash her over the head with an iron bar," said Jackson contemptuously.

DCI Bradley looked at his subordinate irately. Steeples was edgy. He was apprehensive and nervous and Bradley had got him talking. He didn't want his sergeant jumping in needlessly, and ruining any chance they might have of Steeples incriminating himself. "Can we go forward a few days to the 1st of November? You were seen at the Dog and Partridge pub in Langford. Is that correct?" said DCI Bradley.

"I keep telling you Chief Constable; I get about all over the place in my job."

"Do you know a Miss Brenda Howard?" asked Bradley.

"No. Should I?"

"You were with her on the night in question. You were seen talking to two women in the Dog and Partridge pub."

"And what if I did talk to her; there's no law against that is there?"

"Miss Howard was found dead less than twenty-four hours later, and she was seen talking to a man who fits your description," said DS Jackson.

"That doesn't mean it was me. Dozens of men fit my description," said Brooke defensively.

"You don't deny that you were at the Dog and Partridge on the night in question," said Bradley.

"Probably. What if I was? Doesn't mean I killed her."

"We believe the same weapon was used to subdue the victim. Do you recognize this?" said DCI Bradley pointing to a metal object covered with a plastic bag.

"Never seen it before in my life."

"It was found in your trouser pocket when we arrested you," said Bradley.

"Doesn't mean it belonged to me."

"Well if it doesn't belong to you, what was it doing in your pocket?"

"No idea. It could have been planted."

"And why would anyone want to plant that on you Mr Steeples?" said DCI Bradley.

"To frame me for these murders."

"And why would we do that Mr Steeples. We already have a witness that has identified you as her attacker at the Broadlands hotel. We can also place you at the Dog and Partridge at the time of the murder of Brenda Howard and of Mary Warmsley."

"Placing me there isn't evidence that I committed a crime. Anyway you won't find any fingerprints on that," he said pointing to the bar in the bag.

"Who said we had any fingerprints Mr Steeples?" said DCI Bradley.

Brooke realized he'd just made an error.

"How do you know we haven't got any fingerprints?"

"I just assumed that's all," he blustered.

"If you knew there were no fingerprints on the weapon it must be because you wiped them off," said DCI Bradley.

"I've told you, I've never seen it before."

"So you always walk around with an iron bar in your pocket do you Mr Steeples? What's it for ballast, stop you falling over is it?" said Jackson.

Chapter eighty-one

Lizzie went straight to the desk sergeant. "I'd like to see my ex husband please?"

"And who might that be?" said the sergeant.

"Brooke Steeples," said Lizzie. "Please, it's really important.

"I'm sorry love but he's being interviewed at the minute and can't be disturbed."

"I'm not leaving here till I see him. I'll stay here all night if I have too," she shouted.

DS Jackson came out of the interview room to see what the commotion was. "Mrs Steeples what are you doing here?"

"I want to see that bastard of an ex-husband of mine. Does he know his son is due to hang for a murder he didn't do?"

"We're just questioning him at the moment Mrs Steeples; I don't think it will be possible," said DS Jackson.

"I might be able to reason with him," cried Lizzie pleading with the DS.

"Wait here." Jackson went into the interview room and told his boss that Mrs Steeples was outside, and wanted to see her ex.

"Did you tell her that we were in the middle of questioning him, Sergeant?"

"I did Guv but she seemed determined that she might be able to prick his conscience."

"That man hasn't got a conscience. I'll give her ten minutes with him then take him back to the cells."

Lizzie pleaded with Brooke, but it was useless. He was adamant that he wasn't responsible for the murders, and that the police had got the wrong man.

"But what about Jake? He's going to hang for a crime he didn't commit."

"It wasn't me, I keep telling you," he said.

"No like it wasn't you that raped me," she said savagely.

"I never raped you. You were willing. I even paid you if you remember," he scoffed.

"I asked you for money to feed the kids, but you would only give it to me if I said I would go to bed with you. When I refused you dragged me upstairs," she screamed at him.

"She's lying," he said to DS Jackson who was noting every word. "I never raped you. You were always up for it. You were just a slag," he sneered.

Lizzie leapt at him but she was pulled back by DS Jackson. "Ok love come on that's enough. Let's get you out of here." She left the cells sobbing. DS Jackson took her back to the front desk. "Why did you never report that he'd raped you Mrs Steeples?" asked Jackson.

"Who was going to believe me, hey? I'd already been raped by that bastard Joe Warmsley. Not content with just me, he had to go and rape poor Lottie as well. Who'd believe a woman on her own with three kids, they'd just say I must've egged him on," she cried pitifully.

"Bloody hell!" Thought Jackson what that poor woman has gone through at the hands of those two bastards. First, her husband rapes her, and then Joe Warmsley rapes her and her daughter. No wonder the lad was driven to murder. Underneath though he still wasn't convinced that Jake was guilty, especially after what he had just witnessed. He was more certain than ever that Brooke Steeples was the real culprit. "Don't worry Mrs Steeples, we know it's your ex-husband; we just have to get the proof. He won't get away with it you can be sure of that," said DS Jackson.

Lizzie 317 Steeples

"Meanwhile my son is rotting in a jail cell waiting for the hangman to put a rope round his neck."

Chapter eighty-two

Lizzie left the police station sobbing. She was convinced that Jake was going to hang. Brooke had no remorse in him, she thought. He was willing to let his own son answer for his crimes. Brooke had always been fortunate. His parents had covered up for him when he got a young girl pregnant when he was sixteen. Maybe it was the daughter his mother had always craved. When his parents first married, his mother fell pregnant, but the baby girl was stillborn. When Brooke was born about a year later, his mother lavished everything onto him. Nothing was too good for her precious Brooke. As he grew older, he became more and more demanding. If he needed money, he knew he could always depend on his mother. William on the other hand tried in vain to stop his wife from ruining the boy, but to no avail. She always overruled him. In the end, he just gave up, knowing that his son was turning into something evil.

He joined the navy with his fathers' blessing. William thought it would be the making of him. The navy would take him away from the many temptations that were all too easily available and in the hope that it would settle him down.

Through the years, there had always been some irate father knocking on the Steeples' front door. All through his adolescence, Brooke had brought nothing but heartache to his parents' home. He left the navy and returned to his fathers' business. For a short time, he settled down. The day-to-day life as a company rep for his fathers' firm sent him far and wide and hopefully out of trouble. It wasn't long however before he was up to his old tricks. Many were the unsuspecting girls he would entice into his bed. One such occasion he was at the office early, ready to leave on a business trip to London. He walked across the car park to his car, and was confronted by a giant of a man with a not too friendly look on his face. The man stood in front of Brookes' car barring his way. When Brooke asked him what he wanted, the man left Brooke lying on the ground rubbing his jaw. He warned him that if he ever came near his wife again he would do more than just give him a black eye and a fat lip!

He was soon in trouble again. One of the girls at the office had been making eyes at him for several weeks. They had flirted and exchanged pleasantries at the office but nothing more. She was a stunning looking girl, and Brooke decided that she was right for taking. He asked her out for the night. They had a few drinks in a pub and then they went on to a restaurant. Later in the evening, they went on to a club. They had had a few drinks, and decided to go back to the girl's house for a nightcap. The girl said it would be ok as her parents were away for the weekend. Brooke thinking it was a come-on tried to get the girl into bed, but she was having none of it. He had wined and dined her and expected something in return. When she wouldn't oblige, he slapped her across the face, and tried to rape her, but she managed to hit him with the heel of her stiletto and ran out into the street. She raised the alarm but by this time, Brooke had got away. The police were called but thanks to his fathers' intervention, no charges were made. His solicitor pleaded that they had both had a lot to drink, and that the girl was as much responsible for the affray as he was. His solicitor pointed out that he hadn't actually done anything worse than slap her, and the attempt at sex had failed because he was too drunk. He had not actually caused her too much physical harm, stated his solicitor in his defence. In actual fact, he had come off the worse, suffering a blow to his head from the heel of her shoe. The girl decided not to press charges and let the matter drop. She had been more scared than anything else. The police cautioned Brooke and no more was heard of it. Shortly after, much to his relief, she left the company. Such encounters were the norm in Brookes' life until he met Lizzie.

He settled into married life, but not for long. He was soon up to his old tricks, swanning off with a Welsh woman after only six weeks of marriage. Lizzie put up with it until she and Brooke divorced after three years. Even after their divorce, Brooke could never really leave Lizzie alone and was constantly at her door!

DCI Bradley and DS Jackson had the files of all the victims spread out on the desk. They had been through the evidence for the umpteenth time. "There must be something here that will pin that bastard down," said Bradley. "We know he must have been near all of them. That's the only way the lice could have got into their hair," said Jackson.

"What about the cosh Steve?"

"What about it Guv?"

"When we brought him in, where was the cosh?"

"He legged it when Bob Ashcroft went after him. He found it at the side of the railway line."

"He didn't have time to clean it off then?" said Bradley.

"No. Therefore, his prints should still be on it then, Guv; and Bob Ashcroft's as well."

"But there should be something else on it too. There should be traces of blood. Bob Ashcroft managed to hit him over the head with it when they fought in the mill didn't he?" said Jackson.

"Did forensics find anything on Mary Warmsley? I'd like to bet a pound to a penny that those scratches were made by her, not some bloody cat," said DCI Bradley. "I'll get back onto them straight away, Guv. See what they've found."

It wasn't long before Jackson came back his face beaming. "Bingo Guv; guess what? The blood under Mary Warmsley's finger nails is Rhesus negative."

"So, is that significant?" asked Bradley.

"It's a rare blood group Guv. Only one in a thousand have it. If it's come from laddo and he's Rhesus negative we've got him."

"And has he?" said Bradley.

"I'm getting back to forensics to see what they've come up with."

A couple of hours later Jackson was back in the office. "Well," said DCI Bradley.

"I think you might find this interesting Guv," said DS Jackson placing the medical file on the table. "Brooke Steeples' blood group is' guess...?"

"Rhesus negative," said Bradley. He took the file and studied the findings. "Looks like we might have nailed him this time Steve. Let's get him back in the interview room and see what he's got to say for himself this time."

Chapter eighty-three

Brooke was visibly tired. He had dark shadows under his eyes and he had a two-day growth of stubble on his chin. Much of the cockiness had been drawn out of him. Jail didn't suit him at all. DCI Bradley accompanied by DS Jackson entered the interview room where Brooke was already sitting. He looked like a man defeated. He sat with his head in his hands not looking up at the two officers.

DCI Bradley was the first to speak. "Mr Steeples we would like to ask you a few more questions if that's alright with you?" said Bradley. "Would you like a cup of tea, or a glass of water before we begin?" he said.

Brooke shook his head.

"Could you explain again how you got those scratches on your face?" said Bradley.

"I thought that we had cleared that up. I told you a client's cat did it when I went to pick it up," he said.

"Which client would that be? Would you enlighten us?" said Bradley.

"I don't know, I don't remember."

"When did it happen? Can you tell us that?" persisted Bradley.

"A week ago; I'm not sure."

Bradley nodded to Jackson who pulled a packet from the file on the table. "Do you know what these are?" said Bradley pointing to the cellophane packet.

"No. Should I?" said Brooke staring at the packet.

"They are Pediculus Capitis. More commonly known as nits or head lice, to you and me," said Bradley.

"What have they got to do with me?"

"They were found on you, and all of the victims," stressed Bradley.

"You must be joking. I've never had head lice in my life. This is a set up."

"I'm afraid not. Tests prove that all of the victims had head lice in their hair."

"What about my son Jake? He must have had head lice or nits as you call them, when he killed that Warmsley fellow," he said callously pushing the blame onto Jake.

"I'm afraid not, your son was clean. We didn't find any head lice on him." Brooke's demeanour changed as the truth sank in.

"I'd like to take you back to the night Sandra Mason was murdered between the 11th and 12th October."

"I've already told you. I left between ten and ten-thirty, and went straight home."

"That same night Joe Warmsley was in the club. Did you have occasion to meet him or speak to him?" said DCI Bradley.

"No. I'd never met the man."

"That's strange because he was found twenty-four hours later in Charnley's mill with head injuries that matched all the other victims."

"I told you I never met the man," he said edgily. Brooke was beginning to lose his cool.

Bradley pressed on. "When we got Mr Warmsley back to the mortuary and did a full post-mortem examination of the body, we found these," he said pointing again to the packet containing the head lice. "There was no head lice found on your son. The only lice we found were on you and all of your victims," said Bradley. "Are you really going to sit there and let your son hang for a crime he clearly didn't commit?"

Brooke was visibly shaken he shook his head. He started to shake, sobs racking his body. "I knew there was something on those bloody kids. I never stopped itching for a bloody week," he moaned. "I didn't mean to kill her. I was in mood. I'd been knocked back by some woman I met in a pub. I'd seen the young girl in the bar. She'd been drinking and was a bit drunk. I thought that I might have a chance with her. She left the club about eleven o'clock."

"What did you do then?" pressed Bradley.

"I followed her. They went down by the canal."

"They? She wasn't alone?" said Bradley.

"She was with a couple of her girl friends and there was a man as well."

"Who was the man?" said Bradley.

"I think it was the man who the fight had been over."

"Joe Warmsley," exclaimed Bradley.

"Yes it was him."

"Then what happened?"

"The girl said she was going to take a short cut along the canal. Her friends wanted to go with her but she insisted that she would be ok."

"What about Joe Warmsley? Where did he go?" said Bradley.

"He was laughing and joking with one of the women. I thought he had copped off with one of them. I didn't see him until later."

"What do you mean? You didn't see him until later?" interjected DS Jackson looking up from his notes.

"I followed the young girl down the canal for a bit. I caught her up. She was friendly, so we got chatting. She started telling me it was her birthday and that Joe Warmsley had nearly spoiled it. I said not to worry he was gone now. She seemed to like me. We started necking. I kissed her a few times and she kissed me back. I would never have took it further, but she seemed like she wanted to… you know take it further. I started to put my hand up her jumper. She seemed ok with that so I tried putting my hand up her skirt. The next thing I know she's screaming blue murder. I tried to calm her down but she just kept screaming. I guess I just panicked. The next thing I knew, I hit her over the head."

"You hit her over the head with an iron bar?"

"Yes. I panicked."

"This iron bar?" said Bradley.

"I think so," said Brooke his head buried in his hands.

"Then you raped her. What happened next?"

Brooke nodded his head and whispered, "Yes."

"Go on," said DCI Bradley.

"I hid her body in some bushes. I thought I heard somebody coming down the path."

"Who came down the path?"

"It was Joe Warmsley. I thought he'd seen me so I hid behind the bushes. He must have heard the girl moan. When he went over to look, I hit him."

"The girl wasn't dead!" exclaimed Jackson.

"No I don't think so."

"So Joe Warmsley came down the path and you hit him over the head with this iron bar. Was he dead? What did you do with the body?" said Bradley.

"Who's body?" The questions were coming thick and fast, Brooke barely had time to answer.

"Joe Warmsley's body what did you do with it?"

"I hid him near the girl, and waited for a bit. I don't think he was dead. When I thought it was safe I went and got the car. I put Joe in the boot and I was just about to put the girl in as well, when a young couple came walking down the path. It was my daughter Lottie and her boyfriend. I hid in the bushes, then I heard them talking. I heard my daughter say to Frank that she was pregnant. He said that she couldn't be that they had always been careful and taken precautions. She broke down and started crying. It was then she told Frank what had happened. That Joe Warmsley had raped her when she was working at Benson's mill. Frank told her not to worry that he would still stand by her. The next thing they heard the girl moan. They went to see what was up and Frank ran to phone the ambulance. I managed to creep away and get in the car and drive to Charnley's mill."

"You drove to Charnley's mill with Joe Warmsley," said DCI Bradley. "How did you manage that without being seen?"

"I told you, when Lottie my daughter went to phone for the ambulance, the lad went to watch over the girl. While he was there, I managed to move Joe who was behind some bushes into my car. Then I drove to the mill."

"Was Joe Warmsley still alive when you got to the mill?" said DCI Bradley.

"He was unconscious. I was mad as hell at what he'd done to my daughter, plus I thought he'd seen me kill the girl, so I finished him off."

Chapter eighty-four

Thanks to the confession by Brook Steeples to the murders, DCI Bradley and DS Jackson were satisfied that they had got their killer. Brooke had given them details of the other killings, but there were still a lot of unanswered questions that needed answering. Like how did Brenda Howard and Mary Warmsley fit into the scheme of things? They knew that Brenda Howard was a friend of Mary's, but what was the connection? Bradley decided it would be worth another chat with Bob Ashcroft.

"Thank you for coming in again. We know you want to get back to work so we'll be as brief as possible," said DCI Bradley.

"I just want my nephew out of jail as soon as possible," said Bob.

"I would like to take you back to the night in the Dog and Partridge when you thought you saw Brooke Steeples."

"It were definitely him. I'm almost sure."

"This would be the 1st of November?"

"Yeah, I told you I'd gone to look at some acts for the club."

"You say that you are almost certain that it was Brooke Steeples that you saw there?"

"He was over in the corner. He didn't see me."

"Then what happened?"

"I heard these two women arguing an' I remember saying to the landlord, that he might have a bit of trouble on his hands, with the two women I meant."

"Then what happened?" said Bradley.

"The landlord said it was only Mary Warmsley, and that Brenda would look after her. She'd known her for years apparently, worked at the same office or summat," he said."

The pieces were beginning to fit together. Mary Warmsley was a friend of Brenda Howard.

"Go on," urged Bradley eager to hear the rest of the story.

"There's not a lot more I can tell you."

"Why did the landlord say Brenda Howard would look after Mary Warmsley?"

"I told you they worked together. According to what he said; when she were about eighteen or nineteen she were raped, and never really got over it, took to drink. Sent her a bit off the rails if you know what I mean. That's when Brenda started to look after her."

"Did he say who raped her?" asked Bradley, almost sure of the answer.

"According to the landlord it was her brother, Joe Warmsley."

"Did you see Brooke Steeples leave the Dog and Partridge later that evening?" said DCI Bradley.

"Not really. I think he went to talk to them. There were another couple of turns coming on an' I were more interested in them to be 'onest, but I couldn't say whether he left with them or not."

"Well thanks again for your help Mr Ashcroft," said DCI Bradley. "You've been most helpful."

"It's young Jake I want to help. I want that lad out of jail; he's done nothin' worse that belt that bastard Warmsley," he growled.

Bradley was sure he could pin Brooke Steeples down to the Dog and Partridge. All the pieces were starting to fall into place nicely. He needed another look at Warmsley's file.

The file on Joe Warmsley was thick. He had a history of violence from being a youngster. He was brought before a juvenile court when he was ten for setting fire to a neighbours washing, and pushing excrement through her letterbox. At thirteen, he was given six months in borstal for theft from the corner shop. He was still attracting trouble at fifteen, when he was given another six months borstal for assaulting a woman and stealing her handbag and cash. The file was full of minor misdemeanours of various kinds. It wasn't those that DCI Bradley was interested in. Only three years ago, Joe Warmsley had spent three years in Medway Jail for rape and assault. His latest scrape with the law had been a year ago. He had been let off with a twelve month suspended sentence for assault of his girlfriend.

Chapter eighty-five

DCI Bradley and DS Jackson pondered the evidence in front of them. They both agreed that Brooke Steeples was guilty of the murders of Sandra Mason, Brenda Howard, Mary Warmsley and Joe Warmsley. In addition he was guilty of the abduction and attempted murder of Georgina Laycock, and the assault on the nurse at St Mary's. He was also guilty of the abduction of his parents, although they were unlikely to press charges.

They came to the conclusion that both Brenda Howard and Mary Warmsley were the victims of being in the wrong place at the wrong time. After Brooke Steeples had murdered Sandra Mason and Joe Warmsley, he left his usual haunts and started drinking in the Dog and Partridge, unfortunately for both Brenda and Mary who also drank there. The connection between the two women had been the one that had posed both Bradley and Jackson most problems. Further enquiries revealed that Mary had been raped by her brother Joe. She had never really got over it. She began drinking to ease the memory of her ordeal. Brenda Howard had been her best friend at work. She had seen what was happening to her friend, and Mary eventually revealed what had happened to her. She had taken Mary under her wing and met her once or twice a week in the Dog and Partridge pub. Mary had no one else to turn to, and Brenda acted like an unpaid counsellor to her friend; a shoulder to cry on. It was this selfless act of charity that ultimately led to her premature death.

Brooke Steeples admitted he had offered Brenda Howard a lift home after they had dropped Mary off. He took Brenda down a secluded lane at the back of a golf club.

It was there that he raped and murdered her. Afterwards he hid her body in some bushes on Brookdale golf course.

He brazenly went back to the Dog and Partridge pub, because he wasn't well known in the area. Unfortunately, Mary Warmsley had gone in looking for her friend the night after she disappeared. That was the same night that Brooke Steeples was there. He picked her up in the pub and took her back to her place. Mary made a pass at him but he pushed her away. It was then that she recognized him. She tried to get away but he hit her over the head with the iron bar, but in the noise and confusion, the neighbours were alerted, and Brooke made his getaway. Knowing that Mary could identify him, he had to silence her. He waited to see which hospital she was taken to. He later followed her to St Mary's. He found out which ward she was in, when he overheard a woman say how disgusted she was, that there was a police guard outside the same ward as her mother! He hid in a laundry room until it was quiet. The PC on guard answered a call of nature while a nurse was in the room with her. He crept in and knocked the nurse unconscious, and suffocated Mary with a pillow over her head. He made his escape round the back of the hospital and back towards the railway line.

Chapter eighty-six

The Old Dog was the nearest pub to the town centre nick. DCI Bradley and DS Jackson were standing the team a boozy night out.

"Well how does it feel to have cracked the case?" asked Linda downing her beer like one of the lad's.

"You want to go steady with that or you'll be on your back," laughed Bradley to his girl friend.

"Ooh promises, promises," she giggled. "Really though Phil, I've hardly seen you since the start of this case. I was beginning to think that you'd gone off me."

"I know. I'm sorry love it's just that it's taken every spare minute of my time. We knew we had Brooke Steeples a while ago but we just couldn't prove anything. It was only when the lab boys came up with the nits, that we had a chance to nick him. Even that was mostly circumstantial. Loads of people have nits for one reason or another. A decent brief would have made mincemeat out of that. We had to find something else. What really capped it for us was the blood. Rhesus Negative is only found in about one in a thousand people. Once we found his blood on the cosh that Bob Ashcroft belted him with, it was hard for him to wriggle out of it. All three of the dead women had his blood under their fingernails, and there was also blood under the fingernails of Georgina Laycock's as well."

"Those poor women, they must have put up a hell of a fight."

"He's a big bloke. Did a stint in the navy; fit as a fiddle and as strong as a bloody ox. The poor buggers wouldn't have stood a chance," said Phil. "Once he was faced with the evidence, it was only a matter of time until he spilled the beans. He couldn't argue his way out of that. One lot of blood maybe, but not three lots from three different people, and a forth from Miss Laycock where she scratched him as well."

"What'll happen to him now?" asked Linda.

"My guess is he'll go for psychiatric reports. There must be a screw loose somewhere to behave like that."

"If you ask me the bastard should swing for the way he treated those poor women."

"I agree, but these days there are a lot of people jumping on the anti-capital punishment bandwagon. Since that poor bugger, Ruth Ellis hung for a murder that was clearly a crime of passion. Fortunately, it's not up to us. We just catch them and the judge and jury decide what to do with them."

"I hope you are going to take it a bit easier from now on," said Linda squeezing Phil's arm. She aimed a passionate kiss full on the DI's lips that brought howls of ribald comments from the boys in the C.I.D. standing round the bar.

Friday the 13th of November was unlucky for most people. However, for Jake it was the luckiest day of his young life. All the charges against him had been dropped he was free to go. He no longer had the threat of the hangman's noose around his neck. He couldn't believe it had been his own father that had been responsible for the murders. He was shocked that he was willing to let his own son take the blame for his crimes. He knew from an early age that his dad had been a womanizer and treated his mother appallingly. He could never understand why his dad had resorted to the rape of his mother. No matter what fate awaited his dad, he would never forgive him for that. Jake knew that his dad was selfish and had never really cared about his kids, but he found it hard to understand that he didn't regret killing Joe Warmsley. Maybe the father daughter bond had been too strong, and he had feelings after all. Maybe the rape of his sister Lottie had been too much even for his dad to bear. He didn't know if he would ever be able to forgive him. Jake wasn't a spiteful lad, but it was hard to believe he was only weeks from the hangman's noose. The thought had given him nightmares while he was in prison. If it hadn't been for his uncle Bob tracking him down, he might still be there waiting his fate.

Lizzie was in the kitchen, she had made endless cups of tea trying to keep herself busy. She could hardly concentrate. Once the truth had come out, and Jake had been acquitted. She had a million things going through her head at once. Would Jake be hungry? What if his clothes needed washing? How would he feel? He was due home any time now. His uncle Bob had gone to pick him up. She couldn't face going herself. It was the place where Jake was to be executed. The trauma was more than she could face. Lizzie had always believed that her son was innocent, but when the jury had found him guilty, she couldn't believe it. The trauma of the last few weeks had taken its toll on all the family. Lizzie hadn't slept for nights following Jake's sentence. She had hardly eaten, and had lost more weight than her already emaciated body could afford to lose. Lizzie wasn't the only one who had suffered. When she thought that things couldn't get any worse, young Lottie had become so upset that her brother was going to hang; she had lost the baby she was carrying. Lottie was heartbroken. Lizzie had told her that maybe it was a blessing, and that perhaps it wasn't meant to be. She and

Frank were only young, and had plenty of time to start a family of their own.

The car pulled up outside the terraced house in York street. "They're here mam," said Jenny, Lizzie's youngest. Lizzie peered out of the front parlour window. She saw Bob get out first. She almost didn't recognize Jake. He looked so thin and drawn. He looked as though he had aged ten years. His coat that once filled his broad shoulders hung shapelessly on his thin frame, and his trousers hung loosely round his thin waist. Bob held the car door open as Jake stepped out onto the pavement outside his mothers' house. The house that, a short time ago, he was sure he would never see again.

"Go on then lad. Give yer mam a hug." Said his uncle Bob.

"Jake love come here." He stepped unsteadily towards her; the tears were flowing down both their cheeks as she hugged him. "Mam I never thought I'd see you again. Or you two," he said hugging Lottie and Jenny.

"You're here now lad. You're here now, that's all that matters," said Lizzie crushing Jake to her body so hard, that he feared she'd crack his ribs.